Beneat… hand,
Eva shif… distraction.

Did he realize how close he was standing? His knees bumped against hers, rustling her velvet skirts. She could see the individual stitches on his surcoat: satin stitch, chain stitch, making up one of the embroidered lions, the gold thread interspersed with blue. A labor of love.

A bolt of longing shot through her; earthy and visceral. Her mouth parted in a silent gasp, air pleating her chest. His nearness acted like a balm: soothing her frayed nerves, easing out the tension in her back. But in truth, it did far more than that. A kernel of need grew at the base of her belly, slowly at first, like a newborn fire, smoking and spitting, until it burst into flame, incandescent. A wild insanity ripped along her veins, a primal yearning that stretched every sinew in her body to near breaking point, vibrating and aware. If only she could lean into him, rest her head against his chest and squeeze him tight to her. And more.

Meriel Fuller lives in a quiet corner of rural Devon with her husband and two children. Her early career was in advertising, with a bit of creative writing on the side. Now, with a family to look after, writing has become her passion... A keen interest in literature, the arts and history, particularly the early medieval period, makes writing historical novels a pleasure.

Books by Meriel Fuller

Harlequin Historical

Conquest Bride
The Damsel's Defiance
The Warrior's Princess Bride
Captured by the Warrior
The Knight's Fugitive Lady
Innocent's Champion
Commanded by the French Duke
The Warrior's Damsel in Distress

Visit the Author Profile page at Harlequin.com.

MERIEL FULLER

The Warrior's Damsel in Distress

ISBN-13: 978-0-373-29942-3

The Warrior's Damsel in Distress

This edition published by arrangement with Harlequin Books S.A.

For questions and comments about the quality of this book, please contact us at CustomerService@Harlequin.com.

Printed in U.S.A.

The Warrior's Damsel in Distress

To J. Now we are 50! xx

Chapter One

The Welsh Marches—January 1322

'The day grows chill, my lady.' Eva eyed the tall, slim woman at her side. 'Shall we take the children inside now?'

With the sun sinking rapidly, she had climbed with Katherine up the gentle hill from the castle, watching her friend's three young children laugh and scamper up to the edge of the forest, their woollen cloaks bright, vivid, against the dull winter colours. The ground was iron-hard on this north-facing slope. Untouched by the sun all day, frost clung to the long grass, white-fringed, lacy.

Breath emerging in visible puffs of air, the two women had paused at the point where the rough open grassland met the shadow of the overhanging trees, turning back to look down at the castle below. Their elevated position emphasised the castle's dramatic location above the town: perched on a stony outcrop above the river, the jagged curtain wall was built directly on to the limestone cliffs. The low rays of the sun bathed the numerous turrets in a haze of orange and pink, transforming the river cutting through the densely wooded valley into a solid silver ribbon, a flat trail of light.

Katherine's pale skin glowed with the exertion of the climb. She smiled. 'Let's stay out a bit longer, could we? It's so beautiful up here.' She tugged her fur-lined hood up over her silken veil and gold circlet, tucking gloved hands into the voluminous folds of her woollen cloak. She frowned at Eva's thin threadbare gown. 'Are you warm enough?' Worry edged her voice.

Eva laughed, her blue eyes glowing, sapphires of light. 'You must stop this, Katherine, remember? Stop showing concern for me. You must treat me as a servant, a nursemaid to your children, otherwise people will notice, start asking questions. And those people might talk and *he* will find out where I am.' Her voice wavered and she chewed down on her bottom lip, hating the wave of vulnerability surging through her. 'You must behave as if you care nothing for me.'

Behind them the fractious breeze stirred bare trees and a group of large black crows huddled forlornly on a swaying branch, wings folded inwards, brooding outlines silhouetted against the brilliant sky. And through the scrubby outline of trees, the slender curve of a moon appeared, milky white, almost invisible, transparent.

'But I do care about you. You are my friend.' Katherine's voice trailed away miserably. 'I find it so difficult, having to treat you like that, seeing you dressed like this…' She glanced disparagingly at Eva's garments: the coarse strip of linen that served both as a wimple and veil, covering her glossy chestnut hair and winding around her neck, the simple cut of her gown and under-dress, patched in numerous places, the apron tied around her slim waist. No cloak, no gloves. The only reminders of

Eva's past life were the good leather boots and fine woollen stockings hidden beneath her hemline.

'I have no other choice. You know that,' Eva whispered. The children raced around them in a circle, darting in and out of the women's skirts, playing tag, shrieking with laughter as they snatched at each other's clothes, then raced off again.

'You will always be the Lady of Striguil to me, Eva. What that man did to you...'

Eva shook her head, hunching her shoulders forward. Her eyes filled with unexpected tears. 'Please, don't speak of it. I'm here now, thanks to you, and that's all that matters.' Shivering in the icy air, she wrapped her arms across her bosom, aware that the children had stopped running and were pointing at something on the distant ridge. A flash of light on the horizon, reflected by the sun. She took a deep, unsteady breath. Katherine's words had kindled a rush of familiar panic, a surging terror that gripped at her heart, her throat. How long would it be? How long would it be before she could acknowledge what had happened to her without being reduced to a useless, quivering wreck? It had been a whole year now, yet the slightest reminder turned her to a stuttering idiot. She had to be braver, more stalwart, if she were ever to put those awful days behind her.

'Horsemen,' Katherine announced, following the children's pointing fingers. 'Heading this way.' She dropped her gaze, uninterested, retying the loose strings of her youngest daughter's cloak.

Eva narrowed her eyes, bracing her feet wide on the icy hillside: a stance of mock courage. Her skirts swept around her, the biting wind pinning the fabric to her slim legs. Fear trickled through her belly, a chill runnel, as if her mind already knew what she was about to see. She focused on the black figures, advancing swiftly. Not horsemen. Knights. The dying sun bounced off their shields, their chainmail, forcing her to squint. Friend or foe, it was difficult to tell. But whoever they were, why were they here, in this remote corner of the Marches? Her terror grew, lodged in her throat, and her breath stalled.

'There's no other reason they would take that path,' she stuttered out. 'There's nowhere else to go, but here. We need to go back. Now.' Her voice emerged jerkily, low and urgent. 'Come on, Katherine.'

'What is it? What's the matter?' Katherine rounded her brown eyes in astonishment. 'Surely they're only travellers, looking for somewhere to stay the night? They'll find lodgings in the town.'

'Maybe.' Eva's lips tightened warily. 'Maybe not. King Edward has not stopped punishing the Marcher Lords who rebel against him. He is determined to quash them.' Seizing the hands of the two youngest children, she began to stride purposefully down the hill, her generous hem whisking at the ice-covered grass to leave a long dark trail. If she and Katherine walked quickly they would be back within the castle walls before the knights arrived. The horsemen still had to make their way through the forests to the north of the castle and then pass through the soldiers on the town gate. Eva prayed this would delay them long enough for the castle guards to throw the bolts across the gates and keep them out.

Katherine ran to catch up with her, her cloak billowing out like a wing. 'But they wouldn't bother with me, surely?' Doubt shadowed her features. 'A widow, living alone with my three children? And my trusty nursemaid, of course.' She squeezed Eva's forearm. 'The King has long since forgotten about me; he's too busy fighting his battles.'

'But you are his niece and therefore his responsibility. And you are the widow of a rebel lord. You hold the fortunes of three men: your father, your brother and your husband, God rest their souls. You are rich, Katherine, and therefore useful. Remember, I thought the same before Lord Steffen plucked me from my castle. I thought that I was safe.'

But Katherine failed to hear her. She seemed distracted, looking back up the slope. 'Where's Peter?' Katherine's oldest child had an annoying habit of scampering off and hiding at the most inconvenient times. 'Where is he?' Her voice rose, the note shrill and wavering.

'Here, take these two.' Eva handed Katherine her daughters, darting a concerned glance towards the figures on the far hillside, galloping at full pelt down from the ridge. Had they spotted them up here, colourful cloaks pinned against the drab-coloured grass? 'Go now, run, and bolt the gates behind you. Don't let those people in, whatever you do. I'll find Peter.'

Dropping his reins on to the glossy neck of his destrier, Bruin, Count of Valkenborg, twisted his tall, lean body in the saddle and reached for the satchel strapped to his horse's rump, extracting a leather water bottle. Sidling to a standstill, the huge animal pawed the ground impatiently, jerking its head upwards in irritation, iron bit rattling against enormous teeth. Bruin pulled off his helmet, giving it to a soldier riding alongside him, and pushed back his tight-fitting chainmail hood. Vigorous blond-red curls sprang outwards. He pushed one gauntleted hand through them, the icy air sifting against his sweating scalp. The leather glove rasped against his chin. There had been no chance to shave the short hairs from his face in these last few days of continual riding and now his beard glowed red, like the Viking beards of his ancestors. Dragging off his gauntlets, he slipped frozen hands through the chainmail openings across his palms to open his flagon.

'Hell's teeth!' he murmured as he failed to undo the stopper. Clenching his fingers into his fist a couple of times, he encouraged the blood to run through his numb veins. 'God, but it's cold!' Balancing the flagon on the saddle in front of him, he blew into his cupped hands, a hot gust of air, rubbing them together briskly.

Moving his horse alongside his companion, Gilbert, Earl of Banastre, laughed. 'You, of all people, should be used to this kind of weather!' With his face obscured by his helmet, his voice was muffled, an odd, hollow sound.

'What, because I was born across the North Sea? It's warmer over there, I swear. And definitely flatter.' Bruin's grey eyes crinkled at the corners as he smiled, finally removing the stopper with his teeth. Tipping his head back, he gulped the water down with relish, wiping stray drops from his mouth with his chainmail sleeve, the silvery links glinting in the low sun. 'Is Melyn much further?' Tucking the bottle away, he rolled his shoulders forward, trying to relieve the strained muscles across his back. 'We've been riding for a long time.' He yawned.

Gilbert tipped up the visor of his helmet. He sighed. 'The journey would have been a lot quicker if the rebels hadn't burned all the bridges over the river.' White hair straggled out from beneath his chainmail hood. The metallic links, a few flecked with rust, gripped the fleshy folds of his cheeks in a perfect constricting oval. He inclined his head to one side, a questioning look crossing his face. 'But I'm surprised you, of all the knights, should volunteer to accompany me,' he chortled. 'Surely such a task is beneath a soldier of your calibre? That's why the King decided to drag me out of my comfortable retirement and send me to escort Katherine de Montague. Why did you not travel north with Edward? Flush out more of the rebel barons?'

'The King wanted me to go with him,' Bruin replied, shrugging his massive shoulders. 'Even offered me double the normal amount of gold.' His eyes darkened, glittering pewter. 'He's pleased to have me back after...' A muscle flexed in his jaw.

'After your year adrift with Lord Despenser.' Gilbert threw him a brief smile.

Bruin scowled. 'I swear you have the ability to make even the most awful things in life sound good. I was a mercenary, outside the law. Raiding and plundering merchant ships in the Channel.' His mouth tightened, a wave of guilt coursing through him. 'I was out of control after Sophie's death and well you know it, Gilbert. I'm not proud of what I've done.'

Gilbert's eyes flicked over to his younger companion, startled by his blunt admission, the raw desperation in his voice. He had heard that Bruin blamed himself for her death. 'But the King has brought back Lord Despenser out of exile and forgiven him, just as he has forgiven you.' Anxious not to dwell on the subject, Gilbert pushed at Bruin's shoulder with a rounded fist, a friendly gesture. 'It's good to have you back, even if it is just to help me escort Lady Katherine and her children.'

'I came with you for another reason. When my brother heard where you were going, he asked me to accompany you.' Bruin paused. 'He wants me to find someone for him.' Staring out into the lattice of pine trees that clustered each side of the track, his grey eyes adopted a bleak, wintry hue. 'Steffen seems intent on righting past wrongs, absolving himself of all his sins. He's dying, Gilbert.' His voice held little emotion, for he and his brother had never been close. Stronger at birth, Steffen had always been his parents' favourite and indulged as such. Spoiled. As a sickly child, nobody expected Bruin to survive. But he had survived, and when he started to become well regarded for his prowess on the battlefield, drawing congratulations from all around, Steffen's spoiled character seemed to spiral out of control, developing into a deep resentment towards Bruin. He wanted the accolades for himself.

'I am sorry.' The older man drew his grizzled brows together. 'I forgot that you saw your brother at Deorham. He sustained a wound from the Battle of Durfield, I hear?'

Bruin shook his head to clear the memories clouding his mind. He sighed. 'Yes, a head wound. It's a bad one.' He remembered the ragged gash above his brother's ear, blood congealing in the blond-red strands of his hair. 'The physician doesn't expect him to survive much longer. I only hope I can find this woman before—well, in time.' He kneaded idly at the bulk of his thigh, leg muscles bunched and heavy beneath the fawn wool of his leggings. A wave of guilt passed through him. How churlish of him to dwell on their troubled relationship. His brother was dying.

'Someone he loved?'

'I'm not certain. Maybe.' Bruin frowned, a defined

crease appearing between his copper-coloured brows. After their years apart, seeing Steffen again had been a shock. Racked with fever, his brother had thrown him a thin, wan smile from his sick bed. Scrabbling at Bruin's arm, eyes rolling wildly, Steffen had begged his brother to find this woman to ease his troubled mind, to find peace in death. He talked of her dark brown hair, her blue eyes. He also talked strangely, incoherently, about a butterfly, the mark of a butterfly. And he had given him a name: the Lady of Striguil.

'Peter, where are you?' Eva called quietly. A drift of frost-coated leaves littered the twisting track through the woodland. Her feet crunched through them, purposefully. Wrapping her arms around her chest, she stopped for a moment, listening intently. Her face was rigid with cold, cheek muscles stiff, inflexible; the tip of her nose was numb. Where was the boy? Was he watching her from a hiding place, a smug smile pinned on his face as he heard her calling? The sun was dropping quickly now; soon it would be dusk and he would be much more difficult to find.

She hoped Katherine had reached the safety of the castle by now. A great shudder seized her body, catching her by surprise. The sight of those soldiers in the distance, the sun bouncing against swords and shields, aggressive and intimidating, danced across her vision, taunting her. She hugged her arms about her waist, clamping down on another wave of fear. Katherine was probably correct; they were men looking for bed and board for the night, nothing more.

A flash of red snared her vision. A glimpse of colour

between the drab brown, silent trunks. Then a giggle, swiftly stifled, carried down on the scant breeze.

'Peter, you little wretch!' Eva bounded forward. 'Come here!' She could see him now, darting in and out of the oak trees, his sturdy nine-year-old legs skipping over mossy rocks, red tunic flying upwards as he jumped down into a shallow ditch. But Eva was faster, stronger, than the small boy. The past had taught her, taught her how important it was for a woman to be fit and strong, to at least attempt to try to match the physical power of men, although she knew it was impossible. Katherine had mocked her gently, but understood: Eva's need to take herself off every day, to walk and run, to keep her body strong. Now, her feet sprang across the solid ground, nimble and fast, the toned muscle in her thighs and calves powering her forward. Flying along the track, she advanced on the boy's sprinting figure, stretching out her arm towards the bobbing tunic, the tuft of blond unbrushed hair.

'Got you!' Grabbing the frail bones of the boy's shoulder, she spun him around, cheeks flaring with anger. 'For God's sake, Peter, why do you not come when we call you? Do you think this is a game? There are strangers about; we need to return to the castle!'

'I'm sorry, Eva.' Peter hung his head at her sharp tone, shivering slightly. Tears welled up in his eyes, leaking slowly down the side of his face. 'I was having so much fun; I didn't think.'

'Nay, don't cry.' Eva wrapped her arms about his bird-boned shoulders, hugging him. 'I shouldn't have shouted. Let's go back.' Her linen head covering had come adrift as she had run; now she rewound the coarse material about her head and neck, throwing the loose end back over her shoulder.

'Come,' she said to Peter, extending her arm towards him.

He threw her an unsteady smile and took her fingers, gripping strongly. The shadows of the forest deepened steadily: individual trees losing their definition, trunks blurring together into one dark mass. Soon they would be unable to see without a light. Heart thumping, Eva lengthened her stride, dragging Peter along with her, the thistly undergrowth scratching at their clothes. At last they reached the fringes of the forest, the castle lights and town fires twinkling in the valley below. She sagged with relief at the welcoming sight. Of the horsemen, there was no sign.

They scampered haphazardly down the slope, leather-shod feet slipping on the icy grass. Eva lost her footing only once, sliding down on to her side, but quickly rolled to spring up into a standing position once more, pulling Peter with her. He was grinning, loving the adventure. She smiled back, reassuring, but inside her heart was tense, stricken with anxiety. She had had enough adventures to last her a lifetime; she had no need of any more.

A stone wall, four feet thick, encompassed Melyn Town and Castle, an extra line of defence constructed by Katherine's ancestors out of hefty sandstone blocks. As far as most people knew, the only way through this wall was via the town gatehouse, manned day and night by Katherine's house knights. But Eva knew differently. She headed for a clump of hawthorns clustered together at the point where the wall ended at the cliff edge, high above the churning river. Behind these thorny shrubs, laden with red berries, was a narrow door, a secret entrance known only to Katherine's closest confidants.

Pushing back the curtain of ivy, Eva twisted the handle, forcing the stiff iron latch to rise. She clutched Peter's hand. The castle was before them, a short walk away. The moat gleamed with glossy blackness, surface like grease-covered silk, weed-strewn depths treacherous even to the strongest swimmer. Eva's stomach gave a queasy flip; she looked away. A guard walked along the battlements, his burning torch flaring down on to the water, a wavering light. The gatehouse with its two circular turrets loomed up before them, a wooden drawbridge crossing the inky waters of the moat. Even in this crepuscular gloom, Eva saw that the drawbridge was down. Katherine had chosen not to listen to her after all.

'Careful,' she whispered to Peter, crouching down so that her face was on a level with his. 'I would stay here, out of sight for the moment. Only come when I call you.'

'And if you don't call?' A faint whine laced his voice. He was tired and hungry, Eva knew that. But those knights might have come through the town gate already; she had to make sure the castle was safe.

'Then run and hide,' she replied, trying to keep her tone light, jolly. 'I'm supposed to be looking after you and I don't want your mother coming after me in a rage if something happens to you.'

Peter grinned. One of his top teeth was missing, giving him an impish air. 'All right,' he agreed, poking the toe of his boot into a tussock of grass. 'I'll stay here.'

Eva walked slowly up the path towards the gatehouse, heart thumping erratically. The stone walls rose before her, studded with moss, giving the façade a lumpy, diseased appearance. A climbing rose straggled out over the low, pointed arch, bobbing, adrift, ripped from its moorings in a previous gale and never secured again. The silence of twilight crowded around her; only the rippling sound of water from the moat and an owl's lonely hoot hollowed out the dusk.

Fingers brushing stone, she rounded the bottom of one circular turret. The portcullis was up. She peered into the narrow entrance, slightly irritated by her over-vigilant behaviour; she had managed to frighten everyone, both Peter and his mother. Lit by a single torch, the cobbled passageway was empty, leading to two closed wooden gates at the far end that gave access to the drawbridge. A single guard leaned against the sturdy criss-crossed planks, chin hunkered down to his chest and his arms folded tightly, so that his gloved hands could tuck beneath each armpit for warmth.

'John,' she said, recognising him, stepping forward into the torchlight.

His head jerked upwards in surprise. 'Eva,' he exclaimed. 'Finally. The Lady Katherine was concerned. She said you were looking for Peter. Did you find him?'

'I did. He's waiting outside until I call him.' Her shoulders slumped in relief. 'There's no one else here?'

'No,' said John. 'Those horsemen probably found an inn in the town. Or perhaps they were travelling further, maybe to Dodleigh.'

'I'll fetch Peter.' Happiness, coupled with relief, bubbled up in her chest. Spinning on her heel, she strode out of the gatehouse.

Stopped. A hand flew up to her mouth in horror.

A group of knights clustered before the gatehouse, reining in their mounts. Metal bits and stirrups gleamed in the feeble light; chainmail shone. Their approach had been silent, stealthy; they must have slowed the animals to walking pace for the last few yards over the spongy grass. So they had come here, after all.

'John!' Eva called out, her voice stricken with panic. 'John, come here, now!'

The lead horseman lifted his visor, his face lined with tiredness. White hair clung to his creased, sweating forehead. 'Don't be frightened, maid,' he spoke slowly. 'We come in peace.' The three golden lions of the King decorated his red woollen surcoat, gleaming threateningly.

John moved alongside her, holding the flaring, spitting torch aloft. 'Who are you?' he asked. 'What do you want?'

The knight leaned forward in his saddle, gingerly, as if trying to ease some pain. The saddle creaked beneath his weight. 'I trust we have reached Melyn Castle? The home of Lady Katherine de Montagu? The niece of King Edward?'

'Aye, my lord, that is correct,' John answered.

'In that case, I have a message for the lady, written by the King, her uncle, and I have orders from him to deliver it only to her. No one else.' The old knight produced a scroll of parchment from his saddlebag, and waved it at them.

His huge destrier snorted, canting to the right impatiently, revealing the five or six other horsemen behind him. The other men were much younger, bodies sitting lithe and easy in the saddles, not showing any of the aches and pains displayed by their leader. Eva watched as another knight lifted off his helmet, resting it on the saddle before him, turning to murmur something to his companion.

Silver eyes shone below slashing eyebrows; a shock

of brindled hair, wayward, vigorous. And the shadow of bronze stubble across a square-cut jaw. She recognised him instantly. A low cry, unbidden, ripped from her. Her heart smashed in fear against the wall of her chest.

It was the man who had made her life pure hell. The man who had stripped her of all her worldly goods, all her possessions, her livelihood. He had returned.

Chapter Two

Terror loosened her mind, logic unravelling. The ground dropped away, tilted. She staggered back, her arms flying outward, clawing the air, battling some invisible attacker. Her limbs sagged, as if someone had stripped the muscles from her legs and replaced them with wet, useless rope. Shocked, reeling, a sob tore from her throat, a raw, guttural sound that split the air. No, no, not him! How could he have found out where she was?

Eva sprang away from the gatehouse, unthinking, darting back the way she had come with Peter. Pure animal instinct drove her; she had to run, escape. A shudder tore through her at the thought of him catching her again; he would surely kill her this time, after what she had done. She stumbled forward, boots snagging on lumps of tussocky grass, keeping her gaze fixed on the line of oaks beyond the town walls: the forest; her refuge and a place to hide.

Peter's slight figure emerged from behind the shrubs where she had left him, a worried expression on his thin face, flushed red with the cold.

'Go to the castle, now!' Eva gasped out as she rushed

towards him. 'It's me they're after, not you. You will be safe!' Reaching out, she gave him a little push, as if to emphasise her point.

'I want you to come too,' he whined, catching at her sleeve, slowing her step momentarily. His bottom lip trembled.

'No! Do as I say!' Her breath punched out in truncated gasps. Wrenching the fabric from his grasp, she pulled away, biting her lip at the brusqueness of her words. But it was the only way. Peter was a sensible boy; he would understand when she had time to explain the situation. 'Go to the castle now!' His mouth trembled as he turned and began to run. Watching his bobbing flight, her eyes watering against the icy chill of evening, she realised the knights hadn't moved from the gatehouse, clustered around John, talking to him. Was there the smallest possibility that they hadn't noticed her? But she couldn't take the chance, not with that man; she knew what he was capable of. Eva spun on her toes and took off, her step light and quick, like a startled deer.

'Who was that?' Gilbert asked John, turning to watch Eva's flying figure, her wimple white in the gloom. 'I had no idea the sight of us all would be so intimidating!' His mouth turned up at one corner, quirking into a half-smile. 'I hope you believe me when I tell you we have no intention of causing trouble.'

'She's Lady Katherine's nursemaid,' John explained, stamping his feet against the cold creeping up his legs. 'She takes care of the three children.'

Gilbert sighed, leaning to one side of the saddle to ease his aching hip, silently cursing his old bones. The muscles in his neck hurt, his spine tingled painfully, and he couldn't wait to drop out of the saddle and into a hot bath. But the Lady Katherine would need her nursemaid for the journey on which they were about to take her. 'Then I will have to fetch her back.'

'Nay, allow me.' Bruin eased his horse alongside Gilbert's mount. 'My horse is fresher than yours, and...' he grinned, a teasing light entering his metallic eyes '...I'll wager I will catch her in half the time it would take you.'

'I'm not about to argue.' Gilbert smiled wearily at the younger man, holding out his gloved palm in a gesture of defeat. 'I'm too old to be gallivanting around the countryside. But for God's sake don't frighten her. I have no intention of riling Lady Katherine any more than we have to and that includes scaring her nursemaid half to death. Did you see the girl's face? As if she had seen a ghost!'

Bruin rounded his eyes at him, an expression of feigned surprise. He shrugged his shoulders. 'Me, Gilbert? Who do you take me for? Some sort of mercenary who goes around threatening the lives of innocent people, terrifying them out of their wits?'

'Precisely.' Gilbert's voice was gruff. 'You know who you are, Bruin, what you have been. Your time at sea after—after what happened. It's hardened you. But you need to forget that now and tame your ways. Go easy on the girl. She is not your enemy.' He eyed the fleeing figure. The maid was already on the far side of the town wall, almost up to the treeline, a pale outline of flapping skirts against the swiftly darkening hillside.

No, thought Bruin, as he kicked his heels into his horse's rump, wheeling the animal around, *that girl is not my enemy.* Reaching down, he plucked the flaming torch from the gatehouse guard, ignoring the man's protest. Guilt flooded through him. *My enemy is within, like a noose around my neck.*

Lungs bursting, scrabbling for air, Eva reached the trees, leaning against the nubbled bark of a trunk to rest for a moment, gulping precious air back into her body. Blood roared in her ears, thumping horribly. Sweat trickled down her spine, her arms, gathering uncomfortably beneath the linen cloth wrapped around her neck. She had pushed her body onwards, forcing her legs to move faster, harder, and now they ached, the muscles sore and painful. But this was nothing, she told herself, nothing compared to what that man would do to her if he caught her. The urge to wrap her arms around the tree and sink downwards to rest was overwhelming, but she stamped on the feeling, jerking her head upwards, staring into the dark forest beyond. In there, she would hide.

A shout forced her to turn. Her legs shook with fear at the sound, strength sapping. A knight was in pursuit, cantering up the hill at an easy pace, a burning brand shedding a flicking, spitting light across the sparkling steel of his helmet. How had he managed to get through the gate so quickly? Surely his horse was too big to have squeezed through that slight gap? But it was the older knight, she decided, judging from his slow speed. He would never catch her. Whipping around into the shadows, she set off again, feet dancing along a path that twisted and turned through the silent oaks. The glimmer of moonlight gave her just enough light to see by, the track disappearing off between the massive trunks. But if she could see it, then so could he.

She dodged sideways, plunging into a bundle of scrub

and brambles higher than her head. Thorns tore at her skirts, but she fought a way through, pushing aside the lacerating tendrils. She would find somewhere to hide, a place where she could crouch down, catch her breath. Sheltered from the icy air by the tree canopy, the forest floor was muddy, squelching and sucking at her leather boots. Breaking free of the snarling brambles, she emerged into a clearing, the ground mossy and sinking, and she stopped for a moment, listening.

No sound. Nothing. Maybe he had given up on her.

She strode on with renewed energy, with the faintest trickle of hope that she had lost her pursuer, intending to plunge into the darkness on the other side of the clearing. If memory served her correctly, she was at the highest part of the woods; from here the land sloped down gradually to meet the river. She would have to hide herself soon, otherwise she would be cut off by the impassable sweep of water.

Stepping forward, she failed to see the animal trap set beneath a drift of grey curled leaves. Her foot pressed down on an iron bar, releasing a spring on toothed jaws to snap them tight against the rounded muscle of her calf. Pain shot through her leg, burning, visceral; she dropped to the ground, slumping sideways with a howl of pain, clutching at the metal around her leg. Her head spun; waves of dizziness surged behind her eyes, light splintering across her vision. Nausea roiled in her belly. She bit down on her lip savagely, willing herself to remain conscious, tears of agony coursing down her cheeks. It was well known that the townspeople left out the traps in the undergrowth to catch their food. How could she have been so stupid as to leave the track?

Pulling herself upright, leaning forward, she tried to

prise the metal jaws apart, aghast at the blood soaking through her stocking. She tugged ineffectively at the cold metal; her arms seemed to have lost their strength. At her own puny weakness, a sob of sheer outrage spluttered from her lips; her hands dropped to the mossy ground and she laid her face against one upraised knee, weeping softly in sheer frustration. If she were quiet now, then maybe he would never find her.

But Bruin had heard the cry, carried on the wind. A wavering shout, keening, animal-like. The woman he pursued. Wrinkling his long, straight nose, he turned his head from side to side, trying to decipher the sound's direction. Where was she? He had left his horse at the woodland edge; the heavily muscled animal would struggle to make any progress through the dense trees. Springing down, booted feet sinking into the spongy earth, he had followed the track, his long-legged stride light and fast, despite his weighty chainmail hauberk. His hair was bright, a flame against the dark trunks; he had given his helmet to another knight for safekeeping and now relished the freedom from the cloying metal.

Raising the burning brand high in his fist, he whipped the torch around as he walked, searching for traces of the maid's flight on the ground, in the bushes alongside the path: a broken branch, a disturbed scuffle of mud. Piles of decaying leaves deadened his step. He paused, listened, ears tuned to the silence, with an instinct honed from years of fighting, of tracking enemy forces. After that single drawn-out scream there was nothing, nothing but the crackle of the torch, the frantic squeaking of a disturbed mouse as he passed by. In the distance, he could hear ducks calling on the river, the compressed sound strident, disjointed. But although there was nothing to turn him in one direction over another, he sensed the girl's presence, the tense curtailment of her breath as she waited for him to pass. She was hiding nearby, of that he was certain.

The flickering light fell on brambles, torn awry. She had left the path. He plunged through the rent in the undergrowth, thorns scraping against his mail coat sleeves, dragging at the fine red wool of his surcoat. His pace did not falter until he sprang into the clearing and saw what had happened.

Sitting, her whole body hunched forward, folded inwards, the maid appeared to be asleep. Her face was buried in one knee, a slim arm wrapped around her head, as if trying to protect herself. Her other leg lay flat upon the ground, skirts bunched up, the teeth of an ugly metal trap gouging into her flesh. Blood stained her woollen stocking, running down the outside of her leather boot, trickling steadily.

Bruin cursed. Twisting his leather belt so that his sword lay to one side, he dropped to his knees beside her, driving the torch into the muddy ground. Close up, the poor quality of the maid's garments was pitifully evident: a loose sleeveless over-gown constructed from a coarse mud-coloured cloth over a fitted underdress of lighter brown. Threads unravelled at her cuffs, fraying dismally in the light. She wore no cloak, her slight figure trembling in the evening air. He grimaced; his winter cloak was packed in his saddlebags, otherwise he could have draped it around her shivering shoulders. He adjusted the torch carefully so the light was cast over the mess of her leg.

The girl's head rose slowly. The pale oval of her face, wrapped tightly in her linen veil, stared unseeingly at him for a moment, her expression hazy, unaware. In the flaring light, her skin held the creamy lustre of marble, polished and smooth, untouched by blemish or freckle. Her eyes were huge, sparkling orbs fringed with long, velvety lashes that dominated her face; in the twilight, he couldn't see the colour. Then her eyes rounded, her head jerking back in horror, and she started hitching away from him, palms flat on the ground, yanking the trap with her. A chain and long pin secured the trap into the earth; they rattled, clinking together as she tried to pull back, the iron teeth tearing deeper into her skin.

'Stop,' Bruin said firmly, leaning forward to seize her shoulder, to prevent her moving backwards. 'You'll only hurt yourself more.' He nodded down at the rusty trap, her mangled flesh. 'I will take it off.'

'No! Go away! Get away from me, you...you barbarian!' she spluttered inexplicably, wriggling her shoulders roughly from his grip. 'Move back!' With quicksilver speed she grabbed the torch, wresting it from the ground with a strength that belied her diminutive stature, and swung the flame haphazardly in front of his face. Cruel, lacerating pain scythed through her leg at the jerky movement. Bruin lurched back instinctively, to avoid being burned.

Irritation flashed through him. He was used to men following his command immediately, without question, and yet this chit was physically threatening him, ordering him away as if she were the Queen of England! He was tempted to walk away and leave her to fend for herself. Another nursemaid for Lady Katherine's children could be found, surely? But he supposed he ought to try; Gilbert and the rest of the knights would certainly have something to say if he returned empty-handed. Bruin raised both hands in the air, a gesture of surrender, keeping his voice deliberately calm, slow. 'Look, I'm going to help you, don't you understand? I'm not going to hurt you.'

His measured tones reached out to Eva through the dancing panic of her brain. His voice seemed different. And yet it was him, surely, the same man who had ordered her abduction? This man had the same bronze-coloured hair and sharp-angled cheekbones, the square-cut chin? And yet the voice from all those months back, the voice that had shouted and bullied her, had been silky smooth, with a subtle threat to every word. Although he looked the same, this man also spoke with an odd, foreign inflection that hitched his tone with a low, guttural melody, twisting the vowels. But how could she be certain he was not him? She could not afford to take any chances.

'I don't believe you!' she whispered. Her body shook, beset with uncontrollable trembling. The brand wobbled alarmingly in her grip. 'What you did—!' A sob stopped her speech, as she glared at him fiercely, her shoulders sagging inwards. 'Haven't you done enough?'

'What are you talking about?' Bruin growled at her. He sat back in his heels, skin creasing between coppery brows. 'Did you hit your head when you fell? You're not making any sense!' Flakes of snow drifted down between them in a lazy spiral, hissing as they hit the torch flame, one by one.

'How can you forget?' Fear twisted her voice. A residue of tears clung to her bottom lashes, tiny diamonds sparkling. Beneath the ill-fitting gown that she wore, her chest rose and fell quickly. The light slanted across her eyes, revealing depths of the most astonishing blue: like the shimmering sea at noon, shot through with golden streaks.

Bruin's heart jolted oddly and he shook his head, clearing his fanciful thoughts. Something was not right here; the maid spoke as if she were acquainted with him, yet he could swear that he had never met her before. He would have remembered. Remembered those beautiful eyes, that sweet oval face. The precise curving line of her top lip.

'Do you know me?' he asked brusquely. His voice was husky and he cleared his throat. 'Or are you muddling me up with someone else?' Could she have met his brother? It seemed unlikely; his brother had been at the King's side for the past few years and Edward never ventured this far west.

'Do you really need to ask that question?' Her voice was low, halting, as if she were frightened of the answer. The words staggered out of her; she held the muscles in her body taut, almost to the point of collapse, teetering on the brink of unravelling completely.

He loomed over her, this big hulk of a man, tough and intimidating, the man who had terrified her days and nights, until she had finally given in to his demands, exhausted by the days of relentless torment. His hair was more tousled than she recalled, the bronze locks falling forward across his brow. His face was leaner, shadowed furrows slashing down from high cheekbones to his jaw. He was taller.

Wait. Her mind was playing tricks on her. No man would be taller, it wasn't possible. She tilted her head, sticking her pert nose in the air, and frowned. Embroidered across his tunic was a crest that she did not recognise: black and red lions on a gold background, a crown above. Was she mistaken about this man's identity? The frantic beat of her heart gradually slowed, the burning brand in her hand giving her confidence. The flame created an effective barrier between them, preventing him from coming any closer. Doubt sifted through her. 'How did you find me? How? Who told you where I was?' she asked.

His eyes gleamed like pale frost, a glittering icy fire. Her questions made no sense. 'No one told me. You ran away; I followed you from the castle.' Frustration, tightly held, laced his voice.

'Not now,' Eva hissed at him. '*Before*. Who told you?'

'No one told me anything,' he replied bluntly, dismissing her questions with a cool, detached look. 'I have never seen you before.' Uninterest bordered his tone; he glanced pointedly at her leg, the blood on her woollen stocking. 'I need to take this trap off and stop the bleeding.' He leaned forward and she thrust the torch out instinctively, a quick vicious movement. She wasn't sure who this man was, but she had to be careful. There was a crackle and the acrid smell of burning hair.

'Oh, for God's sake.' He made an impatient sound between his teeth, almost a snort, plucking the brand easily from her fingers. He stuck it firmly back into the ground, out of her reach. 'Stop playing games with me.' His voice was laden with deadly intent.

'Go away!' she hissed at him. Vulnerability flooded over her; she wanted to cry at the unfairness of the situation. 'I would rather have the Devil help me than the likes of you!' She pushed at his huge shoulders, the mail coat links rippling against her chill fingers, attempting to shove him away, but he was immovable, an enormous, unwieldy rock. She thumped down on his shoulders, small fists banging ineffectually. 'Don't you dare touch me!'

Bruin chuckled at the maid's ridiculous threats, the false bravado threading her voice. Who did she think she was? She spoke as his equal, yet she was only a nursemaid, a lowly servant. Her feisty, combative behaviour should have made him angry, annoyed, but instead he wanted to laugh. Her shrill tone bounced off him like darts against a drum skin. He couldn't understand why she was so frightened of him and this misplaced fear, obstructive and stubborn, was slowing him down. The quicker he took her back to the castle, the quicker he would be able to undertake his brother's quest. And time was not on his side; Steffen was dying. He needed to remember that.

The snow was gathering strength, falling more thickly now. He blinked away the flakes stuck to his lashes. With gauntleted hands, he grasped the toothed iron hoops and prised them apart with a snap. Muscles bulged in his upper shoulders, rounding out the tight flex of chainmail. Eva sucked in her breath, a sharp, tearing gasp as pain radiated through her calf.

'There was no other way,' Bruin said, watching the tears pool in her eyes. Her cheeks were flushed red, as if the cold air had slapped her.

'Yes, there was,' she bit out, a sob stifling her voice. 'You could have left me alone.' She wrapped her arms tightly around her middle. The teeth of the trap had ripped ragged holes into her stocking, beneath which her skin was purple, bruised with ugly puncture marks, some bleeding heavily. But she was free, free of the awful iron cage. She tried to move her leg, tentatively, but the pain was too great. Unconsciousness threatened, blurring the edges of her mind, hazy fingers of oblivion eager to drag her down.

'Out of the question,' he said, gruffly. 'No one would leave you out here, on your own. Who do you take me for?'

Him. I thought you were him. Eva cleared her throat, nibbling at her bottom lip. But now, she was almost certain he was not the same man. She took a deep shaky breath, the muscles binding her chest and torso relaxing. Failing to answer his question, she wriggled her hips around awkwardly, crawling on to all fours, intending to stand. The gleaming lions on his surcoat wobbled in front of her vision. Nausea roiled in her belly, a sickening lurch. The air around her loosened, shifted; suddenly she found herself incapable of holding herself upright. She began to tip, slowly, sideways.

'Careful.' The man caught her upper arm, supporting her, propping her wilting frame against him.

Her stomach churned dangerously; her forehead was clammy, sheened with a faint sheen of sweat. 'I'm going to be sick,' Eva spluttered out in panic. Oh, God, no. Not in front of him!

'No, you're not,' he responded, his low voice close to her ear, the air from his lungs sifting across her skin. 'Take deep breaths…there.' Grasping her shoulders, he lifted her so that she was sitting on the ground again. His face was alarmingly close, silver eyes sparkling mere inches from her own. 'You've had a shock. That's why your head is spinning. You must keep still.'

Eva clamped her eyes tightly together, fighting the rolling waves of sickness, willing her head and stomach to settle. Snowflakes landed on her face, tickling gently. His hands were heavy on her shoulders; she could smell woodsmoke on his skin and clothes. A strange sensation looped through her chest; the muscles beneath her ribs contracted, involuntarily.

Opening her eyes, she pinned her gaze to a muddy streak across her skirts, mouth set in a straight line, determined to show this man that her nausea, her near-fainting, was merely a temporary weakness and not part of her character. 'Who are you?' she asked through the drifting snow. 'What is your name?'

'My name is Bruin, Count of Valkenborg.'

Not him. Not the same man. Thank God.

Chapter Three

'Valkenborg,' she repeated stupidly. 'I have not heard of that place before...'

'I am from Flanders,' Bruin replied, sensing her tension easing, the fractional wilt in the maid's slim frame. But why would knowing his name cause her any comfort? He was a stranger to her. 'From across the North Sea.'

'I know where Flanders is,' Eva snapped. She raised her eyes to his wild auburn hair. Above the fiery bristles covering his jaw, the determined slash of his cheekbones created shadowed hollows, giving his face a lean, wolfish look. He looked so similar to Lord Steffen, the resemblance was uncanny, and yet, he was not him. Her heart plunged at the intimidating sight of him, but not with fear. With—what? He was too close, too overpowering. His rangy build hunkered over her like a Norse god of old, torch flames touching his skin with a golden patina, his lashes stuck white with snow. The man shed physical energy like shooting stars. Her hands trembled; she tucked them forcibly into her lap to disguise the shake.

Beside them, the light guttered ominously, the flame dipping and sliding, blue-tinged. 'We've tarried long enough. We need to go back to the castle before this light fails,' Bruin muttered. 'And before this wretched snow becomes too deep.' His gaze swept the maid's neatly wrapped wimple, the delicate wrists resting in her lap, her slim calves poking out from beneath her gown: a swift assessment. 'Take your stocking off so I can bind the wound.'

Eva's head jerked upwards, eyes rounding in horror. 'No. I cannot. You know I cannot.' She stuck her chin in the air, bridling at his high-handed tone. 'It would be improper.'

'Improper or not, we have nothing else.' He dragged off his gauntlets, throwing them to the ground. The creased leather made a scuffling sound across the newly fallen snow. 'Unless you want me to do it for you?' He grinned unexpectedly, diamond eyes flashing in challenge.

Damn the man! His big knee was planted heavily in the spreading cloth of her skirts; she tugged at the material ineffectively, wanting to be free of him. Turning away, she lifted her skirts to release the ribbon that secured her stocking top to her thigh, fumbling awkwardly with the fragile ties. The icy air, the large feathery snowflakes, tickled her naked skin. For some reason, she seemed incapable of undoing the ribbon; her cheeks grew hot as she repeatedly failed to release the tight knot.

Strong, sinewy fingers pushed hers aside, tearing the pink ribbon in half and smoothing the stocking down her bare leg, his palm intrusive, shocking against her satiny skin. Eva squeaked in outrage, rocking back at the rough contact as he hauled off her boot and stocking; threw them into the snow. Never, ever, had a man touched her like that! His hand knocked against her toes and she curled them downwards, recoiling at the abrasiveness of his calloused palm. A strange heat staggered through her chest, flexing the muscles of her diaphragm. What on earth was the matter with her? Her mind felt besieged, wooden and loose, as if it were not functioning properly.

'I can do it!' Eva flared at him. 'Stop manhandling me!'

Bruin raised his eyebrows. 'This is hardly "manhandling",' he replied coolly. 'I'm trying to help you.' Ripping lumps of moss from a decaying piece of wood, he packed the wound on her leg. 'And anyway, you're too slow; we'll be sitting in darkness if I let you do it.' Winding the stocking around her leg, he bound it tightly, lifting her leg to wrap the limp wool behind her knee. His movements were deft, efficient, his careful touch minimising the spiralling pain. Tearing the end of the stocking in two to make a knot, he secured the makeshift bandage.

'There,' he said, sitting back on his heels. Snow fell around him, spangled flakes landing on his massive shoulders, dousing the bright flame of his hair, flecking his red surcoat. Seizing her leather boot, he cupped her foot, cradling her heel. 'Shall I put this back on?'

'I'm surprised you even ask me,' Eva replied haughtily. Heat radiated across her exposed ankle. His deft fingers tightened fractionally around her fine bones; tiny darts of heat pulsated upwards from the point where he held her. 'You seem to do most things without asking.'

Ignoring her, he eased the boot carefully around her ankle, securing the wooden toggles that held the pliable leather in place. Eva threw her skirts down over her feet. The damp from the ground had begun to seep through the thin layers of her gown; she shivered. High up in the trees an owl hooted, a lonely drawn-out cry, echoing through the stark, crooked branches. Picking up his gauntlets, Bruin sprang to his feet. He adjusted his belt over his lean hips, bringing his sword around to swing diagonally across his left leg. Semi-precious stones gleamed in the hilt; a strip of red leather, creased and worn, bound the sword handle, a gold circular disc decorated the top. Pulling the torch from the ground, Bruin held out his hand. 'Do you think you can walk?'

'I can try.' Eva hesitated, staring at his outstretched hand, the ridged web of sinew. His nails were clean, clipped short. Since her imprisonment she had actively avoided the company of men, developing a hesitant wariness in their presence. It had become second nature to her, an added protective layer. She couldn't allow what had happened to her once to happen again.

'Oh, for God's sake, take my hand!' A lock of hair had fallen across his forehead; he shoved it back in frustration. What was the matter with her? Why did the maid resist every single offer of help? 'Don't you trust me?'

Her eyes darkened. 'Why should I? I have no idea who you are! You look like a barbarian!' Her gaze flickered over the blond-red stubble coating his jaw, the flick of messy, rumpled hair, the size of him.

'No more than any other knight,' he countered, rubbing his chin ruefully, noting her pointed stare. Maybe he should have taken time to shave before he had started the journey that morning. 'And you seem to have enough of them at the castle.'

Not like you. The thought whipped through her, a streak of fire. This man was young, only a few years older than herself, with every muscle in his body honed, not an ounce of spare flesh on him. Katherine's knights were older, grizzled, barely capable of running for more than a few yards. They had the experience, aye, but were no match for this man's physical ability.

'I'm right to be cautious.'

He sighed. 'I agree, but you can be too cautious. You saw that I came with those other knights to the castle. You have to trust me.'

But I don't trust them either, Eva thought. She sighed. She had little choice in the matter; this man was her only way out of the forest and it was growing late. A snowy twilight drew around them like a dark sparkling curtain. Katherine would be worried. Tentatively, she raised her hand and he pulled her upwards. Tottering for a moment, she placed her full weight gingerly on the damaged leg.

Bruin watched her face pale, her skin grow waxy. 'It hurts, doesn't it? Let me carry you.'

'No, give me a moment. I'll be fine.'

'There's no time,' he responded gruffly. 'Here, hold this.' He shoved the brand towards her, closing her fingers decisively around it. 'Take care not to burn any more of my hair; I have no wish to be completely bald by the time I reach my horse.' Pulling on his gauntlets, he bent down, sweeping her feet from beneath her, one arm under her knees, the other around her back.

'I don't—'

'I don't care.' Bruin cut off her speech, his tone low and forceful. 'You've held me up long enough. We're going back to the castle and we're going like this, whether you like it or not.'

Hoisting her high against his chest, he carried her back through the trees, through the scurries of falling snow. His stride was purposeful and sure, never losing his footing across the lumpy, uneven ground, ignoring the over-arching brambles that clutched and snagged at his surcoat, at the flowing hem of the maid's gown. Sensibly, she had fallen silent, quiet in his arms, but he wasn't fooled by her chastised demeanour. Her shoulder muscles were tense, contracted against his upper arm; she kept her head positioned stubbornly away to avoid touching him, refusing to let it rest. He grinned suddenly; her neck must be hurting like hell with the strain of maintaining her distance from him. Her hip curved temptingly against his forearm, the faintest smell of lavender rising from her skin. His chest squeezed with unexpected delight.

Eva gripped on to the torch, holding the flame out before her like a ship's figurehead, her knuckles white. The memory of this man's over-familiar touch on her flesh was branded on her brain: a scorch mark, throbbing, vivid. The way he had plucked at her stocking. The way his fingers had rasped against her soft skin, leathery and calloused like those of a peasant, and yet he was obviously high-born, a count in his own right. The air shivered in her lungs. The wound on her leg was sore, making her unsettled, unsure of herself.

She gritted her teeth, hating her incapacity to walk on her own two feet, hating the fact that this man had to carry her. His confident domineering behaviour rattled her; his assumption that she would blithely follow his orders, no matter what. She had always been able to look after herself, even more so after what had happened to her; she resented his intrusion, this foisting of unwanted intimacy upon her. His chest pressed against her shoulder, flat plates of hard muscles rippling against the curve of her upper arm, but she was unable to shift away any further, his arms held her too securely. His horse waited on the outskirts of the forest, cropping the few wisps of spindly grass that poked up through the settling snow, jangling the bit irritably between its teeth as they approached.

'We'll ride back,' Bruin announced, shifting his grip on the maid. His short beard scratched against her wimple; she jolted back at the inadvertent contact. 'Hold tight to that torch.' He turned her in his arms, clasping her waist to lift her into the saddle, but to her surprise, he placed her up front, nearer the horse's neck.

'Oh!' Eva said, surprised, rocking forward to grab the horse's mane for balance. Her grasp loosened on the torch; she almost dropped it. She sat with both legs dangling to one side, hip wedged up against the animal's neck. Why had he not placed her in the saddle? 'I thought you said I was going to ride!' Her voice juddered slightly, panic slicing through her veins. A beat of pain streaked through her leg.

'You are. But I'm riding, too.'

'No, no, you're not. You're going to lead the horse.' The words jabbed out of her before she had time to contemplate their impact. He couldn't be near her again; the closeness of him tangled her brain, made her lose her train of thought. He flustered her.

Bruin's chin shot up at her imperious tone, his eyes, mineral dark, glittering dangerously. 'I am riding.' Rummaging in his saddlebags, he extracted a thick woollen cloak, handing it up to her, frowning. 'You give yourself of lot of airs and graces, my girl, for one in such a lowly position. Why, anyone would think you were a noble lady, not a servant dressed in rags. By rights, you should be walking alongside me.'

Eva flinched as if he had hit her. Her mouth snapped shut. She grabbed his cloak with her spare hand, bundling its voluminous folds in her lap, staring rigidly ahead with flushed cheeks. Good God, this man made her forget who she was supposed to be! Not Eva, Lady of Striguil, but Eva Macmurrough, nursemaid to the Lady Katherine's children. She needed to watch her step, remember to behave in a manner appropriate for a servant. 'I apologise if I've caused offence,' she replied eventually. 'Lady Katherine encourages all her servants to be outspoken. She prefers it that way.' Her reasoning sounded limp, pathetic.

'Really.' His response was caustic, disbelieving, silver eyes scrutinising her wan face. He had seen the sudden lurch of her body at his accusation, the flare of panic in her eyes. What was she hiding? Her high-handed manner, the regal tilt of her head—all was out of kilter with her appearance, with the clothes she wore. But then, her feisty, stubborn behaviour matched no other woman he had ever met, ever, in his whole life. The girl was a complete puzzle. 'Well, you'll just have to put up with my unwanted presence.' Sticking his booted foot into the shining stirrup, he sprang into the saddle behind her. The horse shifted sideways under his added weight. 'I'm sorry it will be such an unpleasant experience for you.'

Lifting the cloak from her lap, Bruin laid it around her shoulders, pulling Eva against his hard torso to tuck in the edges firmly around her. She wrenched forward instinctively, unwilling to submit to his control of her, unwilling to let him win. The torch dipped precariously.

'Give me that,' he said, taking the torch from her. 'We can't afford to lose the light.' He gathered up the reins in one hand. 'Do you behave like this all the time? I pity the poor man married to you!' Circling her with his arms, he jabbed his knees into the horse's sides, setting the animal in motion, the jerky forward gait of the animal forcing her to grasp at his arm.

'I'm not married,' she bit out.

In the flickering light, he traced her haughty profile, the stubborn jut of her chin, and chuckled, a long low rumble in his chest. 'I can't say I'm surprised. Your father must be wringing his hands trying to find someone for you!'

The luscious sweep of her eyelashes dipped fractionally. He caught the fleeting trace of vulnerability crossing her face, swiftly masked. 'My father is dead, as is my brother. Killed by the King, fighting to protect their land!' she blurted out, then clapped her hand across her mouth. Why had she not curbed her speech? She rode with a man who had arrived at the castle with a knight wearing the King's colours. It was easy to guess where this man's allegiances lay.

'So your father was a rebel,' he said slowly, ducking his head to avoid a low-hanging branch, steering the horse through the last few trees at the woodland edge and out on to open ground. His eye trailed across the flushed curve of her cheeks, the ebony hair curling out from beneath her linen wimple. 'With his own land,' he added significantly. The saddle leather creaked as he adjusted his weight slightly.

A hot prickling sensation swept up her spine. She had made a mistake. Playing the role of a servant, she should have remembered that her family would have nothing, no land or estates, being entirely dependent on their master, or in this case, Lady Katherine. 'No—no! I meant—his lord's land.'

'I see.' But in truth, he didn't see at all. He had caught the false note in her tone and wondered at it. What was she doing with Lady Katherine? Maybe the chit's mother was living at the castle, too. As he tipped back in the saddle, leading the horse down the snowy slope to the castle, he told himself that the maid was not his concern. He shouldn't care. But strangely, he realised that he did.

'My God, Eva! What happened to you? Where did you go?' Katherine emerged through the arched doorway leading to the great hall, her graceful body silhouetted by the light spilling out behind her. Her willowy slenderness was encased in a sleeveless gown of patterned red velvet, cut low at the sides to reveal a tight-fitting underdress of rose-pink silk. Descending the wooden staircase, set at right angles to the door, she came down into the bailey. At the bottom of the steps, she paused, hugging her arms around her chest to ward off the cold. 'Goodness, it's freezing! We were so worried, especially when Peter came back and told us you had run off into the forest.'

'I'm fine,' Eva said, pinning a wide and hopefully reassuring smile on her frozen face. Her muscles ached from the short journey down the hill, her spine stiff, strained from the constant effort of keeping herself away from the knight at her side. Bruin's arm had roped around her like an iron clasp, winching her continually against his chest. His cloak warmed her; the felted woollen folds lay snug about her shoulders, the fur edging tickling her chin.

Wheeling his horse around to the steps, Bruin reined the animal in, jumping down in one easy movement to land on the snow-slicked cobbles. He handed the torch to a stable lad who came running up. Rolling her shoulders forward, Eva stretched out the tense muscles in her neck, pert nose wrinkling slightly. How on earth was she going to climb down from this enormous horse without landing in a heap at Katherine's feet?

Katherine turned to Bruin. The hanging pearls in her silver circlet bobbed with the movement, gleaming faintly. 'Thank you, my lord, for bringing Eva back. Your men are all inside.' Her breath hazed the air. She tilted her head to indicate the lighted doorway behind her. 'Please, give your horse to the stable lad. Go and help yourself to some food.'

Bruin inclined his head graciously. 'I thank you, my lady. But—' his eyes flicked up to Eva '—your nursemaid has hurt her leg. Is there somewhere I could carry her?'

Lord, no! 'I can walk now, thank you,' Eva interrupted briskly. She had no wish to be beholden to this man any longer than was possible. His powerful presence made her feel vulnerable, weak, traits that she had striven long and hard to erase from her character. She had already said too much to him. Gripping the horse's mane, she slithered down haphazardly, Bruin's cloak clutched to her middle, unwieldy folds gathering heavily around her, the hem falling to the cobbles. She landed with a thump, gasping, eyes watering at the pain radiating up her leg. She willed herself to remain upright, steady, beneath Bruin's glittering gaze. Tipped her chin in the air, proud, resolute.

'What did you do?' Katherine was at her side, holding her arm. Eva flicked her gaze towards Bruin, annoyed by his continued presence, not wanting to talk in front of him.

Interpreting her hostile expression, Bruin smiled, lifting his eyebrows in faint mockery at Eva's obvious rebuff. He passed his reins to the stable boy. 'I see I am dismissed.' He nodded brusquely towards Lady Katherine, ignoring Eva. 'Call me if you need any help.' Climbing the wooden steps two at a time, he disappeared beneath the ornately tiled archway.

'Oh, God!' Eva pressed her palm to her forehead. As the stable lad led Bruin's horse away, she was forced to release her hold on the horse's mane; wobbling slightly, she hopped over to the handrail of the steps, clutching at the polished wood. 'What a nightmare! That man is hell on earth!'

'But handsome, if truth be told,' Katherine said, following Bruin's commanding figure as he vanished into the great hall. 'Why did you run away? What on earth possessed you?' Her breath billowed out like a cloud into the snow-filled air.

Eva swept the loose end of her linen wimple back over her shoulder. 'That man—' she jabbed a pointing finger towards the doorway '—that man looks exactly like that thug who abducted me. Lord Steffen. I wasn't thinking straight; I saw that hair, those eyes, and I thought, my God, he's come back to fetch me, to finish what he started.' Her voice dropped to a fierce whisper. 'Remember, Katherine, I escaped before Lord Steffen discovered the full extent of my inheritance; I suspect by now he's worked out what I hid from him. The man's so greedy; he'll want the rest.'

'He wouldn't come back for you; it's been too long.' Katherine's mouth turned down at the corners. 'He's too busy stealing the riches of other unfortunate heiresses.'

'But I was the only one to escape from him,' Eva replied. 'He's the sort of man who would never forget a slight. He will claim revenge for something like that.'

Shivering, she shifted her feet from side to side, wincing at her throbbing leg.

'I think you need to stop worrying,' Katherine said. 'Let's go inside. Martha can look at your injury.'

'Have you found out why those knights are here?'

'No, I was so concerned about you, I hadn't the wit to ask. The old knight has asked for bed and board, for one night. I assume they plan to travel further into Wales.'

Eva's eyes narrowed to a sapphire glint. 'I don't like it; they wear the King's colours and yet they are bothering with the likes of us. Why?'

Katherine shivered. 'Do you think my uncle has plans for me?' She glanced up at the front of the castle, at the warm glow of light spilling out from the open door, and chewed worriedly on her bottom lip. 'I should hate it—' her breath caught '—if we were taken away from this place.'

'Just be careful what you say in front of them. At least until we know why they are here. Despite our lack of menfolk, they will regard us as rebels to the Crown.'

A sift of vulnerability crossed Katherine's face. 'I hope you are wrong, Eva.' She shook her head decisively, as if dismissing the unwelcome thoughts. 'Now, can you manage, or shall I fetch someone?'

Eva pursed her lips together, staggering awkwardly to the steps. Snow whirled around her, driven into the sheltered bailey on a sharp little breeze. Bruin's cloak dragged on the cobbles, hampering her movement. She swung the wool from her shoulders, dumping the cloak into Katherine's arms. 'Here, have this; I can't move at all!' Placing her uninjured leg on the bottom step, gripping the rail, Eva pulled herself up with grim determination, slowly, one step at a time.

'Eva, this is impossible! This will take all night. Let me fetch someone to carry you.'

'No! You go ahead, Katherine. It won't take long,' she replied stubbornly. She could not allow herself to be carried into the great hall, in full view of everyone, in full view of Lord Bruin's mocking gaze! Sweat gathered along her hairline with the effort of hauling herself up. Katherine remained alongside her, matching Eva's pace until they finally climbed the one shallow step into the great hall.

The raftered chamber was full of people, eating, talking and laughing. Fresh straw covered the flagstone floor; dogs trotted up and down between the trestle tables, scavenging for scraps of food, the occasional bone flung in their direction. A huge fire roared beneath the thick limestone lintel of the fireplace, situated halfway along one white-plastered wall. Giant, ornate tapestries decorated the plain plaster, each one a riot of coloured thread, depicting scenes of hunting, or great battles. Katherine's family crest, the golden falcon of the Montagues, was everywhere: in the ornate bosses set into the curving ends of the rafters, above the windows, embroidered extravagantly across the door curtains, gold thread against blue velvet.

Katherine's hand on her elbow, Eva slumped on to the nearest bench, the peasants alongside nodding briefly at her without ceasing to shove food into their mouths. Their eyes paused momentarily on her wan face, gazes shifting away immediately. A nursemaid was of no interest; she was one of them, a servant of the Montagu family. Peering across the rows of bobbing heads, the faces flushed with mead, Eva checked the knights seated at the top table at the other end of the hall, making sure that he,

Bruin, was as far away as possible. Sitting next to the older knight, his gold-red hair shone out like a beacon. He was laughing at something, tipping his head back. The sinews in his neck wrapped powerfully around the shadowed hollow of his throat, up into his bristly beard. An extraordinary sensation unfurled in her belly, a flickering pang of longing. She couldn't explain it.

'You'd better go up there, Katherine. Leave me now, otherwise it will look strange that you fuss over me so much.'

'If you're sure…?' Katherine hesitated, bundling Bruin's cloak against her middle. 'I'll send someone to fetch Martha; she can help you to your chamber.'

'I'll eat first,' Eva said. 'Please, don't fuss. Just go. And try to find out why those men are here.'

Chapter Four

Gilbert watched Katherine's stately figure move through the great hall. Her progress across the uneven stone floor was slow, as she stopped to engage in conversation along the way: she chatted with the peasants who worked in the fields, the soldiers who kept the castle safe from intruders. She smiled and listened with attention, dropping her head considerately if an older person spoke too quietly, the gemstones on her long fingers flashing in the candlelight as she reached out to touch a shoulder or cup an elbow, before moving on.

'The perfect lady of the manor,' Gilbert said, chewing thoughtfully. 'What a shame I have to take her away from all this.' Reaching for the earthenware jug of red wine, he poured himself another goblet. A bead of liquid spilled from the mouth of the jug as he set the heavy vessel back down clumsily; it landed on the pristine white tablecloth, spreading out in a crimson circle.

'When are you going to tell her?' Bruin speared a slice of pork with his eating knife, depositing it on his pewter plate. The meat was well roasted, crispy. His belly growled; he was hungry after the full day of riding.

'Tonight. But after I've eaten. She'll take the news badly and I have no intention of missing such a fantastic spread of food!' Gilbert patted his stomach. 'But I'll give her two or three days to pack, which means I can avail myself of this wonderful hospitality for a little longer.'

'Two or three days?' Bruin grinned at him. 'Is the King not waiting for her?'

'Edward will meet me at my castle in a sennight.' Gilbert wiped his greasy mouth with a square linen napkin. 'That gives me enough time to travel there with her and the children. Goodness knows how many wagons she'll need. You know what these women are like.'

A wisp of memory snaked out, gripping Bruin by the throat; the sparkling granite in his eyes dulled instantly. No, he thought, no, he did not know what these women were like. He crushed the stem of his goblet, the angular pewter work pressing into the coarse pads of his fingers. He had pushed his own chance away and then it had been too late. His heart pleated in on itself, folding tighter and tighter. For the last year, by his own choice, his world had been reduced to a solely masculine one, harsh and brutal.

'But...of course...' Gilbert spluttered into his goblet, suddenly realising the insensitivity of his words, remembering, too late, what had happened to Bruin. 'I mean...' His kind-hearted voice trailed away, bereft of words.

'It's fine, Gilbert.' Bruin stared bleakly out across the great hall, seeing nothing. Sophie's death, her tragic, pointless death, was well known amongst the circles of nobility, both here in England and across the Channel. After what had happened, unable to deal with the mantle of guilt that hugged his shoulders, the judging glances, Bruin had abandoned King Edward and followed the exiled Lord Despenser into the relentless life of a mercenary, living on his wits, fighting and battling on the open sea, uncaring whether he lived or died. But when King Edward summoned Despenser back to England, he had persuaded Bruin to come back and fight for him again. And he had come, for he had realised that fighting was the same, anywhere. It gave his black soul a reason for existence, even if that existence was as barren and cold as his heart. There was no softness in his life, no feminine fripperies or tinkling laughter. Those things were not for him. Not now. Not ever.

'Did you hear me?' Gilbert's voice nudged Bruin from his thoughts.

'Sorry. What did you say?' He gulped his wine, dragging his mind away from his memories.

Gilbert smiled. 'I see you found the maidservant. What happened to her?'

Bruin forced his mind to concentrate on the present, staring at the food steaming slowly on his plate: roast pork, parsnips, a hunk of crusty bread. 'She was caught in an animal trap and hurt her leg.'

'Unlucky.' Gilbert drew his breath in, sharply. 'But why did she run when she saw us?'

Bruin shrugged his shoulders. 'She says she mistook me for someone else.' He remembered her beautiful eyes, fear dilating the pupils as he approached her. 'Someone who looked like me, apparently.'

'Who could possibly look like you?' Gilbert teased, thumping his pewter goblet down on the white damask tablecloth, chuckling at his own wit. Then his stubby eyelashes flew upwards as he looked at Bruin. 'Apart from—'

'My twin brother,' Bruin finished for him. He rubbed at the coppery bristles on his chin. 'I did think that. It's possible they have seen each other, I suppose,' he continued slowly, 'but I wouldn't have thought they moved in the same circles. And besides, I don't think Steffen even ventured into Wales; he always had his sights set firmly on the English castles. But it doesn't explain why she reacted as she did.'

Gilbert grinned. 'I hate to say it, but it sounds like you completely terrified her. And frankly, I'm not surprised. You're in full chainmail, you haven't shaved…'

Bruin held his hand up. 'Enough,' he said, laughing. 'I know—I'll make an effort for the morrow.' Disquiet threaded through him. He had no wish to go around scaring women; Gilbert's words hung on his shoulders like a chastisement. Had his time as a mercenary changed him that much? Fighting and plundering had given him a warped sense of satisfaction; at the time, he was out for revenge, but against whom? He didn't know. All he knew was that Sophie was dead and that it was his fault.

Gilbert raised his goblet in welcome as Katherine climbed up to the dais. Half-rising from his seat, he bowed his head respectfully as she approached the table. Bruin and the other knights followed suit. She slipped in beside Gilbert, handing Bruin's cloak across to him. 'Here, my lord. Thank you for bringing my nursemaid back to me.'

'It was nothing,' Bruin murmured. Eyes, as blue as a kingfisher's wing, leapt across his vision. His heart jumped at the memory. He scanned the hall, the throng of heads and bodies. He had watched her limp through the door, leaning heavily on her mistress, but then she had disappeared into the throng of people. He would have noticed if she had left; the only way out of this hall was by the main door, or through a curtained alcove set opposite to him, presumably leading to bedchambers above. Every woman in the place seemed to be wearing identical white wimples, drab-coloured dresses.

'Now, my lords,' Katherine said, as a servant pushed the heavy oak chair beneath her and she snapped a linen napkin across the red velvet of her gown. 'Mayhap you would like to tell me what you are doing in such a remote corner of Wales.'

A dryness scraped Eva's throat; her tongue, big and unwieldy, stuck to the roof of her mouth. She had been chewing a lump of bread for what seemed like hours, unwilling to swallow, worried that she might choke. Her eyelids drooped; all she wanted to do was climb the stairs to her bedchamber and fall into a deep, dreamless slumber. And forget.

'Hey, Eva!' A young lad to her right elbowed her sharply in the arm, laughing. 'You should go to bed! You're falling asleep at the table!'

She jolted her lolling head into an upright position, staring hazily at her plate of uneaten food. 'Help me, then,' she said to the boy. 'I've hurt my leg; I need to lean on you to reach the stairs.'

He jumped up with a puppy-like willingness, springing back over the low bench. Eva eased herself up carefully, grabbing at the boy's fragile-boned shoulder. She kept her actions deliberately slow, gradual, not wanting to draw any attention from the top table. The last thing she wanted was for Katherine to come rushing down to help. Or him.

Her movements seemed laboured, unwieldy. The long trestle tables, the flaring torches, swam before her vision. Objects seemed hazy, edges blurred and undefined. What was the matter with her? All she had to do was reach that curtain across the doorway. The boy moved forward and she hopped to keep up with him, pressing down on his shoulder, injured leg raised up behind her.

Pushing the curtain aside, she dismissed the boy. A thick rope curved up along the wall of the spiral stairs; that would serve her now. She would crawl on her hands and knees if need be. Her progress was painfully slow, but at last she reached the next floor, hopping along the corridor to the bedchamber she shared with Katherine and the children.

Clicking up the iron latch carefully, she pushed inside, lurching clumsily across the polished elm floorboards to her truckle bed, tucked neatly against Katherine's large four-poster bed. The chamber was dim, lit only by a single candle in an iron sconce, the flickering flame casting uneven shadows across the bumpy plaster. Over by a charcoal brazier, glowing with hot coals, Katherine's three children slept, their small bodies bundled beneath huge furs. Angling herself down awkwardly, Eva lowered herself on to her bed, checking the bandage around the wound. Much as she hated to admit it, her leg seemed much better after Bruin's deft handling. His cool, strong fingers grazing her skin.

There was a muted tap at the door and Martha came in, carrying a jug of hot water. 'The mistress bid me bring this to you.' Her eyes flicked to the lone guttering candle and she clicked her tongue in irritation. 'Ah, I should have brought you another light.' An earthenware bowl sat on an oak coffer; she poured the steaming water into it, glancing at Eva. 'What happened to you? They're saying in the hall that the big knight hunted you down.'

Her heart lurched at Martha's choice of words. The

girl was young, with a sense of the dramatic. Her plump hands dunked a linen washcloth into the bowl; it swirled around, absorbing the water. 'I hurt my leg, that's all,' Eva replied shortly, an involuntary shiver coursing her slim frame. Hunted down. It had certainly felt like that, to hear that man's shouts, the bulk of his body thrashing through the undergrowth, pursuing her. If it hadn't been for that wretched trap, she would have escaped him easily.

Martha's eyes rounded. 'They're saying he was an outlaw, at sea with the exiled Lord Despenser.'

Her heart jolted. Lord Despenser. A knight known for his cruelty, his barbaric methods. 'That doesn't surprise me.' And yet, this knowledge of his past did surprise her, for although the knight had treated her in a brusque, matter-of-fact manner, he had been considerate. Up to a point.

'Let me look.' Martha approached the bed. 'Lift your leg up on to the coverlet, so I can see it more clearly.' Eva raised her leg. Martha eyed the stocking bound around Eva's calf, the limp fringes of moss poking out. 'Did you do this?'

'He did,' she admitted reluctantly. A pair of silver eyes startled her vision; she hunched forward uncomfortably. How could that man, that stranger, affect her thus, when he wasn't even near her?

Martha untied the knot, unravelling the woollen stocking with care. Three wounds gouged Eva's pale flesh. 'Mother of God,' Martha said, 'it looks like you have been bitten by a dog. I bet it hurts.'

'Not as much as it did.' The bleeding had stopped, thank God.

'But the wounds look as if they might close up on their own? I'll clean it for you; put a new bandage on. I don't think you need stitches.'

'I agree. I have some salve that will—'

The door slammed back on its hinges. Katherine stood beneath the lintel, breathing heavily, her brown eyes furious. 'He's only gone and done it again!' she cried out, marching into the chamber, flinging herself across the bed. Her slender feet, encased in leather slippers, swung clear of the floor. The gold beading worked across each slipper toe gleamed in the shadowed light. 'That man—will be the bane—'

'Hush, Katherine.' Eva put a warning finger to her lips. 'Don't wake the children.' Reaching up, she touched her friend's sleeve. 'What is it? What's happened?'

Katherine's face crumpled, about to cry. Then she took an unsteady breath, drawing herself upright, smoothing one palm across the outspread velvet of her skirts, as if to calm herself. Spots of colour burned her cheeks. 'Those knights downstairs,' she enunciated slowly, 'those knights have been sent by my dear uncle, the King, to escort me back to Lord Gilbert's castle.'

'But why?' Eva whispered.

'I am to be married.' Katherine raised her head listlessly, her sable eyes enormous, worried. 'Like you said, Eva, I am a wealthy widow; how could I possibly be allowed to keep all that money to myself? Edward wants to reward those men who have shown the utmost loyalty to him—and I—I am that reward,' she finished bitterly. 'Damn him! I knew this life couldn't last! How I wish I were not related to him!'

'He can't do this, Katherine. He can't force you!'

But Katherine was nodding sadly. 'He can, Eva. He is the King and my guardian. If I disobey, he will take my children away and throw me into a nunnery. Or worse, he might even kill me. The way he has been behaving lately, the methods he has been using to punish people who go against him, I wouldn't be surprised. You of all people should understand this, Eva. How men can make your life a living hell!'

With a swift tilt of her head, Eva indicated Martha's silent figure, a warning to her friend to stay quiet. The servant hovered by the oak coffer, the washcloth hanging between her hands, beads of water dripping into the bowl. Martha's eyes were avid, alive with curiosity, drinking in her mistress's words like an elixir.

'Martha, go. Do not repeat a word of what you have just heard to anyone.' Katherine's eyes were hard, stern. 'Otherwise I will dismiss you instantly.' Collecting the bowl and jug from the coffer, the maid ambled from the chamber, slopping water as she walked, trailing glistening spots across the wooden floorboards.

Both women remained silent until the door closed. Eva gripped Katherine's hand. 'I can't let them take you like this. Not after everything you've done for me. There must be something we can do.'

Katherine's chin drooped to her chest, a forlorn, disheartened movement. As if she had given up already. Dry sobs racked her body; the pearls in her filigreed silver circlet trembled. 'And there's something else, Eva,' she said, her voice low.

'What is it?'

'That knight who brought you back—Lord Bruin.' Katherine lifted her head, defeat dulling her eyes. 'He's asking about the Lady of Striguil.'

Eva slept fitfully, tossing and turning beneath woven blankets. Katherine had taken a long time to settle; she had helped her undress, brushing her hair with an ivory comb, plaiting the shining strands into two long braids for the night. Now she could hear Katherine's regular breathing from the high bed beside her, her friend's slim frame relaxed into a deep sleep against the goose-down pillows.

She stared into the shadows of the chamber, eyes straining with tiredness. With the candle extinguished, only a faint light emerged from the charcoal brazier, one hot coal emitting a feeble glow. Her leg throbbed, but less so now. After Katherine had climbed into bed, she had cleaned the wounds herself, applying salve and re-bandaging her leg.

Katherine's words churned in her mind and refused to let her sleep, worrying at her like a dog with a bone. Why, oh, why would Count Bruin be asking about Striguil? And, more specifically, asking about her? Before Katherine had gone to sleep, she had taken pains to reassure Eva that Lord Bruin had discovered nothing about Eva's true identity. At the table, still reeling from the news of King Edward's plans for her, Katherine had informed Bruin that she had never heard of the name Striguil, let alone a lady who resided there and he had seemed to be satisfied with that.

The simple lace at the neck of Eva's nightgown tickled her chin and she pushed the fabric away, turning her head towards the window. Her braided hair rustled against the straw-filled pillow. Her mind scuttled fruitlessly down one path after another, chased by a pair of silvery eyes, a hard, determined mouth. Through the rippled glass, light from the rising moon tipped over the window ledge and stretched down into the chamber, pooling on the floorboards like milky liquid. How on earth could she and Katherine extricate themselves from this mess?

Beneath the window, a bundled lump on one of the

low pallets shifted around, then sat up, furs falling off young shoulders. Alice. Golden hair fell down in a tumbled mass over a white nightgown; Eva's heart panged with guilt. While she was downstairs, Martha had put the children to bed, obviously forgetting, or simply not bothering, to braid the girls' hair. The child made a small mewling sound, reaching out towards Eva.

She threw back her blankets, welcoming the distraction of the child from her own troubled thoughts. Tentatively, she placed her weight upon her injured leg, please to find it was less painful now. She moved with a hitching, but bearable gait across to Alice, kneeling down beside the pallet bed.

'What's the matter, darling?' she whispered, placing her hand on Alice's head. The child's golden hair, exactly like her mother's, was silky beneath her palm.

'I feel sick.'

Eva peered into Alice's face. The child's skin was pinched, drawn, but at the same time, flushed with a leaden colour. She placed her palm against Alice's forehead. Her skin was hot. Very hot.

'You lie down, Alice; I will fetch some water.' Straightening up, Eva removed the furs from around the child, leaving a single sheet. Alice had a fever, not unusual in someone of her age, but she needed to be cooler, before her temperature raged out of control. She would go down to the kitchens, fetch some water from the well. 'Don't wake your mother,' she whispered. 'I'll be back very soon.'

Seizing a blanket from her own bed, Eva flung it around her shoulders. She took the candle from the bedside table, touching the wick to the flame within the charcoal brazier, watching it flare. The chapel bell had tolled midnight as she had lain awake with her troubled thoughts; everyone would be tucked up in bed now, especially on such a chill, snowy night. Katherine would have given the guest chambers to the visiting knights, chambers on the other side of the bailey, a lengthy distance away. And thank goodness for that, she thought with relief, as she pulled the door open.

As she stepped forward, her toes collided with a large bulk lying across the threshold.

Chapter Five

Eva stopped. Fear scythed through her, her muscles tensing. She slithered her foot back along the floorboards in a gradual movement, eyes running over the shadowy outline below her. One of Gilbert's soldiers lay curled across the threshold, surcoat rumpled around brawny thighs, a creased leather belt around his hips. His broad sturdy back was curled towards her.

Breath snared in her chest. She hesitated, poised in the door frame. Frustration pulsed through her; Lord Gilbert obviously believed that Katherine and her children would try to slip away in the middle of the night. He was taking no chances, placing this guard across their door. The man was definitely asleep; she could hear his deep, steady breathing. Could she step over him without waking him up? She had no wish to be seen in her nightgown, hair uncovered and in braids, but Alice's temperature worried her. To dress appropriately would waste more time; she needed to fetch water for the child now.

Lifting her bare foot, she stepped over the sleeping body, careful, hesitant, her nightgown filming over the man's tunic, gauzy hem rustling across the expanse of red wool. With both feet on the other side of him, she paused, glancing down to check that he still slept.

Eyes of granite watched her, twinkling in the candle flame.

Lord Bruin, the knight who had brought her out from the forest. Eva recognised him instantly. 'Not you again!' she blurted out, exasperated. Anger pulsed through her, blazing, irresponsible; lifting her skirts, she kicked out towards his stomach with her good foot, a childish gesture, instinctive and wilful. She never reached her target. A lean hand snaked out, grabbing her ankle, powerful fingers grinding into her delicate bones.

'You've quite a temper on you, maid,' Bruin said softly, pressing her foot back to the ground, releasing her. He sat up, running his fingers through his vigorous bronze curls, hitching one shoulder against the door frame. He had shaved; the lines of his square-cut jaw were revealed, the raw slanting contours of his cheekbones. His sculptured features held a sensual beauty which drew her gaze; her heart jolted treacherously. Bruin folded thick, muscled arms across his chest. 'You would do well to keep it in check or it will bring you trouble.'

'It's the way you are treating us that's making me annoyed,' she said, bridling at his words. The memory of his thumb on her ankle taunted her: a heated imprint, tantalising. She clutched at the blanket across her chest, a self-conscious gesture, heart bumping erratically. Hot wax dripped from the candle across her knuckles. The pain bit into her skin, then subsided, the wax cooling swiftly. 'Can't you leave us alone for one moment?'

'And let you run away with your mistress? No doubt she has told you the news?' Again, that strange lilt to his voice that tickled along her veins, entrancing them. Excitement stranded through her; she stamped hard on the feeling with grim determination. Who was this stranger with dangerous, flinty eyes who had intruded so brutally on her quiet hidden life? A man who reminded her constantly of her previous tormentor. She wanted him out, away. Gone.

'Aye, she has.' Eva rolled her feet against the chill wooden floorboards; she had forgotten her slippers. A draught whistling along the corridor chased beneath the hem of her nightgown. Beneath the new bandage, her wound throbbed, pain radiating across her shin. 'But there was no need to post a guard across our door. She has no intention of going anywhere.'

'Why wouldn't she after what she's just been told?' Drawing one leg up, Bruin rested his hand on his knee. Moonlight streamed through the bedchamber door, the limpid rays highlighting his ridged and calloused palm, the corded sinew winding across the top of his fingers.

She glared at him archly. Was he trying to trap her into saying something she shouldn't? His words surprised her; it seemed inconceivable that a man such as this, a man that spoke of war and battles, should understand Katherine's predicament.

'Because it's impossible,' Eva replied, her voice subdued. Her velvet lashes fluttered down, masking her eyes. She shook her head, glossy plaits rippling like wide satin ribbons. 'Lady Katherine knows she has no choice; the King is her uncle and she must do his bidding.' She chanted out the words, the correct answer for the circumstances.

'But you would run in her position, wouldn't you? You would take that chance.'

Jerking her head up, Eva frowned. His speech sounded

too personal, as if he were prising apart the thoughts in her head. She wanted to rebuke him for his intimacy, but she held her tongue, repressing the words she wanted to say, scared of saying too much. She watched a gob of wax trail down the candle, the guttering flame. 'What does it matter what I think, what I would do? It's different for me, I'm only the servant.' She threw him a false, brittle smile.

'Are you?'

A hollowness besieged her heart, belly plummeting. During her whole time living with Katherine, not one person in the castle had guessed her true identity. She kept a close guard on herself, careful and measured at all times, moving through her days at the castle like a ghost, a wraith of her former self, unnoticed. A half-life. But this man, with his silver glance that seemed to see her thoughts, forced himself beneath her well-constructed defences, made her forget who she was supposed to be.

'Of course I am!' she ground out, snapping the blanket more securely around her shoulders. Fear skittered through her veins.

'Then where are you going?'

'Lady Katherine's youngest child has a fever; I must fetch water for her. Her temperature is too high. And you are holding me up.'

Bruin sprang to his feet, the swiftness of the movement shocking her, his shoulders filling the doorway. 'I'll come with you.' The black and red lions emblazoned upon his tunic gleamed out like a threat, intimidating.

'There's no need,' Eva responded haughtily, tipping her head back to stare into the angular lines of his face. Without a beard, he seemed more dangerous somehow, the honed angles of his face exposed. He towered over her in the moon-soaked shadows. Eva considered herself to be quite tall for a woman, but annoyingly, her head scarcely topped his shoulder. 'Besides, Lady Katherine and her children might slip away if you come with me, so you'd better stay here.'

Bruin heard the note of sarcasm in her voice, and chuckled. 'What, and have you slip away instead?'

Her eyes widened, long, curving lashes kicking up towards the perfect arch of her brows. 'I would never leave Lady Katherine! Why do you think I would do such a thing?'

Bruin inclined his head fractionally. His eyes sparkled over her like diamonds. 'Let's just say that I don't trust you.'

'But I'm nothing to you, or anyone else for that matter. I'm not important,' Eva protested, knuckles white and rigid around the candle. 'Why not go and pester the maidservants downstairs? Why do you persist in plaguing me?'

Because there is something about you that doesn't add up, Bruin thought. *You protest too much about your insignificance.* He remembered the way Katherine had supported her, helping Eva to her seat in the hall; how they had murmured to each other, heads together, not like servant and mistress, but more like friends. Everything about the chit made him suspect she was not a servant: her behaviour, her voice—the refined elegance of her beauty, the translucent quality of her skin. Her hair, like ebony silk, bound into two neat braids on either side of her head.

His chest seized. One of Eva's plaits fell forward, snaking across her shoulder, her chest, the curling end tied with a thin leather lace, swinging down across her nightgown. And through that fine, gauzy fabric, revealed by the treacherous moon spilling through a distant window, he could see the perfect delineation of her shapely legs, her thighs, before they disappeared up beneath the blanket. His stomach muscles tightened, taut, aware.

Jaw hardening, he whipped his gaze away, signalling to another knight further down the corridor. 'Hey, you there! Guard this door!' A huskiness curled through his voice, lowering the timbre.

'But I told you—' Eva began to speak. He hadn't answered her question.

'Come on.' Bruin ignored her, plucking the candle from her fingers. He clasped her elbow to guide her along the corridor.

At his commanding touch, Eva dragged her arm down to detach herself from his grip, a deliberate action, forceful. 'No, I can walk unaided, thank you.' The pulse at her throat beat in rapid momentum, her pale skin sheened in moonlight.

'Can you? You had to ask that boy for help when you left the great hall.' Bruin dug his thumb into his sword belt, eyeing her sceptically. The gemstones in his sword hilt winked and glittered, vaguely menacing.

So he had watched her leave then. Those fearsome eyes had followed her, observing her every move while she, unaware of his scrutiny, had stumbled awkwardly towards the stairs. The thought filled her with dismay, worry threading her veins. She must be more careful if this man watched her so closely.

'The wound's not deep; it feels much better now,' she answered him tersely. 'It was good of you to tend to it.' But she looked away from him as she said the words and started walking off down the corridor, unable to meet his iron-hard gaze.

Bruin laughed, following her limping gait, the awkward lift of her hip as she countered the soreness in her leg. 'Are you thanking me?' Her swinging plaits tormented him; he wanted to grab them, haul her back against his body, savour those pliant curves against his own. The urge swept through him, wild and traitorous. What would it be like, to pull that lithe, slim body against his? To wrap his limbs around her, kiss her? But he knew. His groin pulsed treacherously, tightening, his breath punching out in surprise. Her beauty drew him, entranced him, chipping away at his self-control, his sadness—like sunlight burning through fog, a magical heat against the frozen lump of his heart.

Acknowledging his question with the briefest of nods, Eva continued to walk forward, eyes fixed on the end of the corridor, her nose stuck in the air. Annoyed at her impudence, Bruin shot his hand out, closing around her shoulder to halt her, spinning her around. She gasped at the swift, unexpected movement. The blanket gathered in gentle folds around her neck, emphasising her sweet face, the plushness of her mouth. Above the point where her fingers gripped the blanket, the white-lace edging on her nightgown peeked out, the neckline dipping down to reveal the top swell of one breast. For one insane moment, he wanted to touch his fingertip against the delicate hollow of her throat, to feel the satiny push of her breast against his palm.

Eva glared at him, then saw the latent heat gathered in his eyes, the flash of desire, of intent. Her stomach muscles puddled to a giddy whirlpool, looping dangerously. She had never lain with a man, yet she recognised the savage promise in his eyes, those dark sparkling orbs that whispered of places unexplored. Places she had never been. Every nerve in her body thrummed, strung with anticipation, an expectancy of—of what?

Bruin's head dipped fractionally, the etched curve of his mouth looming down to hers. The air between them thickened suddenly, solidifying, adopting a soporific, dreamlike quality. Blood hammered in her veins. The rope of her resistance, once tightly bound, now creaked and strained. She was unable to move, feet bolted to the floor, captured by his sparkling gaze.

Then, as if from a distance far away, a child cried, a frantic series of sobs, high-pitched, frightened.

Eva cursed, shoving petulantly at his chest. What in God's name had she been thinking? Loitering beside him, beside this—this oaf, mesmerised like some foolish dimwit! 'Can't you hear?' she hissed at him. 'Alice needs me! Stop holding me up like this! What are you doing?'

What was he doing? A fiery insanity had gripped him, turning his loins to pulp. He had been about to kiss her, to run his mouth across those plush, rosebud lips. To delight in the velvety patina of her skin. This wasn't him; he didn't behave like this. Why, he hadn't even touched Sophie during their brief betrothal—if he had, things might have turned out so differently. Bruin's heart turned over at the memory, a tide of cloying sadness flooding through him. Disgusted with himself, he released Eva's shoulder. His fingers shook. With a curt nod he indicated that she should go ahead, his arm dropping to his side.

The kitchens were warm, the fire in the cooking range smouldering gently, banked up for the night with great squares of peat. Flickers of glowing light shone out through the cracks in the turf, reflecting against the pots and pans hung by their handles inside the huge fireplace. An oak table, the boards well-scrubbed to a bleached lightness, dominated the room, earthenware and pewter dishes stacked upon it in piles, ready for the morning. Next to them, Bruin secured the candle in a pool of wax. The flame cast his substantial figure into a huge black shadow on the wall behind.

The well was in the corner: a circular hole covered with a wooden lid, a rope handle in its centre. A wooden pulley sat alongside, secured to the floor, used to pull the bucket up. Favouring her injured leg, Eva walked over to it, bending down to drag the lid to one side. The stone flagstones froze the soles of her feet, numbing the skin. Annoyance shimmered through her at Bruin's continued presence, at her own foolish behaviour towards him. As if a man should affect her thus! She was tired, that was all, tired and upset by what was happening to Katherine, and he wasn't helping matters by following her about. But she must behave in a manner appropriate to a servant; much as she disliked it, she must follow his orders. Taking a deep breath, Eva straightened to work the handle on the pulley that would lower the leather bucket down to the water level, a black shining disc far below. She jumped as Bruin moved beside her, his arm jostling her shoulder.

'Here, let me,' he said, pushing her away from the wooden handle and lowering the bucket rapidly. The bucket hit the water with a violent splash.

Eva moved back, folding her arms tightly across her bosom, her whole manner bristling and defensive. She bit her lip, holding back the words she had been about to say. That she could have done it; that, as the servant, she *should* have done it.

He turned his head, as if he read her mind. 'I know you could have done this. But as I am here, you may as well let me help you.'

Let me help you. His words flowed around her like a balm, as if he'd wrapped her flesh in a coat of downy feathers. When was the last time anyone had said something like that to her? Since the deaths of her father and brother, she had been alone, used to fighting her own battles, used to standing on her own two feet. Her mother had died when she was a small child, drowned on the return from the island shrine of St Agnes. Eva scarcely remembered her. The oddness of the situation struck her: to have someone step in and offer to perform a task for her. She just wished it wasn't him, this man, with his striking hair of reddish-gold, who towered over her and drove her knees to pulp.

'When do you and Lord Gilbert plan to leave?' she asked.

Bruin turned the handle. The rope coiled slowly, creaking, wrapping around the horizontal spindle set across the well. The full bucket, water slopping down its sides, emerged from the dark hole, moving slowly to the top. 'Gilbert plans to leave in a couple of days. That should give you and your mistress time to pack. But I am travelling on further, into Wales.' At the back of his neck, his chainmail hood lay in rippling, metallic gathers against his surcoat.

'Why, where are you going?' she blurted out, then ducked her head quickly, staring at the floor. Curse her own outspokenness!

Bruin laughed. 'Nosy little thing, aren't you?' Unhooking the bucket, he hefted it into his right hand. 'I'm looking for someone. Did Lady Katherine not mention the name to you?'

Eva shook her head, her heart pounding. She knew what he was about to say, to ask. The less interested she appeared in the whole matter, the better.

'The Lady of Striguil. Do you know her?' His eyes swept over her, sparkling, intense.

Eva stared at the water trickling down the bucket sides, strings of bright water, like silver thread. His words reverberated through her consciousness: her real name, tangled in his lilting accent. Air scoured her lungs; she willed herself to keep her features schooled, neutral. She must not give herself away. Perspiration gathered in her armpits. 'No, I'm sorry.' Her voice was calm, steady. 'Why are you looking for her?'

'My brother said he thought she lived around here—this area, anyway.' Bruin's wide, generous mouth was set in a straight, grim line. 'He wants to see her before...' he stopped for a moment '...before he dies.'

His brother? For a moment her mind was numb; then her thoughts skittered, shifted, scampering to slot the blocks of information into place. Bruin's bright hair, honed features, those granite eyes. Oh, God, no. No! Please don't let it be... 'Who—who is your brother?' The question staggered out of her.

'Lord Steffen. Steffen of Wyncheate. He has a castle there and several holdings in the area. Have you heard of him?'

Her knees buckled in terror and she lunged for the table, masking her stumble. Seizing a couple of linen cloths to take up to the chamber, she held them against her belly like a shield. No wonder she had mistaken this man for her persecutor; their looks were similar because they were related: they were brothers! But even as her legs failed her, her heart flared with treacherous hope, fledgling, unsteady. If Bruin's brother was the man who had terrified her days and nights, then it sounded as if he was about to leave this earth. About to die. And if he died, then, she would be free of him for ever.

'No.' Eva twisted anxiously at the bundle of clothes, nerves shredding. 'No.' Her response was monotone. The effort of keeping her voice steady made her head throb.

'I could have sworn you did,' Bruin said, swinging the bucket as if it were a bag of feathers as he walked towards her. His silver eyes gleamed like knife blades. 'Back in the forest, you were frightened of me. You said that I reminded you of someone else and I think that someone else was my brother. You see, we do look very alike. Steffen is my twin.'

'I had no idea who you were!' she flashed back at him immediately, instinct guiding her words. 'A knight armed to the teeth, dressed in chainmail, chasing me up the hill! I thought you were going to kill me!'

'But you thought I looked familiar,' he repeated, drawing his brindled brows together.

Why did he not leave it alone? He was like a dog with a bone, nipping and worrying at the few words that she had uttered. Why had she even offered him an explanation for her fear? She should have kept her mouth firmly shut. 'And I told you, I was mistaken,' Eva replied coldly.

Ripping the candle from its bed of cool wax, she hobbled towards the archway leading to the dank shadows of the stairs. Bruin caught her elbow, holding her back. His mouth dropped to her ear, brushing the lobe with a gust of air. 'And I'm telling you, Eva, that I don't believe you,' he said. 'I think you have seen my brother before.'

'No.' In the wavering candlelight, her features were white, stricken.

He let her go and she staggered up the steps back to Katherine's chamber, his words skittering about her brain like a flock of startled crows. She climbed too quickly; the wound on her shin throbbed and pounded. Bruin was behind her, pursuing her, a wolf at her heels, hefting the bucket against his chest. He could not find out her real identity. He would haul her straight back to his dying brother and there was no way in the world she wanted to face him again. Lord Steffen. The Devil incarnate. That man would take his revenge on her even as he was drawing his last breath on earth. God in Heaven, it didn't bear thinking about.

If only she could manage not to give herself away for a couple more days, then Bruin would leave this castle and travel on further into Wales, and she would accompany Katherine and the children to Lord Gilbert's castle. And then Lord Steffen would die and she would be able to live a normal life once more.

Chapter Six

Alice's fever was worse. The small child thrashed beneath the linen sheet, moaning incoherently. Her delicate face was bright red, sheened with sweat. When her eyes opened for a moment, they were wild, unfocused. Concerned, Eva dropped to her knees beside the low pallet bed, ripping the sheet up and away from the child's body. The material was soaked with sweat. Thinking only of the child, she let go of the blanket around her shoulders and it fell down to the floor, pleating about her slim hips.

'I need to cool her down, quickly,' Eva muttered, almost to herself. All worries about Bruin discovering her identity flew away as she observed the plight of the child. She plunged the flannel into the bucket of water that Bruin had placed on the floor beside her. Wringing it out, she bent forward and placed it across Alice's forehead, then her cheeks. The generous, square-cut sleeves of her nightgown hung down, the light from the charcoal brazier shining through the flimsy fabric. The shadowy outline of her slim arms was revealed. She pushed back her sleeves, annoyed, as they continually fell forward about her wrists, hampering her movements, small white teeth worrying at her bottom lip.

'That's not going to help,' Bruin said. His low voice shocked her, piercing through the mantle of her anxiety. Standing behind her, sentinel-like, he crossed his arms over his chest.

'You should go,' Eva said, without looking at him. She pressed the flannel to Alice's neck, to the pulse beating frantically in the vulnerable hollow of the child's throat. 'You shouldn't be in this chamber. It's not seemly: Lady Katherine sleeps just over there.' She jerked her head in the direction of the four-poster bed, the quilted curtains drawn tightly around.

Bruin ignored her. 'A wet flannel will not bring down the girl's fever,' he said bluntly. 'It's raging too high.'

Eva pushed the linen square back into the bucket, her mouth tightening to a stubborn line. 'I've treated fevers this way before,' she replied testily, flicking an irritable glance in his direction. 'What would you know, anyway?'

'Quite a lot, as it happens,' Bruin replied evenly. 'Soldiers fall ill in battle all the time and not only from their wounds. We don't have the luxury of a physician; we rely on each other's skills to treat each other.'

'What would you do, then?' she asked grudgingly, sitting back on her heels with the air of defeat, the flannel hooked between her slender fingers, dampening her nightgown.

'The night air will help,' he said. 'I would carry her outside.'

'But that's madness; it's freezing out there!'

'Precisely. The very thing to bring down her temperature. If you don't do something soon, she will start losing consciousness and then—'

'I do know that!' Eva blasted back at him, worry tearing her voice. Frustrated, she threw the flannel into the bucket, watching the cloth swirl and sink. Her eyes burned with exhaustion; she was struggling to think logically. She hated the fact that this man, this foreigner with his silver-grey eyes, seemed to be dealing far more competently with this situation than she. She hated to ask for his help. But with the child's life at stake? 'Very well, then.' Eva sighed in defeat. 'Do it.'

Bruin moved down beside her, ladling his hands gently beneath the child, lifting her high in his brawny arms. Eva caught the heady scent of him as his arm brushed hers: the woodsmoke imbued in the weft of his surcoat; the fresh, invigorating smell of his skin. Alice moaned, her head lolling against the big man's shoulder. Sweeping up the fallen blanket, her makeshift cloak, Eva moved ahead of him, lifting the iron latch on the door, opening it with a sharp click. Her bare toes peeked out from the swinging hem of her nightgown.

He noticed. 'Eva, put something on your feet. You'll freeze out there.'

He spoke her Christian name with a sensual ease, implying a familiarity that did not exist. Was it the first time he had spoken her name? As she turned back into the chamber, her cheeks burned, and she placed her palms to her face, trying to cool her skin. Her calf-length leather boots lay discarded by her pallet bed and she shoved her feet into them. The coarse leather scraped her heels. Bruin spoke to the guard outside Katherine's door and the man moved aside to allow Eva into the corridor. Skirting the soldier, Eva forced her injured leg to stride at a normal pace and followed Bruin and the child down through the great hall. The soldier at the main door removed a lit torch from an iron bracket and handed it to her. Bruin was already outside.

Snow filled the inner bailey, whirling, spinning down in chaotic spirals. A dense, oppressive cloud had obscured the silvery light of the moon, weighing down like a sturdy lid on the courtyard, the shadowy outlines of the gatehouse, the crenellated ramparts. Fat, feathery snowflakes landed on the cobbles, settling fast, veiling the ground in downy white. They touched Eva's face, glancing against her swinging braids, leather laces securing the curling ends, tumbling down the threadbare fabric of her nightgown. The wisps tickled her skin like the flick of a moth's wing as she moved beneath the arch of the main door, holding the torch high.

Bruin stopped at the top of the steps and turned towards her; the torch flame flickered across his jaw, highlighting its tough sleekness, the taut pull of flesh across his cheekbone. 'There's no need to go any further,' he announced. Caught in his brawny arms, Alice appeared so fragile, so vulnerable, her thin legs poking out like pale sticks from her nightgown, narrow feet dangling. Bruin glanced down at the child's face, lifting one large hand to brush the snow away from the child's hair, her closed eyes.

'Oh!' Eva blurted out, then clapped a hand across her mouth, trying to stifle the sound. An arc of inexplicable longing pulsed through her, her eyes widening in surprise at Bruin's gentleness towards Alice, that brief, careful touch against her forehead, the considerate way he cradled her in his arms. The gesture seemed incongruous, contradictory somehow, when contrasted against his stern, battle-ready appearance: the shining chainmail, the embroidered coat of arms glinting on his surcoat, the jewelled sword swinging at his hip.

He tilted his head to one side, his gaze questioning. 'What is it?'

'No, no it's nothing,' she responded awkwardly. How could she tell him that the way he held the child made her crave his touch, stirring a rickety newborn need within her belly, a yearning for those strong tanned fingers to brush against her own skin, to drift against her hair? How could she explain such an odd notion? There was a time before her captivity, a time when her life was different, when she might have welcomed such feelings, but now? Now she shunned male attention to the point of rudeness. She shook her head quickly, quelling her scandalous thoughts. Her mind played tricks on her; she was exhausted and worried, that was all.

'It's obviously something,' he said. 'Tell me. I can take it, good or bad.'

'The way you're holding Alice,' she replied hesitantly, making up the words that would deflect him from her true feelings, from asking any more questions. 'You obviously have children of your own.'

His chin jolted upwards as if she had hit him, eyes deepening with a sudden, powerful emotion, blank holes of utter anguish. He gripped the child, jaw flexing taut and rigid. Despair, raw, undiluted, crossed his features, swiftly masked.

What had she said?

'I do not.' He bit the words out, his tone harsh and stinging. The torch flickered, spat, a shoal of fine sparks raining down to the snow-covered planks.

'I'm sorry,' Eva whispered, focusing on the gold whip stitches forming one of the lions on his tunic. 'I had no intention of prying.' The fine embroidery wobbled before her eyes. His reaction had been unnerving, frightening even, the change in his behaviour so swift and devastating. What had happened to him to cause such a response? Had he lost a child, was that it? She placed her hand against Alice's silky forehead, eager for distraction. Already the child seemed quieter, more settled; her skin was a better colour now; the bluish tinge was gradually disappearing from around her mouth.

Bruin's chest sagged, a long slow breath leaving his lungs. As Eva's neat head bowed over the child, he shut his eyes momentarily, trying to gain some control over his rattled thoughts. They spilled through his mind like a thick, coruscating liquid, whipping up the fires of guilt, dragging him down. Why could he not forget? The image of his fiancée, still slim in those first few weeks of pregnancy, her beautiful face screwed up in anger at their last terrible argument, another man's child in her belly. Why could he not have forgiven her? Why was he unable to suppress his anger and accept her baby as his own? If he had, then Sophie might still be alive.

He sighed, shifting Alice's slight weight in his arms. All this domestic idleness was making him think too much. He needed to take off again, to throw himself back into the civil war between the King and his rebel barons. To ride with the Devil at his heels, to wield a sword and hurl his mace, to fight until exhaustion dragged him under to a heavy dreamless sleep; that was the life he had known since Sophie's death. Fight, eat, sleep—it was what he needed now. His brother's illness and unexpected request had pulled him away from that life; the sooner he returned to it, the better.

'She is cooler,' Eva said, tipping her face up to his, her

expression bright and hopeful, eager for him to say something, to break this interminable silence. Her previous question lingered between them, colouring the air. She hitched one shoulder awkwardly beneath his penetrating stare, unwilling to say anything further, or provoke him.

His grey eyes sought hers and held them, drawing unexpected strength from the midnight-blue depths. He saw the concern cross her eyes, the worry that she had, once again, overstepped the mark with her earlier words. But it was not the maid's fault; she had spoken in innocence, unaware of the impact her words would have. He had reacted badly.

'It's me who should be sorry,' Bruin found himself saying. 'Your words took me by surprise, that's all.'

She nodded briskly with relief, thankful for his reply, even if he had failed to explain his reaction. It was enough. Even though she barely knew him, even though his brother was the man she feared most in the world, somehow it mattered to her that she had not offended him. The circle of the torchlight gathered the night around them. Her heart thumped fractiously, the beat unsteady. Instinctively she stepped back, her heel bumping against the stone step across the doorway. 'Shall we go in?'

'Yes.' Bruin inclined his head, the snowflakes melting rapidly in his brindled hair, darkening the locks to a deep bronze colour. The delicate flakes landed on the sculptured curve of his cheek, the generous outline of his mouth. A heady fluidity, intoxicating, snared her body, holding her in thrall, a puppet beneath his silvery perusal. She frowned, a small crease appearing between the sable arches of her eyebrows, pleating her fine skin.

Pivoting slowly on her heel, she took a couple of halting steps to reach the main door, lifting the torch high.

Sparks showered over the glossy ebony of her braids, tumbling across her blanket-covered shoulders. Carrying his light burden, Bruin followed her, his long, decisive stride bumping into Eva's back as she suddenly stopped, fumbling to turn the unwieldy door handle.

'Oh, Lord! This stupid door!' she cursed, rattling the circular handle irritably, the wrought iron chill against her fingers. Bracing the child with one arm, Bruin reached around Eva and turned the handle with a swift, easy click.

'There,' he said, as the door swung inwards, squeaking on rusty hinges. Eva marched quickly inside and he smiled suddenly, amused by her stubborn, obtuse reaction to the fact that he had helped her, once again. She obviously couldn't stand the sight of him. Watching her, being with her, his guilt drained away, easing the vice-like grip around his heart. He made to follow her, then realised his boot was planted heavily on her trailing hem. Eva had no idea, continuing to move forward. The neck of her nightgown pulled downwards, dragged by his boot.

'Oh!' Eva gasped, feeling the fabric pull away from her shoulder. The neckline was loosely gathered, threaded through with a ribbon, which, as usual, she had neglected to tie. Clutching frantically at the front of her gown, she prayed the thin material wouldn't rip. The blanket slipped to the floor. 'Bruin, move your boot, now!' she cried out. 'Set me free!'

The skin on her shoulder was like silk, a luminous marble, polished, glimmering. Bruin swallowed, his mouth dry, scratchy. What would happen if the material dipped even lower, fell to her waist even? In his mind's eye, he traced the ridged delicacy of her spine, the curved indent of her waist, her softly flaring hips—then his eyes sharpened, iridescent points of light. Across the flat blade of her shoulder was a blotchy mark. He wondered if it were a bruise—had she hurt herself more than he had thought in the forest? Leaning closer, he realised it was a birthmark, a raised red blotch staining her satiny skin. It looked like a butterfly.

A butterfly.

His mind scrabbled for meaning; Steffen's words staggered through his memory. The mark of a butterfly. He touched the reddened skin, tracing an outline. Eva sucked in her breath, outraged by his impropriety. 'What is this?' he demanded. His calloused pad burned her flesh. A curtness entered his voice, like the edge of a scythe biting into her.

What was he talking about? Eva was hunched forward, bending at the waist, trying to pull the flimsy gown up to cover her naked shoulder. She almost threw the torch at the lone knight standing respectfully in the hallway. He took the light, returning it to the iron holder, then stepped back into the shadows.

'Bruin—!' she called out, exasperated, ignoring his question. 'Take your foot off, please!' Snowflakes blew in through the open door, pinpricks of ice against her skin. She wriggled beneath his heated touch, trying to dislodge him. Blood pumped erratically through her veins, flustering her. Embarrassment hazing her mind, she twisted around, intending to wrench the gown from beneath his foot. But he was too heavy, immovable, and the fabric was too flimsy to risk such a manoeuvre. Exasperated, she felt her elbow bump against poor Alice, a sleeping barrier between them. Chagrin flooded through her as she crossed her arms over her bosom, defensive beneath his sparkling gaze. 'Bruin, we must take Alice—'

'What is it?' he demanded. The etched curve of his mouth was inches from her own, his breath sifting across her skin.

Her head knocked back; she forced herself to concentrate on his words. His glossy eyelashes were long and black, a surprising contrast to his bronze-coloured hair. Silver streaks striated the grey of his eyes, radiating out from peat-black irises. He must be asking about her birthmark, although she couldn't think why.

'It's only a birthmark,' she replied grumpily, deliberating keeping her tone neutral, uninterested. 'Now, will you let me cover myself?'

'Who are you?'

The brutal swiftness of his question shocked her, as if he had brought his fist against her ear. 'Why, the same person as I was a moment ago,' she replied carefully. What had happened? His eyes, orbs of lustrous glass, were pinned on her face, scrutinising every nuance of her expression, watching her reactions closely. He was waiting for her to slip up, to say the wrong thing.

And in that moment, she knew it was over.

Her carefully constructed life, with all its safeguards and secrecy, the hiding and disguise, all had come to naught. The silent prayers that she sent heavenwards daily, to guard and protect her from the vengeful wrath of this man's brother, lifted away from her like scorched leaves dancing above a fire, curling rapidly, shrivelling away to a black cinderless nothing.

'You know,' Eva said. Her voice was dull, resigned. 'You know who I am.' There was no query in her tone; she was simply stating a fact. There was no point in pretending any more.

Bruin nodded, his mouth set in a fixed grim line. He

should have been triumphant. How quickly he had managed to find the woman his brother was desperate to see again. He could deliver her back to Deorham, where his brother lay on his deathbed in a borrowed castle, and be on his way, back to Edward and his battles. But, as he watched the brightness leach from her eyes, like a veil descending to shadow her whole demeanour, he wanted with every fibre of his being for it not to be true. 'Aye,' he said, eventually. 'You are the Lady of Striguil.'

She wanted to weep.

Alice barely opened her eyes as Bruin laid her back down on the crumpled sheets of her pallet bed. Kneeling on the floor, Eva pulled a sheet and a single blanket over the child, tucking them in around her. The fever had abated; Alice's skin was cool and dry. Eva patted and fussed with the top of the blanket, unwilling to rise and face Bruin. Panic grew steadily in her throat, a hard, unwieldy lump; her hands shook as she smoothed the creases from Alice's covers.

Bruin leaned down and cupped her elbow, lifting her to her feet. 'The child is settled now, Eva,' he said firmly. 'Or should I say my lady? I need to talk to you.'

Eva's mind reeled with exhaustion. 'Now?' she asked, a forlorn note curling her voice. 'Can it not wait till morning, at least? I need to sleep, just for a little while.'

Bruin thought of Steffen, stricken with illness, his urgent need to beg this woman's forgiveness before he died. A wave of disquiet passed through him. He knew what his brother was capable of; why, he had been the very first witness to his brother's volatile behaviour. Eva was plainly terrified of him. Unanswered questions clamoured in his brain, rolling in swiftly. How had Steffen known about the birthmark on her shoulder? A birthmark on her naked skin. Had he lain with Eva? His stomach hollowed out. Resentment flashed through him, vicious and brutal, a savage coil of inexplicable jealousy.

His eyes moved across Eva's pearly skin, the smooth curve of her cheek, her sweet, tip-tilted nose. Her slender frame drooped, wilting with fatigue. Shadows hollowed out beneath her shimmering blue eyes, thumbprints of violet. Shame flooded over him. His questions could wait. He was behaving like an ogre, as if he were still at sea, looting ships full of precious cargo, slashing his sword at anyone who stood in his way. Her unblemished femininity, her tough vulnerability, had crept beneath his mantle of self-contempt, prising the thick crust upwards. 'You do need to sleep,' Bruin agreed. 'We will talk on the morrow. I will be outside the door if you need me.'

So I can't escape, Eva thought, as the door clicked shut behind him and she fell on to the wobbly, creaking bed. She was so tired, she didn't really care. Her body and mind were numb, devoid of fear, devoid of logic. Tomorrow her brain would be clearer and she would think of a way out of this mess. There was no way Bruin was going to take her back to see Lord Steffen. And that was that.

Chapter Seven

'Katherine?' Eva whispered, parting the quilted curtains around the four-poster bed. She had waited long enough to wake her friend. Lying in her truckle bed, anxiety churning in her mind, she had watched the night recede and the glazed windows flood with pale silver, the colour sliding to iridescent gold as the winter sun rose slowly. The scent of lavender, delicious, fragrant, filled her nostrils as she planted her knee on the fur coverlet and crawled over to the sleeping form of her friend. Katherine lay on her side, her blonde head supported by two downy pillows, the blanket edge pulled up to her chin. Her braided hair trailed across the covers, gilt ropes glinting in the shadows.

'You need to wake up,' Eva whispered urgently.

Katherine's eyes opened. 'What is it?' Her voice was halting, croaky with sleep. Hitching up against the pillows, she stared at Eva, her expression befuddled. A ray of sunlight streaked through the opening in the curtains, striking Katherine's pale skin, making her squint. 'Is it the children?'

'No—well, Alice had a fever in the night, but she's

much better now.' Eva had checked on the child before waking Katherine. Alice's skin had been cool; she was sleeping calmly.

'Why did you not wake me?' Katherine lifted herself higher against the pillows. 'I would have tended to her.'

'She's fine.' Eva pursed her lips. 'I—we—managed to bring the fever down. She seems a lot better this morning. A few sniffles, that's all.'

'We?' Katherine tilted her head, curious. 'Who helped you?'

'Oh, God.' Eva's heart plummeted with the full impact of what she was about to say. She shook her head miserably. 'Something awful has happened. Lord Bruin helped me with Alice. When I went to fetch water for Alice, he was lying across the door, making sure that we wouldn't steal away in the night!' Her voice rose, chest heaving with half-sobs. 'I couldn't shake him off, couldn't get rid of him! He followed me everywhere. And then—then he saw the birthmark on my shoulder—' Pressing flat palms to her eyes, Eva willed herself to slow her breathing, to stem the rising tide of panic in her chest. 'He knows who I am.' She stared bleakly at Katherine. 'He came with the other knights, but not to fetch you. It was me he was searching for all along—he was sent by Lord Steffen. His brother.'

'Sweet Jesu,' Katherine cursed. 'He must have told Lord Bruin about how distinctive the mark is. How on earth did Lord Bruin manage to see it?'

Eva took a deep, unsteady breath. 'The back of my nightgown slipped down. When he was carrying Alice back inside.'

'You were outside with him? In your nightgown? Eva, have you taken leave of your senses?'

Eva rubbed her eyes viciously, driving away the tears. Katherine's criticism was justified; her behaviour had been inappropriate. 'Alice's fever was so high, I was worried for her. All I wanted to do was cool her down, in the fastest way possible. I know I shouldn't have gone with him, but I had to stay with Alice. If she had awoken and seen him…' A pair of silver eyes flashed across her vision; her belly dipped, then hollowed curiously, but not with fear.

'I shouldn't have said anything,' Katherine interrupted. 'You did the best thing for my child and for that I thank you. The bad news is that Lord Bruin knows who you are. Has he any idea what his brother did to you?'

Eva lifted her shoulders, a resigned shrug. 'I have no idea. I don't know how close they are. But he probably does, otherwise why else would he do his brother's bidding? Lord Steffen is ill, apparently, and wants to beg my forgiveness before he leaves this earth. I don't believe a word of it. I think it's a trick. He wants me back so he can find out the full extent of the fortune I hid from him. I still have the ruby of Striguil. And that's what he wants.'

'You cannot go back to that man.' Katherine released a long, slow gust of air, her manner decisive. She plucked at a speck of lint on the fur cover. 'You need to escape from here, before Lord Bruin takes you away. Take yourself up into the moorland and the mountains. Vanish.'

'It will be difficult to escape.' Eva jerked her head towards the door. 'He's out there now.'

Katherine smiled slowly, her brown eyes lighting with optimism. 'There is always a way, Eva. Remember, I know this castle like my own children's faces. I will think of something. We can surely stall him for a little while.'

The strings of panic braced around her chest eased

slightly. 'If I have to run away, it means I cannot come with you and the children to Lord Gilbert's castle.'

'Come to us later, Eva. When that awful man is dead and you are safe. We will be all right, believe me. Goodness knows what the King has in store for me, probably some crusty old knight who can't hear properly.' Eva grimaced. Katherine was deliberately keeping her tone jaunty, light-hearted, despite being ordered around by her powerful relatives. Her situation was as desperate as Eva's.

'Come on, we need to dress and go down to the great hall to break our fast.' Through the covers, Katherine nudged Eva with her knee. 'And there's no point in you wearing those awful rags any more. Your identity has been discovered. You are the Lady of Striguil and must dress as such. You can wear one of my gowns.'

'Well, well, who would have thought it?' Gilbert said slowly, as he reached out for a crusty bread roll. 'The little nursemaid turns out to be a noble lady. I would never have guessed.' He chewed thoughtfully, nodding his thanks to a manservant who was pouring ale into his empty goblet. He licked his lips greedily as the golden liquid rose to the brim. 'Are you completely sure she is the woman your brother is looking for?'

'I am,' Bruin replied, splaying his tanned fingers across the pristine white tablecloth. He had left one of the other knights at Lady Katherine's door while he had gone back to the guest chamber to wash and then down to the great hall to eat. He still wore his chainmail beneath his surcoat and the iron rivets chafed uncomfortably against his neck. In a moment he would run upstairs and bang on the door of the ladies' chamber, wake them up if need be. He wanted to travel back to Deorham as soon as possible. As soon as Eva was dressed and had broken her fast.

And yet an inexplicable reluctance continued to bother him at the thought of taking her back to Steffen, of forcing her to face up to a man of whom she was quite clearly terrified. He ran his fingers up and down the angular stem of his goblet. Questions, doubts, roamed in his head. Why was the chit in this castle, hiding under the wing of Lady Katherine, when she was a rich noblewoman in her own right? And, more importantly, why did he even care? She was nothing to him; he had known her for one day and yet he had known his brother all his life. Despite their fractious relationship, he felt he owed Steffen his last dying wish. All he had to do was escort her there and then he would be on his way.

'God in Heaven!' Gilbert barked out, spluttering crumbs of bread across the table. 'Who is that?'

At the opposite end of the hall, the quilted curtains had parted. At this early hour, only a few people ate at the trestle tables below the dais. Their breath pumped out, white mist in the chill air, as they cleared their plates, chatting idly to each other. The fire in the enormous hearth was newly lit, the flames spitting reluctantly against the chunks of damp wood, doing little to heat the huge cavernous space. Around the fireplace, the air was thick with acrid smoke.

Lady Katherine moved out from the shadows of the stairwell, her step graceful, elegant. Her tall slim frame seemed to glide across to the top table, her trailing hem catching at the fresh straw spread across the flagstones. Another lady followed, of a more diminutive stature, her dark glossy hair bound by a gold-filigreed net set with pearls. The filaments winked and sparkled in the sunlight that streamed down through the hand-blown glass in the windows.

'My God, it's Eva,' Bruin blurted out, recognising her. Shock rattled through him. He gulped at his ale hurriedly, placing the vessel back down on the tablecloth with a thump. Ale splashed down the goblet. If he had thought she was beautiful in the forest, shivering amidst the snowflakes, tears smearing her mud-streaked face, it was nothing compared to the woman walking towards him at that moment. Her gown was of green-patterned velvet, fashioned with low, open sides to the hipline, revealing an underdress of pale green which hugged the curving indent of her waist. Tight-fitting sleeves encased her slim arms, a row of tiny pearl buttons closing the fabric from wrist to elbow. In contrast to Katherine's gown which gathered up beneath her chin, befitting her status as a wealthy widow, Eva's neckline was round, simply cut, emphasising the fragile hollow of her throat. A silver circlet, decorated with large hanging pearls, was secured on her head, above the gold net that contained the heavy coil of sable-coloured hair.

'Sweet Jesu,' murmured Gilbert. 'What a beauty.'

Bruin's tongue moved thickly, cleaving to the roof of his mouth. He took another quick sip of ale, his belly gripped with unravelling desire. What was the matter with him? He had seen many beautiful ladies before; brought up and trained as a knight in King William of Hainault's household, he had been amongst them at court every day. But there had been no women around him recently: his body numb with grief, he had preferred the hard, uncompromising life on a ship at sea.

He had been away too long. That was it. How else to

explain the way he cleaved towards Eva as if he were beneath a spell. He itched to touch her, gripped with longing, poised to take, to lay her on the ground and wrap his muscled limbs around hers. To sink into her. His mind darkened; nay, he was not like that, not some marauding bastard to rape and pillage without a by-your-leave. He would do well to keep his feelings under control, for both of their sakes.

'I bid you good day, my lords.' Katherine threw a terse smile towards the two knights as she slid into the high-backed chair beside Gilbert. Her flaring silk skirts rustled against the arm of the chair. The men rose in unison, bowing formally; she flapped her hand impatiently at them, indicating they should sit back down. Smoothing her ruffled gown over her knees, she turned her large brown eyes on Bruin. 'I hear that you were very helpful with my daughter last night?'

Slipping next to Katherine, as far away from Bruin as she could possibly manage without it appearing rude, Eva bent her head over her plate, the shining pewter blurring before her eyes. A maidservant set an oval dish of meat pottage down on the table, her arm inadvertently brushing against Eva's shoulder; a bolt of fear rushed through her. Steam rose from the pottage as panic stirred her veins, but she clamped the feeling down, refusing to allow it to take hold, to take over. Terror would rob her mind of cool, thinking logic, the ability to work her way out of this mess. For the moment, she must pretend to submit meekly to Bruin's plans, so he would not suspect her plot to escape.

Dragging his eyes from Eva's downcast demeanour, the smooth cheek dipping down to the plush corner of her delectable mouth, Bruin forced himself to look at Katherine, to acknowledge her previous comment. 'Aye, your child was burning up; I carried her outside.'

'It seems to have worked.' Katherine smiled graciously. 'She is much better this morning.' A manservant walking along behind the row of chairs with an earthenware jug leaned over and filled her goblet with ale. The smell of malted barley scented the air, mingling with the smoke from the fire.

'I'm glad of it,' Bruin replied, his voice hardening. 'No doubt Lady Eva has told you what else happened last night?'

A small frown pleated the skin between Katherine's pale eyebrows. She nodded carefully in response. Sitting between the two of them, Gilbert, his spoon poised before his mouth, eyed them both with a puzzled expression.

'You have known of Lady Eva's identity all this time?' Bruin's eyes shifted across Katherine's face with a flinty, challenging stare. Hearing the iron determination in his voice, Eva hunkered down further in her seat, trying to make herself smaller, invisible almost. Perspiration gathered in her armpits.

Katherine tipped up her chin, a swift, delicate movement, her fawn eyes widening with a flicker of hostility. 'I did. What of it?'

'Only that you lied to me when I asked you of her whereabouts. As the King's niece, I would have expected you to be honest with me.'

'You are a stranger. I was protecting her.' She shrugged her shoulders, playing with the stem of her goblet. The sapphire in her heavy silver ring sparked out like blue fire.

'Why?' Bruin shot back. 'What are you protecting Lady Eva from?'

'I do believe that it's none of your concern,' Katherine replied coolly. She laid her palm flat against the hollow of her throat, an unconscious gesture of defence. Her other arm slid over her belly, as if she were guarding her body from his incisive gaze.

Caught between the two of them, Gilbert cleared his throat ceremoniously. 'Er… Bruin, I think…'

'It is my concern. I suppose she's told you that I intend to take her to see my brother? It looks to me like you have been hiding her, for some time it would seem. I want to know why. Is it to do with Lord Steffen?' Bruin's eyes were pinned to Katherine's face. She fidgeted uncomfortably in her seat, plucking at a stray thread on the lap of her gown, small teeth worrying at her bottom lip. Glancing sideways, Eva saw the despair flashing across Katherine's features, her unwillingness to reveal her friend's secrets.

'No, please, stop this!' Eva jumped up, wincing as her hip knocked painfully against the edge of the table. 'Stop bullying her! Katherine does not deserve your scolding.' Her eyes, the colour of a turquoise sea, shimmered with anger. 'She has enough to deal with without having to answer countless questions about me. She has done everything in her power to keep my identity hidden, and now you've come along—' Eva spluttered to a halt, searching for the correct words.

'—and spoiled your little game,' Bruin finished for her. His silver gaze glittered over her, fierce and intimidating.

'How dare you!' Incensed by his mocking tone, Eva thumped her fist down on to the table. Her goblet, the loose cutlery, all shook and rattled with the forceful vibration of the movement. If she had been any nearer, she would have smacked his smug, self-confident chin with the flat of her hand. 'A game? Is that what you think this is? So it's a game when I dress in rags every day and go about my tasks as a servant of Lady Katherine. You think I do that for my own enjoyment?' Her voice rose steadily, tremulously, driven on by flaring rage. Half-turning in her seat, Katherine laid a comforting hand on her arm. A warning. Gilbert's mouth adopted a hanging slackness, his eyes bulged out of his pudgy face, a dull ruddy colour suffusing his fleshy cheeks. Bruin sprawled back against the chair back, big shoulders wedged against the carved wood, his eyes intent on her face, their pewter depths predatory, expectant.

'Oh, dear Lord, you have no idea, do you?' Eva said, almost spitting the words out. 'You sit there, calmly asking questions with that sneering look upon your face, and yet you have no idea. What sort of man your brother really is.' Her blood pulsed hotly in her veins, drumming hard in her ears; anger controlled her now, whipped up by Bruin's mocking stare. She wanted to wipe that scornful look from his face, his arrogant expression. He thought he knew it all, and yet he knew nothing at all. Hysteria bubbled in her chest, a whirlpool gathering strength, fuelled by temper, caution scattered, tossed chaotically like fine seed from a peasant's hand. The tiny voice in her head that told her to tread carefully, to hold back, vanished completely.

'That man dragged me from my home in the middle of the night and locked me in a tower. He kept me in there, threatened me, starved me—' Eva jabbed the air with a closed fist '—until I signed all my holdings over to him. The castle, lands that had been in my family for generations—all of it went to him. Your precious brother!' Her chest heaved with suppressed sobs. She had the briefest satisfaction of seeing Bruin's reaction to her words, saw him hunch forward, mouth tightening to a terse, grim line, before the tears began to run down her face, dripping from her neat chin. She dashed them away furiously. This wasn't supposed to happen; she wasn't supposed to cry in front of him.

'Hush now, calm yourself.' Katherine rose to comfort her. Eva batted her friend's arms away, jewelled tears spinning out from her face.

'No—I need—I need some air,' she gasped out, fighting her way out from between the unwieldy chairs, staggering from the table to fumble blindly through the thick curtains at the back of the dais. The corridor beyond was shadowy, dank, lit by a single, unglazed window at one end. Eva darted towards the square of light, throwing her belly across the slanted stone sill, leaning out, gulping in the crisp morning air.

What had she done?

Exhausted by her outburst, the rage drained from her. She slumped forward over the windowsill, her body spent. Spots of colour burned her cheeks, a dusting of fire. A breath of wind snagged her veil, a white wing blowing out. Far below, the brown river churned, the spiralling flow powerful and relentless. The temptation to clamber over the sill and plunge down into those muddy waters gripped her; she could let the river carry her away, away from all this to a safe, hidden place.

For a large man, Bruin moved with exceptional quietness, the sound of his footsteps barely discernible in the corridor behind her. His hand curled around her shoulder, resting lightly.

'Go away,' she croaked, her eyes focused on the river,

the undulating wavelets, crested with white froth. 'Forget I said anything.'

'That would be difficult,' he replied, 'as the whole hall has been entertained by your tirade. I doubt anyone will forget that in a long time. That was quite a performance.'

His words stung, nipped at her. Eva whirled around, peerless skin streaked with tears. In the shadows, her hair shone, like the polished colour of chestnuts. 'Why are you being so cruel? You think this is all an act? For God's sake, Bruin, I'm telling the truth!' Tears surged, threatening once more. She closed her eyes, wanting to block the piercing cruelty of his eyes, clamping her lips together to control the trembling of her bottom lip. Grinding her fingers into the sill, she clawed at the stone for support. 'I told you the truth,' she said again.

Guilt sliced through him. He was being mean, bullying both Lady Katherine and then Eva to reveal their secrets. But he suspected if he had asked them nicely, they would have provided him with evasive, half-hearted answers. Fobbed him off with bright words and airy phrases. And he had wanted the truth. A shudder of disquiet coursed through his large frame. Had his brother's vicious streak finally climbed out of control? He remembered the fear he had felt as a child. Steffen always had to win, at everything. Every game, every sword fight. His competitiveness had been exhausting, turning the most playful game sour.

A wave of sickness passed through him, a thousand questions burning in his brain. He knew, deep in his heart, that Steffen was entirely capable of treating a woman so badly. He had seen it before, in Flanders. The way he used them, discarded them when he was bored. 'Are you sure?' Bruin asked, his voice hoarse. He sounded wretched. 'Are you sure it was my brother?'

Shivering, Eva straightened up, winding her arms across her bosom. The velvet sheen of her gown rucked up beneath her crossed forearms. 'Oh, yes,' she confirmed in a shaking voice. 'It was him.'

Chapter Eight

Her silent gesture knocked into him with the force of a crossbow bolt. His chin jerked up, a ruddy flush covering his cheekbones. Eva's aquamarine eyes fixed warily on Bruin's face, watching for the slightest change in his hard expression, desperately wanting him to believe her. A welter of emotions ricocheted through him; he should have been outraged, incensed by Eva's accusation, but strangely, he was not. She was telling the truth. He saw it in the trembling of her bottom lip, in the fearful guarded way she held her body; had seen it yester eve in the forest, when she had thrust the flaming brand into his face, mistaking him for his brother.

The silence between them lengthened; an icy breeze whipped through the passageway from the open window. Eva bunched her fingers into tight fists at her sides. It was evident from Bruin's lack of response that he didn't believe her. 'It's all right. I don't expect you to believe me. But it's the reason I don't want to go to Deorham with you.'

He came towards her, tall frame filling the constricted space. The toes of his boots knocked against her own, hidden beneath the flowing hemline of her gown. He cupped her shoulders. 'Eva, I believe you.'

'Really?' Through the gloom, the diamond glitter of his eyes pierced her soul. She clung to them, grasping their brightness like a lifeline.

Beneath his hands, the bone structure of her shoulders was fragile, a delicate cage; absent-mindedly, he rubbed one thumb against the cloth of her dress. 'I do,' he confirmed. 'My brother has lived in England for many years now; before seeing him at Deorham, I hadn't seen him since—' he stopped, unwanted memories crowding his mind. Steffen telling him what had happened to Sophie, a smug little smile crawling across his face; Steffen holding out Sophie's wet shawl, the ends trailing in the mud '—since we trained as knights in Flanders.' Shame washed over him, vile and coruscating. He stared over Eva's neat head, the gleam of her circlet and through the window, to the washed-out blue sky beyond. A buzzard hovered above the flood plain, feathered wing tips ruffling upwards in the stiff breeze as it fought to keep itself steady.

Beneath the solid weight of his hand, Eva shifted, sensing his distraction. Relief flooded through her; he believed her. Fear, that leaden cloak draping her shoulders, fell away, leaving her light, aware. Did Bruin realise how close he was standing? His knees bumped against hers, rustling her velvet skirts. She could see the individual stitches on his surcoat: satin stitch, chain stitch, making up one of the embroidered lions, the gold thread interspersed with blue. A labour of love.

A bolt of longing shot through her; earthy and visceral. Her mouth parted in a silent gasp, air pleating her chest. His nearness acted like a balm, soothing her frayed nerves, easing out the tension in her back. But in truth, it did far more than that. A kernel of need grew at the base of her belly, slowly at first, like a newborn fire, smoking and spitting, until it burst into flame, incandescent. A wild insanity ripped along her veins, a primal yearning that stretched every sinew in her body to near breaking point, vibrating and aware. If only she could lean into him, rest her head against his chest and squeeze him tight to her. And more.

Her head knocked back at her own shocking thoughts. Never before had a man made her feel like this, or think like this. She had to step away, move back from him, before she made an utter fool of herself. 'Thank you, Bruin. Thank you for believing me,' she stuttered out. She placed her palm against his chest, a gesture of gratitude. Taut muscle ridged beneath her splayed hand. To her surprise, he gripped her fingers, holding them tight to his ribs when she would have pulled away.

'What did he do to you?' He stumbled over the question, tongue thick and awkward in his mouth, not wanting to think the worst. If Steffen had raped her… His mouth twisted savagely.

Eva dipped her head, biting down hard on her bottom lip. Silver discs, engraved, studded the worn leather on Bruin's sword belt; they swam before her vision. 'I said it all in the hall,' she murmured in a thin brittle voice. 'Don't make me talk about it again.'

His jaw was rigid; a muscle twitched below his cheekbone. His grip was strong. 'Tell me one thing,' he said. 'Did he—did he take advantage of you?' For some insane reason, the question was of the utmost importance to him.

Eva tipped her face up, skin gleaming like a pearl in the shadowy half-light. 'You mean, did he rape me?' she replied bluntly. 'No, he did not.' Although Lord Steffen had threatened her with it, she remembered, if she had continued refusing to sign the papers.

'Then how did he know about your birthmark?' The words stumbled out of him. 'Steffen told me to look for it. When would he have seen that?'

'He didn't. The maidservant who attended me told him about it,' she explained. 'He did allow me to have the occasional bath.'

Thank God, Bruin thought. 'How could he have done such a thing to you?' he murmured roughly. Fuelled by a need to comfort, his other hand lifted, wanting to erase the fleeting look of emptiness, of utter desolation, that tracked across her breathtaking features. His thumb slid over her cheek, tracing a warm arc. The texture of her skin was like silk, a polished whisper against his calloused pad. His touch drifted to her mouth, brushing the fullness of her bottom lip.

'He wanted my money and that's all there is to it.' Eva shuddered, but not with thoughts of Steffen. 'He didn't want me; he had enough women around him to keep him happy.' Her heart raced as Bruin's fingers tingled against her skin. Her blood thickened, pooling dangerously. Move away now, she told herself. Move away before it's too late. Her breath snared, laced with desire; her pupils dilated, black pools radiating outwards to flood the sea-bright colour of her eyes. The exquisite sensation of his touch captured her body, held her prisoner. If she moved, Bruin would stop. And she had no wish for him to stop. Her lips parted, air rushing out from her lungs, expelling the faintest whimper, an echo of desire.

Bruin heard the small sound. Recognised it for what it was. Rushed on by a growing need, his self-control splintered. Tilting his head, he leaned down, touching his lips to hers. He roped his brawny arms around her back, winching Eva against the broad heft of his frame. His mouth roamed along the delicate seam of her lips, a trail of fire, of sweet sensation. The fire spread downwards, flushing the sensitive skin of her torso, diving deep into the secret recesses of her belly, and below, ricochets of liquid desire arching through the very core of her.

His big body crushed against her and her back flexed beneath the pressure of his chest, the hard, flat plane of his torso as he gathered her close, bracing her body against the stone window sill. His knee nudged between her thighs; she arched beneath him, muscles slackening. Beneath the insistent torment of his lips, her mouth parted and he groaned, deepening the kiss, his tongue darting into that sweet hollow. Time flew away, suspended in an airy bubble, a dream that encased them both.

'Eva?' Katherine's voice called out into the corridor. 'Eva, where are you?'

The weight of Bruin's body vanished immediately. Eva found herself lying against the sloping window sill, nay, sprawled, like a wanton, a woman of the night, her breath emerging in quick, truncated gasps. Beneath her dress, her breasts throbbed, tingled with awareness. Scowling, Bruin yanked her sharply to her feet. The muscled planes of his face were tight and hard, his expression inscrutable.

'Oh—there you are!' Spotting the two figures at the end of the corridor, Katherine moved towards them in a gracious sweep of her skirts. She frowned, sensing the unspoken tension in the air between them. 'I hope you're not upsetting her again?' she barked at Bruin, folding her arms imperiously across her bodice.

Eva's face was flushed. Desire shimmered in her eyes, violet-blue. Seeking stability, her arm flew out, touching the wall lightly for balance. 'No, nothing like that,' she stammered hurriedly, scrambling to answer for both of them.

'Eva has told me everything,' Bruin explained coolly, his long eyelashes dipping briefly as he turned towards Katherine. He was composed, his face set into stern lines. The angled light from the window highlighted the golden tips of his tousled hair. Nothing about his demeanour suggested what had happened a moment before: his body sprawled across hers, lips devouring, seeking. Eva frowned at him, resenting his composure. How could he recover so quickly? Flames of yearning licked through her veins, like the aftermath of a storm.

'Everything?' Katherine frowned, her brown eyes darting quickly to Eva. Out on the window ledge a pigeon cooed, the rounded sound echoing through the arched window space.

'He knows about—his brother,' Eva confirmed.

Katherine's fair eyebrows flew upwards and she glared stonily at Bruin. 'I can't quite believe that you and he are related,' she said slowly. 'Since your brother came into the employ of the King, his behaviour seems to know no bounds. The things he has done.' Her voice trailed away; she shrugged. 'He's made a habit of preying on young heiresses, dividing their fortunes between himself and the King. And my uncle supports him!'

Bruin grimaced, the memory of the childhood games with his brother twisting in his gut. 'I cannot speak for what he has done, but I am sorry for it.'

Katherine inclined her head, acknowledging his apology. 'So you can see why Eva cannot come with you. Why she cannot see him again. She must come with me and the children.'

'I disagree.' Bruin shook his head, a firm distinct movement.

'Wh-what?' His words struck Eva like a thunderclap. She staggered back against the wall, her shoulder grazing roughly against the unyielding stone. 'But I told you what—I thought you believed me about what happened!' she cried out.

'I do believe you,' Bruin said calmly, tucking his thumbs into his sword belt. His voice was low, melodious. 'But despite what he has done, my brother is dying. I cannot refuse to grant him this last request. I know it will be difficult for you, but I will be there.'

Eva's face paled. Her mouth pinched together, ringed with white. As if he had slapped her. Her flesh, lithe and malleable from his kiss, now tingled with apprehension. His kiss had been a jewel, a luxurious gift that she had accepted gleefully, foolishly, with all the naivety of an innocent; now, with his abrasive announcement, it was as if he ripped that gift away, leaving her open-mouthed and gasping.

She clutched at Bruin's forearm, her oval nails digging into the links of his chainmail. Fear pulsed through her. 'I cannot.' Her voice climbed with panicky shrillness. 'I told you. Lord Steffen is lying to you. What if he isn't dying at all—?'

'I saw him,' Bruin said, his voice slicing through her speech like a steel blade. 'The blood was running from his head, his breathing shallow. Do you think I don't know when someone is on the brink of death? I have seen it often enough. Eva, you need to be ready to go before the noon bell. I will be with you the whole time. Nothing is going to happen to you.'

Every word he spoke exacerbated her terror, so that it

rose, mountainous and forbidding, paralysing her mind. She couldn't think logically. 'Katherine—?' In consternation, Eva pulled away from Bruin, plucking at her friend's sleeve.

Katherine folded her cold hand within her own. Her brown eyes challenged Bruin. 'How can you force her to go through with this? After what she has endured at your brother's hands?'

Bruin sighed. 'I will look after her, I promise. And bring her back to you after we have seen Steffen. You have my word on that.'

Katherine was silent for a moment. 'So there's nothing I can say or do to persuade you from this course of action?'

Bruin's pressed his lips together. 'Nothing.'

Fingers of terror gripped Eva's heart, clawed into the very soul of her. Everything she had known for the last year or so, the restricted, ordered life that she had built for herself after the horror of her captivity, had been thrown up in the air, disordered, topsy-turvy. As if she were standing on a raft, tossed by unpredictable waves, the wooden planks slowly disintegrating beneath the churning power of the water until at last she disappeared into those sunlit green depths.

And all because of him.

Mouth tight with mutinous dislike, she scowled at Bruin, trying to summon up any last remnants of courage. For if there was a time to be brave, to stand up for herself, then surely it was now. She felt betrayed. Where had the man gone, the man that moments earlier had held her safe in his burly arms, and touched his lips to hers? Eva straightened her spine, lifting her chin towards Bruin. 'Well, I don't care about your plans for me,' she announced boldly. 'I am not going to Deorham; I am not going to see Lord Steffen again and that is final.' She pinned her wide blue eyes on Bruin, her expression hostile, acerbic. 'You will have to drag me there, kicking and screaming, against my will.'

'Then that is the way it will be,' Bruin replied. There was no softness in his eyes.

'Eva, I don't see how you can avoid travelling to Deorham with him.' Katherine was on her knees beside the oak coffer. The carved lid was flung back against the plastered wall. Katherine pulled out another gown, folding the velvet cloth expertly: sleeves tucked inward, skirts pleated neatly. Rising to her feet, she carried the bundle over to the travelling trunk and laid the gown inside. Silver embroidery decorated the generous hem: a trailing chain stitch worked into leaves and flowers winked in the sunshine streaming through the chamber windows.

'He has no idea what his brother is capable of,' Eva replied, hollow-eyed. Her own small bag was already packed with her few possessions.

'It does sound like Lord Steffen is capable of very little,' Katherine replied softly. She fiddled with the gown in the trunk, tutting beneath her breath, adjusting the skirts so that the fabric lay flat. 'You heard Lord Bruin: the man is on his deathbed.'

'And I do not believe it,' Eva whispered, biting down hard on her bottom lip. 'That man will do anything, even fake illness to gain what he wants. He knows I have the ruby and he wants it. That's why he's asked his brother to find me. I am the only person who knows where it is.'

'But even if Lord Steffen is pretending to be ill, Lord Bruin has said he will protect you, Eva.' Straightening up,

Katherine planted her hands on her hips. She stepped over to the window, glancing down to the snow-dusted grass where the children played. A drawn-out shriek echoed up from below; leaning closer to the wobbly, hand-blown glass, Katherine frowned. 'Remind me to speak to Peter; he's being too rough with those girls.'

'I will go down to them,' Eva said.

Katherine stalled her. 'No, it's nothing serious. Martha is with them. Besides, now everyone knows who you are, you can be my nursemaid no longer.'

Eva pushed her palm up against her forehead. 'How I wish that man had never come here; he's ruined everything!' A pair of silver eyes mocked her. The sensual curve of his bottom lip. Her heart jolted, edged with resentment. 'Lord Gilbert has guards posted at every door, but there must be some way out.'

'You are determined, aren't you?' Katherine threw her a smile. 'I bet you'd even jump from that window and swim away down the river, if it meant you never had to see Lord Steffen again.'

'I've done it before,' Eva said in a small voice. Fear snagged her chest at the memory: the walk along the battlements with one of Steffen's soldiers, her delighted exclamations at the sunshine, the panoramic views, all to put her guard at ease. To him, her slight figure posed no threat. She had shoved at his chest, leaping up on to the stone parapet and then—jumped. The dank green waters of the moat had closed over her head and she had struck out underwater, deaf to the shouts above. Eva was a strong swimmer; after what had happened to her mother, her father had made sure of that. Thank God, for it had saved her.

'Of course,' Katherine replied quietly. 'I had forgotten.'

'My God, that's it,' Eva said. Her mind leapt on the idea with quicksilver clarity. She knew what she must do. 'The rope and pulley from the kitchen storeroom. There may not be a boat at the bottom, but there is a narrow shoreline to walk along. I can go that way!'

'Have you gone completely mad?' Katherine's voice rose shrilly. 'I only said such a thing in jest! Listen to me, Eva. Scrap any notion of escape, for that man, Lord Bruin, is sure to catch you, one way or another. Why can you not trust him to protect you?'

Eva hesitated. A pair of frosted eyes, challenging, intimidating, loomed before her. Firm lips claiming her mouth, her sigh of release, of desire. Hot colour flooded her cheeks. 'Because I've never had to rely on a man, or need a man's protection. And I'm not about to start now.'

'Then maybe you should,' murmured Katherine.

'And what if I end up imprisoned again?' A shudder permeated Eva's voice.

'I think you underestimate Lord Bruin.'

'Why do you leap to his defence?' Eva replied petulantly. 'Anyone would think you are on his side.'

Katherine flinched. Her mouth pursed into a grim, straight line, and she began ruffling through the stack of children's clothes piled on the bed furs, her movements quick and agitated. She snapped the fabric through the air; dust motes swirled, golden specks catching the light. 'I don't think you are in a position to choose.'

Eva glanced at her friend's tense expression, disquiet trickling through her. She was being mean and thoughtless. 'I'm sorry,' she said. 'You have been so kind to me and here I am, thinking only of my own salvation. You have so much to bear at the moment.'

'I don't blame you for trying to think of a way out.'

Katherine's smile was stiff. 'Given what you have been through, it would be strange if you did not. But I do not want you to kill yourself in the process.'

'But I have to try to escape,' Eva replied. 'You know me well enough. I must try.'

Katherine nodded, her slim shoulders slumping with an air of resignation. 'So be it,' she said. 'In all honesty, I expected nothing less from you.' Clutching Eva's elbow, she gave her a little push towards the door. 'You must go. But promise me—that you will come back to me and the children.'

Tears rose in Eva's eyes. 'The worst thing about all of this is leaving you. You have done so much for me.' She threw her arms around Katherine's tall, elegant figure. 'Thank you for being my friend and for helping me when I had nowhere else to turn.'

Heart lodged uncomfortably beneath her ribs, her leather bag slung over one shoulder, Eva crept down the steep stairs. She wore a hooded cloak belonging to Katherine over her green-velvet gown; the long train slipped down the steps behind her, a slippery, insidious sound. Her leg was less painful today; the skin around the wound was knitting together. No doubt Bruin planned to come and fetch her from the chamber at the noon bell. By her estimation, she had time to reach the kitchens without meeting him.

And yet. The man was fearsome, unpredictable. He wouldn't care about any bell, or any time that he might have told her. He could run up this stair and fetch her at any time he chose, demanding that they leave. Her breath snared. The angled steps, worn, dipped from years of tramping feet, fanned out from a stone column that ran like a spine up the centre of the stairwell. She stumbled, fingers flying to the rope banister for support.

The kitchens were busy; along the trestle table, servants chopped vegetables, kneaded rounds of dough, the yeasty, fermenting smell permeating the air. Flour dust rose, hazing the air. Heaps of peelings, apple cores, carrot tops, littered the well-scrubbed planks. A great cauldron hung on an iron chain over the fire, the contents bubbling furiously, steam billowing out. Interested eyes turned towards Eva as she entered, covert glances sliding away quickly as the servants marked her rich, expensive garments.

'Eva?' the cook said tentatively, wiping her floury hands on a cloth and coming towards her. Her sleeves were pushed back to the elbows, revealing strong muscular forearms; her face was flushed, perspiring from the heat of the fire. A look of consternation crossed her fleshy cheeks. 'Forgive me, my lady… I mean, Lady Eva.' Holding her patched skirts up, the cook bobbed into a brief curtsy. 'We're all a bit surprised. We had no idea that you were—that you were a—a lady.'

'Greetings, Maeve.' Eva gripped the cook's thick hands. 'I'm still Eva underneath all this. A title doesn't change people.' Her voice lowered, threaded with urgency. 'Listen to me; this will sound strange, but I need your help. Can you find two men to lower me down on the winch in the storeroom?'

Maeve's sparse eyelashes flew upwards in shock.

Eva rattled on, wanting to explain. 'I must leave the castle and leave it now, without—without Lord Gilbert's soldiers finding out. I'm in trouble.' A pair of sparkling eyes chased across her vision and her heart pleated inwards, creasing with fear. What would Bruin do to her if he found out she was trying to leave? Would he beat her, as his brother had done? A shiver rippled down her spine, unsettling, and she threw a quick, worried glance behind her as Maeve seized her arm, steering her towards a dark corridor.

The storerooms were on a floor below the kitchens, the castle provisions of beer and ale stacked along both walls, round wooden barrels arranged in neat rows up to the vaulted ceiling. At the far end was an opening that faced out on to the river, the tall arch framing the bright blue sky. Two men, breath puffing white in the icy air, operated a heavy wooden winch, one turning the large handle that wound up the rope on a spindle, the other reaching out to grab and swing the barrel into the chamber. Maeve walked towards them, her thick arms jabbing the air as she explained Eva's situation in low, urgent tones. They listened with bowed heads. Then their faces sprang up in shock and they looked towards Eva with grave concern.

'But, mistress, it's not possible! It's too dangerous!' The older servant, his beard thick and springy over his wide jaw, addressed her directly. 'We're too high above the river!'

'It's my only option, I'm afraid,' Eva said, walking forward with quick, neat steps. She lifted the long handle of her leather bag over her head and shoulders, feeling the weight of it settle against her back, diagonally across her chest.

'But you might fall,' said the other man. Sweat coated his brow from the effort of pulling in the barrel, thin wisps of blond hair sticking to his forehead.

'Believe me, it's a risk I am willing to take,' Eva said, desperation lacing her voice. 'I am strong; I will be able to hang on. All I ask is that you lower me down.'

'Please, Giffard,' Maeve prompted, jostling the older servant's elbow. 'She'll be able to do it.'

'Then stand on the barrel and hold tight,' Giffard advised. He held on to the rope and the younger servant eased the barrel still firmly attached to the winch rope to the edge of the opening.

'God speed, mistress,' Maeve said. Her fleshy face creased into a worried smile.

Eva climbed on to the barrel, grabbing the thick rope. The coarse flax whiskered against her bare hands. 'I'm ready,' she said. The younger servant shoved the barrel outwards and into the open air, where it swung slightly before bumping gently against the stone wall. The rope creaked and strained beneath the load. A stiff breeze rising up from the river caught her veil, blowing the material chaotically around her head. The older manservant released the winch slowly and she began to move downwards, her heart pounding rapidly. She kept her eyes pinned to the huge stone blocks that made up the exterior wall of the castle. Her fingers ground into the rope, her knuckles white, aching with the effort of holding her own weight. High above her, in the periwinkle-blue sky, a circling buzzard shrieked.

Eva was halfway down when the rope stopped with a sudden jolt. She swung violently, bouncing in the air. An angry roar bellowed at her from above, muffled curses raining down. If she looked up she knew she would see Bruin's face, savage with rage, at what she had tried to do. Fear slid through her like liquid poison.

Chapter Nine

'Eva! You little wretch!' His voice hammered down.

The barrel bounced and swung, then slowly started rising again. Her hands clawed the rough, whiskered rope. Bruin had ordered the servants to raise the wooden cask! She glanced down, her eyes watering with the cold, the slip of shingle beach where the river boats moored to unload provisions for the castle shimmering below her. Was she near enough to let go of the rope and jump down? Was she brave enough? Her belly flipped with queasy fear. The drop was only about ten feet, but landing on the hard-packed stones could break her leg or worse. But if she made an effort to push herself back and jump into the river, the deep water would break her fall.

She glanced up, horrified. From the arch of the storeroom, Bruin glared down at her, his jaw set with grim determination, his mouth hard, unrelenting. His hair flowed out like fire, flaming bronze in the raw, unforgiving sunlight: a Norse god of old, a Viking raider. My God, she thought, her heart plummeting, he looks exactly like his brother. It could have been Steffen staring down at her in that very moment. And he was waiting for her, watching as she slowly rose towards him. He looked like he wanted to kill her.

Her whirling mind tipped, fled along irrational paths. The thought of his wrath, of what he might do to her, far outweighed any risk of flinging herself into the churning water. Terror drove her. She had no time to waste. A stiff, truncated cry tore from her lips; pushing her boots sturdily against the wooden cask, she flung herself out and backwards, hands relinquishing the rope. Her cloak spread out like a wing around her as she fell, the hem curling in around her legs, her feet bobbing helplessly in the limpid air.

And then she smacked into the water, skirts catching around her ankles, hampering her attempts to kick her legs out. She knew how to swim; her father had made certain that both her and her brother had the skill after what had happened to their mother all those years ago, but she hadn't reckoned on the heavy garments pulling her down. She sank, the churning, freezing water enveloping her. Struggling blindly in the sucking flow, she shoved her arms down, fighting to keep her head up. Sunlight danced on the surface, disorientating her. Water filled her nose and mouth, making her splutter and choke; she fought for breath, caught in a powerful vortex of water. She wasn't going anywhere.

And then a hand seized her hood, hooking into the neckline of her gown, big knuckles grazing the bare skin beneath her sodden hair, hauling her backwards. She howled in outrage, stretching her arms forward, thrashing at the water in a desperate attempt to try to swim away, pumping her legs out and back. But she couldn't move. The hand gripping at her clothes would not allow it. Bruin's hand. She wanted to weep. How had he managed to reach her so quickly?

'Come here!' Bruin roared at her, his substantial frame dipped low across the bow as he dragged her, kicking and struggling, towards the boat. 'You foolish woman! What were you trying to do?'

Two men rowed the boat, adjusting the oars constantly to keep the vessel steady in the brown, choppy flow. Lying flat, hooking his toes over the seat in the boat, Bruin stretched his arms out, seizing Eva's shoulders, then her waist. Feet kicking out wildly, she struggled against his powerful hold, wriggling furiously.

'God, will you stop fighting me!' he shouted above the rushing sound of the river. 'You are not going to escape, do you hear me?' Exasperated, he managed to hoist her out of the water, dumping her in the bottom of the boat, gasping and sodden. Fuming.

'You cannot get away with this!' Eva hissed at him. 'Treating me like a...' she paused, struggling to find the words '...like a sack of grain!'

The corner of Bruin's mouth quirked upwards. 'A sack of grain would be far easier to deal with.' His tone was dry, mildly scathing. 'For a start it doesn't talk back.' Water droplets spotted his red surcoat, the metallic links of his chainmail sleeves. 'What on earth possessed you to jump into the water?'

'To get away from you, of course! From what you're making me do!' Eva replied. She thumped her fists down on the planks beneath her, annoyed for not having succeeded. 'You had guards posted on every door; it was the only way out.' Her veil and circlet had disappeared; a good portion of her hair had come adrift. The tangled strands rippled down in curling tendrils, glossy seaweed across her green-velvet gown. Touching her hips.

Bruin cleared his throat. In the clear, undiluted sunlight, his hair shone like golden filaments, ruffled by a sharp little breeze. 'You could have been killed,' he said slowly. Fear shot through him, a visceral pulse of pure, undiluted terror. Echoes of the past. What if he had been too late, what if he had pulled her, limp and lifeless, from the surging river? He leaned forward, his face looming close to hers. 'It was stupid and thoughtless. Don't you ever, *ever* do that again!'

The boat rocked violently, caught in a vicious eddy; Eva's hands flew out, clinging to the sides of the boat to keep her balance. 'It's not likely now, is it?' she replied sarcastically. Her teeth started to chatter; her words juddered out through frozen lips. The wet fabric of her hood gathered lumpily around her neck, water trickling over her damp cheek, behind her ear. 'I've ruined my one and only chance of escape. You won't let me out of your sight now.'

Her voice held a forlorn note. In her lap, her hands trembled, like white, upturned flowers rocked in a fierce breeze. Beneath her bulky cloak, her gown, sopping with water, clung to the luscious curve of her hips and thighs, the sweet indent of her waist. A bluish tinge played across her mouth. Despite her fighting talk, she reminded him of a hunted animal, cornered, broken, with nowhere left to turn.

'Row us to the shore, now!' Bruin ordered the men and they nodded, turning the vessel expertly in the current, steering a bouncing path across the river. Eva stared numbly at her knees, beaten, exhausted. Her eyes paled to a shimmering turquoise, the light leaching from her face. Guilt swung over him. He had driven her to this; he had made her so desperate to escape the trip to visit Steffen that she had been prepared to jump into the river. To risk her own life.

A tendril of hair stuck to her cheek; Eva pushed it away with a shaking hand. Snow dusted the opposite bank of the river, the land rolling upwards to a copse of trees. The strength of the current had been too great for her; she never would have managed to reach the other side. Shivering, she wrapped her arms across her belly, her chin jutting out in grim determination. The stark, dancing light bounced up from the waves, lapping the boat, reflecting against the gold-threaded embroidery on Bruin's tunic. 'How did you manage to reach me so quickly?' she asked resentfully.

He had to admire her courage, despite her foolishness. What other woman would have done such a thing to avoid him? Maybe he should let her run and lie to his brother about having found her. But he was in no doubt that while Steffen was alive, his brother would find others to track her down. Steffen was used to his orders being followed; it was not in his nature to back down. The thought of another man searching for Eva made him feel acutely uncomfortable. A surge of protectiveness flooded through him, sudden, surprising. He shifted his hips, adjusting his position on the wooden seat. His reasoning made no sense.

'I climbed down the rope and into the boat,' Bruin explained. 'The men were already there, about to row out to you. They thought you had fallen.' A muscle twitched in his jaw. 'Little did they know the truth of the matter.'

She flinched beneath his silver-bright perusal. Drew her knees up to hunch herself into a tight bundle, trying to control her erratic shivering. 'I told you I didn't want to go with you! I told you I didn't want to see Lord Steffen—ever again. But did you listen? No, you did not.' Her voice was shrill, punctuated by short gasps, aquamarine eyes flaring over him with irritated hostility. She caught the musky tang of his breath as his eyes levelled with hers; her chest quivered, flexed in response to his nearness. The memory of his mouth from before.

'And I told you, you have nothing to fear from Steffen, that I would protect you. Why do you not trust me?'

'Why would I?' Eva spat back, staring moodily at the slatted boards beneath her boots. 'You're his brother, you are connected by family. I am nothing to you.'

On the contrary, he thought with a jolt. You are most definitely something. *Someone.* Someone I don't want to let go of, just yet. The thought thwacked into him with the force of a crossbow bolt, stunning, unexpected, allied with a flicker of hope. Newborn and tentative, but, aye, it was there: hope. He cared about Eva, he realised, cared about what happened to her. The air stuck in his throat and he frowned, glancing away across the river, the wide choppy expanse. A flock of seagulls circled over a flat meadow that ran down to the water's edge and he watched their wheeling progress for a moment, heard their lonesome, mewling cries. What was it about this woman that captivated him, held him in such thrall?

She sat before him, half-drowned, stockings peeking in sodden folds beneath her hemline, tumbling hair plastered chaotically around her head. Most women would be in tears by now, hysterical, clinging. Not Eva. She refused to give up, or give in to him, battling stubbornly for any ounce of freedom she could find. Her stance was defiant: spine pulled straight, shoulders set in a determined line. Her rare courage drew him, like a beacon in the darkness.

'I would not leave you at the mercy of any man, let alone my brother, whatever it is you think he might do,' replied Bruin eventually. Squinting against the brilliant light across the water, he realised the boat had almost reached its destination: a tiny inlet that sat below the gatehouse of the castle. Oak trees clustered along the bank, bare branches dusted with snow sweeping low across the water, frilled ends sketching the shallows. The boat grated against the shingle, a rough, discordant sound, as the men manoeuvred the vessel on to the stones.

Standing up, Bruin placed his foot on the edge of the boat and sprang out, boots crunching on the loose gravelly stones. As the men secured the oars in the rowlocks, he barked a few words at them and they began running through the trees back to the castle, the sunlight streaking down through the dark grid of criss-crossed branches, striking patches of white snow on the brown earth. Bruin watched them go, then turned back to Eva sitting proudly in the boat. 'Now, my lady, will you come with me to Deorham?'

Eva pursed her lips, feeling her strength drain away. 'I suppose I have no choice.'

'No,' he said bluntly. 'You don't.'

She stood up slowly, her legs wobbling, almost giving way. Her wet gowns pulled heavily on her shoulders. 'So be it,' she stuttered out, reluctantly. He had won. Her brain, scrambled by her dunking in the river, seemed void of solutions to her predicament. She couldn't think of a single one.

'And no more attempts to escape?' A taut muscle flexed in the hollow of his cheek.

'I promise,' she replied meekly. Her eyelashes fluttered down, a gesture of compliance.

Bruin wasn't fooled. Despite Eva's acquiescent behaviour, the demure flick of her velvet eyelashes, he had no intention of believing her. Ignoring her squeak of protest, he gripped her waist, lifting her shaking body out of the boat. He placed her beside him and she staggered a little. Water streamed from the ends of her hair, the long strands plastered lovingly to her curves like silken skeins. Like a mermaid, he thought, a fairy creature from a story long ago, fey and ethereal.

The material of her gown clagged uncomfortably against her chest and belly, the chill cloth prickling her forearms. 'I have to change,' she announced. 'I can't travel like this. I need to go back to the castle.'

Bruin's mouth set into a firm line. 'No, Eva, I'm sorry. We've wasted too much time as it is. The men have gone back for the horses and some clothes for you.'

'But…'

'No, Eva.'

At his brusque refusal, her eyes flared with annoyance; she pursed her lips, folding her arms belligerently across her chest. 'What gives you the right to treat me like this?' Irritation laced her tone; she plucked viciously at the fabric stuck wetly to her thighs.

'No right at all,' he replied amiably. Beneath the trees, his features appeared hewn, as if from wood: craggy and angled. And yet his mouth held a surprisingly generous curve. 'Other than the fact that I made a promise to my dying brother and I aim to fulfil it. In whatever way possible,' he finished, ominously.

'In whatever way possible,' she repeated slowly, turning away with tears in her eyes. 'Riding roughshod over people's rights and opinions, determined to have your own way. How like your brother you are.' Condemnation dripped from her voice. 'I'm surprised you didn't march me to Deorham in the middle of the night, with your knife at my throat!'

Dark streaks clouded his eyes, muting the silver. 'Is that what Steffen did to you?' Nausea rose in his gullet.

'No,' she admitted. 'No, he didn't do that. He threatened all sorts of things, to scare me, but he never carried them out.'

'I am sorry you had to endure such things.'

'Are you? Then why are you dragging me back to my persecutor? If you're sorry?'

A dull flush covered Bruin's cheeks. He sighed. 'You know why, Eva. I've known my brother all my life; I've known you a couple of days. There is such a thing as loyalty, despite what he has done. And, yes…' he held up his hand as Eva was about to speak '…I do believe what you told me about him, but I also believe that he needs to be able to ask your forgiveness before he dies.'

Eva glared down at her boots poking out from her skirts, the leather stained dark from the water. She knew what Bruin said made sense, that she couldn't deny a man, any man, his last dying wish, but she also knew how clever and manipulative Lord Steffen could be.

Bruin's eyes slid over her lowered head, the defiant glitter in her eyes. 'Eva, you have to know when to stop fighting.'

'Give in, you mean.' Her voice was bitter.

'If you want to call it that, then, yes,' he replied calmly. Through the trees, the filtered light danced on his shoulder, patches of shadow. 'You're not going to survive much longer in this world if you keep behaving like this.'

'Like what?'

'Like you're invincible. Speaking your mind when it would be better to remain silent. The physical risks you take...' he shook his head '...why, even a man would baulk at them.'

She jerked her chin up. 'You don't understand, do you, Bruin?' Her voice adopted a dangerous lilt, a shrill note of discord. 'I've had to be like this.' She kicked petulantly at a small stone, watching it skitter away to the water's edge. 'When my father and brother were killed, I was left everything that my family owned. I managed the estates, with the help of good bailiffs. My servants were happy, everyone was happy...'

'And Steffen took it all away from you.' Disgust rose in his mouth, a sour taste.

'Yes.' She angled her gaze up to him. 'He took it all away from me, but not without a fight.'

He shoved one hand in his hair. 'Most ladies in your position would have given it to him without argument. Surely that would have been easier?' And safer, he thought.

'Is that what you would have done?' She glared at him archly. In the limpid light, the skin in the hollow of her neck gleamed with a pearl-like lustre. The pulse in her throat beat rapidly. What would it be like to place his fingertip on that very spot, feel her blood race beneath his touch?

Bruin tilted his head to one side. 'No. No, I would not have. But then, I am a man. I can fight my own battles.' He stuck his thumbs into his sword belt.

'It shouldn't make a difference.' Her tone was tight, laced with bitterness. 'Your brother picks on the wealthy unmarried women, the rich widows. Daughters and wives. In my case, I think the King condoned his behaviour because it's seen as fit punishment for being related to a rebel. I'm not the only one, Bruin. Lord Steffen has ruined other women's lives, too, stripping them of their lands and wealth. Their dignity. Did you know that?'

Bruin rolled his shoulders, frowning. 'I did not.' What, he wondered, had his brother become? Had Steffen's childish competitiveness, his petty jealousies, developed into something far uglier? He knew that Steffen had resented his own skill as a knight, particularly when it drew praise from the King, but had this resentment grown into something far crueller and more widespread?

Eva's mouth twisted, eyes glittering with unshed tears. 'I've fought for what I think is right, Bruin, not just for me, but for all the other women who have suffered at his hands. It was time for someone to stand up to him.'

Her words gouged into him. If he had stood up to his brother as a child, then maybe Steffen wouldn't have gone on to torture and humiliate such innocent woman as Eva. 'You were brave to do such a thing, Eva.' He paused. 'Steffen—can be unpredictable.'

She threw him a sharp look. It was the first time Bruin had referred directly to his brother's character. 'I had to try,' she whispered. Her shoulders sagged downwards, her small frame wilting beneath the harsh reality of his words.

He watched the fight drain out of her, vulnerability sifting across her face. His hand caught her icy fingers, a gesture of apology, before his fingers dropped away. 'I'm sorry it has to be like this, for your sake.' he murmured.

'It doesn't matter,' Eva replied. 'I'm not entirely stupid. I do know how this world works and where women are placed within that world.' She threw him a wan smile. 'We are at the bottom of the pile.'

Bruin dipped his head, about to speak, but she placed a hand on his chest, stalling him. 'The men are back,' she said, raising her tone with a false jollity. Her pronouncement sounded inane, cutting through the intensity of their previous words. She fixed him with her brilliant blue gaze, opening her eyes wide in innocent question. 'What do you want me to do?'

He grinned at her unexpected meekness. Taking the pile of clothes from the manservant, he handed them to her. 'Go and change in the bushes over there.' Bruin nodded at an area of low vegetation. 'And make sure you stay where I can see you.' A ruddy colour dusted the top of his cheekbones as he realised the implication of his words. 'I mean—well, not all of you, obviously.' God, her beauty made him stumble over his speech like some callow youth.

'Obviously.' Her response was dry as she marched off in the direction of the bushes edging the woodland. Ducking behind a thick scrub of holly, she peeped over towards him. 'Can you still see me?'

'Yes,' Bruin muttered hoarsely. He turned abruptly to check over the bridles and saddles of the new horses from the castle stables, acutely aware that, barely a few feet away, Eva was removing every stitch of clothing.

Roughly following the line of the river, the route to Deorham led north out of the sweeping valley that had been Eva's home for the last few months. Her sanctuary. Already she missed Katherine's calm, easy company; it felt strange, unusual to be away from her friend, away from the simple routines of domestic life, the tolling of the chapel bell that structured the day, the playful shrieks of the children. She hoped and prayed they would be safe and happy, that King Edward had not arranged some ogre of a husband for his only niece, Katherine.

The clear, settled weather held; although the air was chill and snow lay on the ground, the sun shone brightly, hot against her spine. The cold weather had turned the mud on the track into hard, unyielding furrows, easier for the horses. Ice sparkled down from the trees, glittering like tiny crystals. Occasionally, the earthen banks alongside the track rose steep and high, plunging them into shadow, branches bending over the space to create a dank hollow, laced with brown, brittle ferns.

The dry clothes imbued her with a renewed energy; behind the thicket of bushes she had changed every last scrap of clothing, scrubbing her wet skin briskly with the linen towel that someone, supposedly on Katherine's orders, had placed in the leather satchel that was now strapped to the rump of her horse. Her chemise and undergarments, her stockings, even her leather boots had all been replaced, the wet garments handed back to the servants who were returning to the castle. Her new gowns were of fine wool: a blue dress over an undergown of pale cream. She recognised the hooded cloak as one of Katherine's, swinging out in voluminous pleats from her shoulders. The warm layers enveloped her, gradually driving out the icy chill of the river from her body.

Her horse was docile, but lively and responsive to the touch of her knee, or twitch on the reins. At Striguil, she had ridden out on a daily basis, inspecting the crops in summer, checking the food and hay stores in winter. Before they had set off, Bruin had asked her if she could ride, and before he could help her, she had stuck her foot into the stirrup of the chestnut mare and swung herself up easily, side saddle, her right knee crooked before her. Bruin had grinned, a quick flash of praise, and she had blushed stupidly in the glow of his approval.

Now, he led the way along the stony track towards the ridge that marked one end of the valley. She had no choice but to follow him; Bruin had attached a leading rein to her horse. He didn't trust her, understandable after what she had tried to do, but still annoying. Sighing, she studied the broad expanse of his shoulders, his red surcoat straining over bulky muscles. A quiver of delight rippled through her belly, but she quashed it swiftly, pursing her lips together with an acceptance of the inevitable. After his earlier words, a small part of her believed that he was on her side; she must hold on to that thought, for now there was no option left to her but to trust him. Trust that he would protect her against Lord Steffen.

Chapter Ten

The sun was beginning to drop as Bruin and Eva finally crested the ridge at the head of the long valley in which Katherine's castle was situated. They had been unable to follow the river for the last mile or two: the bank was too steep and rocky for a track to run alongside, so the path had deviated upwards instead. The horses had climbed a rocky zigzag path, their step sure and slow, a strengthening wind catching at their manes, fanning the coarse hair out across their noses. Brilliant gorse, shining yellow, gathered in clumps along the track, spilling abundantly down the steep hillside. Trees became increasingly sparse, branches contorted, until at the top there were none, only a vast plain, empty but for patches of stiff, fawn-coloured grass, blown sideways.

Eva's stomach rumbled. She shifted awkwardly in the saddle, drawing one gloved hand through the arm slit cut into her cloak to surreptitiously rub her belly. Easing forward, she stretched out the cramped muscles in her back. Despite her horse being led by Bruin, the lengthy ride was taking its toll; she was out of practice and her limbs started to protest. Her hip bones ached. Her eyes watered, aching with the continual squinting against the glaring sunshine, the vivid blue sky. The breeze scoured her cheeks. But the exertion of the ride, combined with the new dry clothes, had warmed her after her time in the river, and for that, she was thankful.

Below them, the countryside flattened out. Down to their right, the river wound a steady course, hugging the low hilly contours, studded with clumps of bare-branched oaks. To the left the flood plain extended across flat pasture, bisected by hedges. And ahead in the distance, a higher range of hills, tops covered with orange bracken, their looming bulk shimmering on the horizon. Pulling in his reins, Bruin slowed to a stop. His knee nudged hers as her horse moved alongside him. Silently, she envied his energy, the superior physical strength that no doubt would keep him riding all day. She knew she was holding him up, being tugged along by the leading rein, but she was glad of it. Because the slower they went, the more likely Lord Steffen was to die before they reached Deorham.

'Why have you stopped?' Eva asked. 'Are you lost?' Her horse stood slightly higher on the slope than Bruin's, dropping its head to rip up the sparse, short grass.

'No, I know the way,' he answered. 'But I thought we would rest for a moment.' In the harsh, unrelenting light, his cheekbones seemed cast from stone, angular in his tanned face. Dark bronze bristles hazed his chin, lending him a saturnine, devilish look. Catching her quick glance, he rubbed a rueful hand across his jawline. 'Aye, I had no time to shave, but you can spare me the reproving look. If you remember, I had other things on my mind this morning.'

Eva grimaced, flushing at the memory of their kiss in the shadowed hallway, ducking her head to study the line of silver discs that decorated her bridle. His firm mouth moving over hers, searching out the softness, flirting with her innocence. Her body splayed beneath him. Her stomach hollowed out with insensible yearning. 'It was a mistake,' she replied sharply. 'I was upset. I wasn't thinking straight.'

'I wasn't talking about that.' Amusement etched his tone.

'What—oh!' The colour on her cheeks deepened to a rosy red. 'You mean my escape.'

'Why, what did you think I meant?' he asked, raising his eyebrows innocently, although he knew to what she was referring. He hadn't forgotten the kiss: the luscious pliability of her feminine curves; her sweet mouth.

'Nothing. I thought you meant that.' She twisted the leather bridle with irritation—what was the matter with her? She was usually adept at maintaining a haughty aloofness, a sneering disdain, around men, even more so since her time with Lord Steffen. And yet with Bruin? Every glance, every smile, even the slightest brush from his arm, made her heart sing stupidly, an unsteady desire knocking through her, incandescent, unsteady. Why, oh, why did it have to be him? This man, larger than life itself, with his wild brindled hair and diamond eyes. Her body cleaved towards him with a treacherous determination that she seemed powerless to control. Staring grimly at the pale flickering grass, she waited for Bruin to move off. She would do well to put such thoughts out of her head, and concentrate on the journey ahead.

'Do you want to eat?' Bruin asked mildly. 'You must be hungry after all that exertion this morning.'

'You don't have to keep referring to what happened,' she snapped. The wind whipped at her veil, a chaotic spiral of silk, and she raised one slim arm to push it back, holding the flying end with her fingers. Beneath the diaphanous material, her hair was still wet, cold droplets trickling down behind her ears, down the elegant column of her neck. She had pinned her hair up into a loose bun with the few remaining hairpins that had survived her plunge into the river. 'I know you think it's a tremendous joke that I would try such a foolish thing, but you can stop gloating now. You caught me.'

Her spine was drawn straight, mouth pressed into a hostile line, every inch of her body radiating a prickly, combative energy, a taut readiness for a fight. She had agreed to come with him peacefully, but he suspected their journey would be anything but easy. 'I was only teasing, Eva.' He held his palms up, a gesture of apology. 'And I do have some food.' The edges of his generous mouth curved upwards.

His quick smile punctured her crabbiness. Her tight-lipped expression eased, appreciating his easy camaraderie, his efforts to dispel the tension between them. Without waiting for her reply, he swung down from his saddle, jumping down into the bristly grass.

'I have bread and cheese, and a flagon of mead,' he said. 'Is that enough to tempt you down from your horse?' He reached up for her, swinging her light weight down beside him. Her leg muscles screamed in protest and she winced. He frowned as the pain flashed across her face. 'Your leg?'

'No, my leg is fine. It's just that I haven't ridden for some time,' Eva replied ruefully. 'I'm not used to it.'

He chuckled, removing his gauntlets to release the buckles on the saddlebag at the back of his horse. 'It will become easier,' he reassured her. 'Here.' He handed her a pie filled with chunks of meat, vegetables. 'Eat quickly, otherwise we'll freeze standing still like this.' His eyes moved over her face, her cheeks slapped bright red by the icy wind. 'Are you warm enough?' Reaching over her head, he pulled her voluminous hood forward. 'There,' he said, with an air of satisfaction, 'that should keep the wind off you, at least.'

'Why are you being like this?' Eva glared at him suspiciously. A wary look crossed her aquamarine eyes. The fur edging on her hood ruffled around her ears, brushing the curve of her cheek.

'Like what?' Bruin said through large mouthfuls of pie. He ate with relish, obviously hungry. 'I'm trying to be nice.' He swept the stray crumbs from his mouth with his thumb. 'Eat your food.'

Eva wrinkled her pert, tip-tilted nose, delicate crinkles appearing between her eyes. 'That's just it. You being nice. They said at Melyn that you were an outlaw.'

A flinty rawness crossed his face, extinguishing his smile. 'What makes you ask that?'

'Something the maid said to me. Is it true?'

'Those days are long gone now. It's a time of my life that I'm not proud of.'

'Then why did you do it?' she persisted.

'Eat your food, Eva…' he sighed '…and stop plaguing me with questions.'

'Well, at least I can see now why you behave the way that you do.'

'You think I behave like an outlaw?' Noticing a raised spot on his horse's fetlock, he crouched down, running an experienced hand across his destrier's leg. The side split of his tunic fell open, revealing woollen leggings pulled taut across the thick defined muscle in his lower thighs.

'You did. You were a thug when I first met you.' Eva picked at a loose flake of pastry. 'Now you're offering me food, helping me down from my horse. Asking me if I'm warm enough.'

'I'm a knight, Eva.' His voice rumbled, flint-sharp eyes glittering with undisguised amusement. 'I've spent the last year fighting for the King, living in a makeshift camp with hundreds of soldiers. Forgive me if my manners aren't quite up to your high standards.'

She flushed. 'My standards aren't that high. But you've dragged me about with so much a by-your-leave, forced me to do things I don't want to do...'

He stood up slowly, resting his hand on his destrier's neck. 'Not everything, surely?'

She read the silent question in his eyes, flushed deeply. The kiss in the corridor, of course. Her lungs emptied of air, nerves bunched tight with tension. The kiss to which she had responded without restraint would have given her body to him in a moment. He hadn't forced her at all. A rush of heat spread over her chest, rising up into her neck. 'No,' she admitted truthfully, 'not everything.' Her eyelashes flew up, gaze sparking with memory. His lips grinding down on hers.

'We both enjoyed it.' Bruin bent to adjust his horse's girth strap. 'No harm was done.'

Eva flinched, stung by his callous dismissal. She should forget the encounter, cast the memory away. 'That's what I mean,' she replied. 'You take what you want and you do what you want, without thinking of the consequences.'

If he *had* taken what he had truly wanted, then she would be more than cursing him now. What would have happened if Lady Katherine had not appeared? Bruin slapped the reins irritably against his horse's neck, stunned by the direction of his thoughts. He was drawn to Eva's quiet beauty, aye, by that ethereal light that shone out from the perfection of her delicate features, but was this—whatever it was between them—purely physical? Mayhap he should bed her now and be done with it. But the thought sickened him and he turned away from it. He was not that sort of man, never had been, even in his darkest days.

Stuffing the muslin cloths that had wrapped the pastry back into his saddle bags, he glanced at the lowering sun. 'You'd better eat up, Eva. We need to find lodgings before night falls.'

The castle at Goodric, where Bruin intended to stay that night, lay at the conjunction of two massive river valleys, the jumble of buildings sprawling out across the flat meadowland. One river cut through a field beside the castle, running shallow and fast, the lowering sunlight glinting on the sparkling water. Trees cast long shadows across the lumpy ground, still flecked in places with the white tongues of frost. The sun was setting fast, going down in a shimmering display of pinks and oranges, streaking the translucent blue sky.

Bruin slowed the horses to walking pace through the foul-smelling, muddy streets of the small town that clustered around the outer walls of the castle. In this twilight hour, the temperature dipping rapidly, few people were about; those that were scarce gave them a second glance, keen to reach their own dwellings before darkness fell. Woodsmoke hung heavily in the air, filling the narrow streets, stinging their eyes. Through cottage windows,

Eva glimpsed families huddled around their open fires, jostling together. Laughing.

'Have you been to Goodric before?' asked Bruin, steering their horses across a low wooden bridge that ran directly to the studded oak gates of the castle.

Eva shook her head. 'No, our lands were to the south of Katherine's. We had little occasion to venture further north. My father and brother may have visited, but not me or my mother, obviously.'

'Why "obviously"?'

Eva stared down at her gloved hands on the reins. The daylight was dimming so quickly, she could scarce see the creased leather any more. 'My mother died when I was little, not above five or six years old.'

'I am sorry.' Bruin's eyes gleamed in the bluish light, chainmail sparkling across his hefty shoulders like a cloak of stars. The enormous hooves of his destrier thudded noisily against the wooden planks of the bridge. Beneath them, the waters of the moat were inky blank, the surface like a viscous skin, impenetrable.

'Nay, it doesn't matter, Bruin.' She hunched down into the encompassing sweep of her woollen cloak. 'I can't really remember her at all. I was so young.'

'How did she die?'

'She drowned.' Eva hitched herself up in the saddle, leaning forward slightly to relieve the strain in her lower back. 'It was the reason why my father insisted that my brother and I learned to swim. My mother couldn't; she was returning from visiting the shrine of St Agnes—it's on a small island just off the coast—and the weather turned bad as she was coming back. The boat overturned.' She clamped her lips together suddenly, sensing she had blurted out too much; why on earth would Bruin be interested in her family matters?

'What happened?'

Eva traced his profile in the limpid twilight: the strong, aquiline jut of his nose, the whipcord strength in his neck, highlighted by the glistening chainmail hood pushed back on to his shoulders. 'Her manservant survived, but was unable to rescue her.' She paused. 'In a way, she saved me. Because she drowned, my father made sure I could swim.'

'Which is why you had the confidence to jump into the river at Melyn. Because you thought you could swim away from me.' He studied his gloved hands, remembering his shock as he watched Eva fly backwards through the air, cloak flapping. 'You must have been desperate to do something like that.'

'I was,' she confirmed. Her eyes hollowed out in the twilight, huge dark pools in her pale face, haunted by memories. The long lonely hours locked in a damp turret at one of Steffen's castles; fear plummeting her heart as she heard his boots climb the stairs. Then the crunch of Steffen's fingers around her own as he forced her to sign parchment after parchment: agreements to hand over her lands.

Bruin saw the sadness cross her eyes; the flick of pain. She had endured so much, he thought, and not only at his brother's hands. The loss of her family, all that she had held dear to her. An overwhelming desire to look after this woman swept over him. To stand by her side and fight her battles for her. To gather her in his arms, and hold her tight. 'Promise me you'll never do anything like that again,' Bruin murmured.

His voice was a husky whisper, sliding through her veins like silk. A possessiveness coloured his tone, but then she wondered if she had imagined it. For why would Bruin say such an odd thing? Surely she was merely a problem for him, a problem that would be solved when he delivered her to his brother. But he sounded like he actually cared for her.

'Bruin? Good God, man, is that really you?' Lord Goodric, one of King Edward's most trusted nobles, raised his tankard of mead and bellowed out across the great hall towards them. 'Come here and share a cup with me! You are most welcome here.'

Unsure what was expected of her, Eva hesitated in the doorway, half-hidden behind the padded curtain that hung to one side of the arch. The cloth smelled of lavender, freshly washed. Bruin was beside her, his arm pressing into the rounded softness of her shoulder. His fingers dug beneath the folds of her cloak and clasped her gloved hand, squeezing it. Heat tingled up her arm. He held her hand firmly as they walked towards the top table, across the double-height hall and up the steps. His assured grip gave her confidence and she drew strength from his fingers, her heart dancing a perilous tune beneath his touch.

Lord Goodric sat alone at the polished wood table, leaning on his elbows, the steward who had announced their arrival now standing respectfully behind him. Goodric was older than Bruin; grey strands rippled through his blond hair, cut square across his forehead and shaved close to the base of his neck. Rolls of crumpled parchment spread out around him, covered in sprawls of spidery words. As Bruin and Eva approached, he half-rose out of his seat, bowing. 'Bruin, how long is it since I've seen you? When was our last campaign together? Was it Tutfield? Or Skenfirth?' Whipping his head around to the servant, he clicked his fingers impatiently. 'Fetch mead and cups, now!' The servant scuttled off in the direction of the kitchens, through a narrow door at the back of the dais.

Bruin grinned. 'I can't remember, my lord, but it's been too long. I appreciate you giving us bed and board at such short notice.'

'Anything for you, Bruin. Anything. Stay as long as you like. But I'm surprised you're not with the King now. He's intent on subduing the rebels. I hear they've been fighting further up the river, to the north.' Goodric slumped back down in his seat. 'Sit yourself down, anyway, and your good lady as well. Introduce me, Bruin. When on earth did you find the time to marry?'

Eva stumbled forward, her toe tangling in the hem of her dress. Bruin gripped her hand, keeping her upright. Colour blazed across her cheeks and she opened her mouth to correct Lord Goodric. But Bruin turned slightly, pushing her into the nearest seat. He quirked an eyebrow at her: a warning. *Trust me*, his eyes said, as he wedged her down, a firm hand on her shoulder.

'This is Lady Eva,' Bruin confirmed, not correcting Lord Goodric's mistake. He threw his tall frame into the ornately carved chair, crooking his elbow on the armrest.

Lord Goodric hitched forward so he could gain a better view, his bloodshot eyes raking across the delicate oval of Eva's face, the elegant line of her neck, slim shoulders. 'My, my, Bruin, you did well for yourself, didn't you? What a beauty.' He tipped his fleshy chin towards

Eva. 'My wife and daughters will be delighted to meet you later, my lady, at the evening meal. I apologise for them not being here at the moment. They are travelling back from Raglan.' He pressed a hand to his forehead, wincing dramatically. 'Four daughters and none of them yet betrothed; I wouldn't wish it on anyone. Give me a battlefield any day.' He shoved irritably at the parchments spreading across the table. 'Take these away, boy!' he snapped. 'And pour us all some mead. You look like you could do with some, my lady.'

Eva hitched uncomfortably in her seat at Lord Goodric's words. Although she still wore her cloak and gloves a great shiver seized her, rattling through her slim frame like a gust of freezing air. Why would Bruin say such a thing, that she was his wife? It made no sense, because surely it made no difference? Maybe he thought it would offer her greater protection. The revelation poured through her like an elixir, a balm. Comforting. She revelled in the delicious feeling, the feeling of being able to rely on someone else, for a tiny moment.

The servant moved between them, collecting up the parchments with a studied efficiency, pouring the mead into pewter cups and setting a large platter of honeyed oat biscuits on the table. 'I can have more food brought out if you wish?' Goodric offered, gulping mead from his cup, wiping stray droplets from his mouth with his sleeve.

'Nay, this is sufficient, thank you,' Bruin answered.

'Well, then…' Goodric cleared his throat noisily '…how about some rest after your journey? Forgive me, but your wife looks like she could lie down for a while.'

Bruin's eyes swept over Eva's wan face, her swaying stance. 'Aye, she has had a lot to deal with today,' he replied, his explanation deliberately vague. His silvery eyes glittered over her. Her heart jolted in response, but not with fear.

'Then I will have some hot water sent up.' Goodric clapped his hands decisively.

Chapter Eleven

'What on earth possessed you to say such a thing?' Eva hissed at Bruin as they walked side by side from the high dais, following a maidservant.

'What thing?' Bruin paused, letting her precede him into the dim stairwell. Up ahead, the maidservant held a flaming brand, lighting the stone steps spiralling upwards. They were difficult to see in the shadowy half-light. Eva placed her gloved hand on the rope banister and climbed a few steps. She stopped, twisting around to answer him, expecting him to be below her. But he was on the step below, the difference in their heights putting his sculptured features on a level with hers, shockingly close.

'You know.' Eva touched her veil self-consciously. A shudder rippled her voice. 'The thing about me being your wife!'

Bruin tipped his broad chest forward, his mouth a mere fraction from the downy cushion of her cheek. A delicious scent radiated from his warm skin: heated wax and woodsmoke; the earth. Desire pleated her heart; the rigid trap of her throat snared her breath. She would not move back, or turn away. She could not. Her body seemed enslaved, hopelessly tangled in the heady power of his presence.

'Wait until we are alone.' One big hand splayed across the slender curve of her waist, urging her to continue. Eva baulked at the familiar gesture, even as her belly looped with excitement. She lunged forward, too fast, tripping over her skirts in a desperate attempt to create some space between them.

'Careful,' Bruin said, seizing her elbow as the steps loomed up in front of her face. He yanked her upright. 'This light makes it difficult to see where you're going.'

'You don't have to make excuses for me,' she flashed back grumpily, wrenching away from his loose hold. 'We both know it's these damned skirts, curse them! Katherine's so much taller than me.' Gathering up the front of her skirts, she lifted them high above the steps, knowing that she lied. She blamed the clothes, when all the time it was him, Bruin; he was doing this to her, making her act like this, like a woman who had seemingly lost the power to think, or look after herself. Who stumbled around like a fool.

Behind her, Bruin chuckled.

'I'm glad you think it's funny.' Eva fixed her eyes on the maidservant bobbing ahead. 'You try wearing clothes like these for a day and then you'd realise!'

His eyes traced the slim, elegant curve of her hip that nudged against her dark blue cloak, the graceful tilt of her head as she climbed before him. They were bickering like an old married couple, he thought. And he was enjoying it, enjoying being with this feisty woman who had barrelled into his life as if from nowhere, who wanted nothing from him but to be left alone. But he had no intention of leaving her. He was glad that his brother had sent him to find her, glad of that excuse that meant he could remain by her side. For every moment in her company meant that the cold, shuttered wings of his heart stretched out a little, the pain of memory easing gradually.

The stairs opened out on to a long corridor. Low windows, free of glass, lined the left-hand side; light and air swilled through the space. Wooden shutters had been dragged open for the daytime; no doubt they would be shut when night fell properly. Shadows dappled the wood-planked floor in broad rectangles. The maidservant opened a door to reveal a sumptuous guest chamber: a four-poster bed hung with velvet-brocade curtains, red and gold, with furs piled on sweet-smelling linen. Colourful tapestries lined the cream-plastered walls. Heat radiated throughout the room; a brazier glowed in one corner, lumps of charcoal flickering brightly.

'My lady.' The maidservant bowed her head, dutifully standing by the door, allowing Eva to walk into the chamber.

'Thank you,' said Eva, pulling off her leather gloves as she stepped over the threshold. Her tired eyes fell on the bed; she longed to throw herself upon it and fall into a heavy, dreamless sleep. 'This is delightful.' Ducking his head beneath the thick oak lintel, Bruin came into the room behind her. Eva wrinkled her brow at him, then addressed the maidservant. 'Mayhap you could show Lord Bruin to his chamber now?'

'My lady?' Concern flickered across the maidservant's blunt, heavy features.

'My wife speaks in jest,' Bruin explained. 'We've had a tiff and she wants me gone.' His granite eyes twinkled. 'What can a man do?' He grinned conspiratorially at the young maid. 'This chamber is perfect, thank you. If you could send up some hot water…?'

'Of course, my lord, at once.' Blushing deeply beneath his attention, the girl bobbed a swift curtsy before disappearing out into the corridor. Bruin shut the door behind her, shooting the iron bolt firmly across the wide wooden planks.

'What are you doing?' Eva squeaked at him, scrunching her leather gloves between her fingers. 'You need your own chamber, don't you? We cannot stay here together.'

The mineral darkness of his eyes drifted across her lovely face, the worry creasing her smooth brow. 'But we have to, Eva. We are supposed to be married, remember? And I have no intention of arousing any suspicion by having two separate chambers.'

'But what on earth made you let Lord Goodric think we were married?' A melancholy note entered her voice. 'I don't know why you said it.' She sat down miserably on the bed, skirts and cloak spreading around her, hems splattered with flecks of mud from the journey. She lifted her hand, fiddling with her circlet, her veil. 'Why did you?'

He folded his arms across his chest, moving to stand before her, muscled legs planted firmly astride. The leather on his boots was scuffed, cracking slightly. 'Because I can protect you,' he explained quietly, 'if people think you are my wife. As an unmarried woman, you are vulnerable, even with me here, in a next-door chamber. It's better this way.'

'But it means we have to share a room,' Eva whispered, pressing one hand to her mouth, the other tight across her stomach, cupping her elbow, defensive. Her pupils dilated, huge black pools obscuring the blue of her eyes.

He almost laughed out loud at the dread in her voice. 'Is the prospect really that awful?'

Smoothing the rumpled silk of her veil, she settled it on her shoulder, fussing with it. Her hair smelled of river water, an earthy freshness. 'I don't know,' she replied in a tired little voice. 'I've never done it before. I don't make a habit of sharing chambers with men.' Especially men like you, she thought, her eyes travelling up the sturdy brace of his legs. The close cut of his fawn leggings revealed heavy, defined muscles that disappeared at mid-thigh, beneath the hem of his surcoat. She looked away, her throat dry, desperate for liquid. No, she thought, her blood beginning to race, the prospect of sharing a room with him wasn't awful at all; it was exciting, exhilarating, and that was what she was worried about.

'Look…' Bruin sighed '…I have no intention of offending you in any way. But you must believe me when I tell you that sharing a room is far safer than being apart. It's you and your safety that I'm thinking of here, nothing else.'

'As long as that's all it is,' she blurted out, flushing. Her eyes shimmered, a vivid turquoise.

'What are you implying?' He thrust his jaw forward, brindled brows drawing together in a deep frown.

Raw colour stung her cheeks. She leaned back on the bed, balancing herself on outstretched arms. Her small hands splayed across the furs, delicate bones ridging her fingers. Her cloak parted, falling away to reveal the lithe elegance of her body encased in the richly decorated fabric of her gown. The firm span of her waist, flaring down to curving hips. 'I—well—' She stuttered to a halt.

What had she been implying? That he would ravish her in the middle of the night? Plunder her sweet flesh and rob her of her innocence? Her breath picked up speed, emerging in sharp little gusts. 'Nay, it's nothing, Bruin. I'm not sure it's a good idea, that's all.'

'You can trust me,' he said slowly. But even as he spoke the words, a newborn lust ignited in his belly, a flare of lightning, streaking through his veins, untrammelled, haphazard. It would take just a fraction of a moment for him to step forward and push her down, to throw up her skirts and bury himself in her sweetness. Sheer, undiluted lust pulsed through him, throbbed at the base of his groin. He cleared his throat hastily, glaring up at the velvet canopy above the bed, the endless pleating, dredging the depths of his self-control. He could do this, he told himself sternly; he could keep himself in check around her.

'How can I trust you?' Eva chewed fretfully at one of her nails. 'I have no idea what kind of man you are. Your brother's character is all I have to judge you by.' The pearly twilight silhouetted his burly frame, the wild strands of his hair rippling around his head; she was unable to see his face clearly. 'I don't know who you are at all.'

'I'm nothing like my brother,' he rapped out, scowling. 'I haven't treated you badly, have I? I've treated you with respect.'

'Yes,' she agreed. 'But how can you be so different from your brother? I don't understand it.'

Bruin sighed. 'It may have something to do with our childhood, but I can't be certain.' The straw-stuffed mattress creaked, crackled as he bounced down on the bed, pulling off one leather boot, then the other, throwing them on the floor. Woollen leggings crushed against his thick calves, his big feet clad in fawn wool. 'When we were born, I nearly died. I was so weak my parents doubted my survival. And growing up, I was no match for my brother physically; in any game, he would always beat me.' His tone was blunt, matter of fact. 'I suppose my parents indulged Steffen because they thought he was more likely to make it to adulthood.'

Eva's gaze slid over his broad shoulders, the muscled heft of his chest. Bruin, weak? It seemed impossible, somehow. 'So he was spoiled and indulged as a child. That shouldn't turn him into a monster.'

Balancing one foot on his knee, Bruin kneaded his stockinged toes with strong fingers. 'No,' he agreed, 'but there was always an edge to Steffen, a need to be at the top of everything, a need to win.' He shook his head. 'I'm not sure what has happened to him, but from what you are telling me, it sounds like he has been given too much power by the King.'

'And that power has gone to his head.' She was nodding now; everything he said about Steffen was making sense. As twins they might look the same, but their characters were completely different.

'Precisely. Steffen is nothing like me, Eva. You have my word on that.' Throwing himself back against the pillows, he stretched his legs across the bed, half-closing his eyes with pleasure. 'God, that's better,' he murmured. 'I haven't taken those off in a while.'

His woollen-clad toes brushed against her hip, a strangely intimate gesture. Horrified, Eva hopped up. A flush crept over her neck, climbing up her throat, and she pressed one pale hand to her skin, hoping to mask the flood of heat, heart thumping. Bruin seemed to cover the whole bed, his leonine head propped up against the linen pillows, the pretty lace edging incongruous against the hard, tanned lines of his face. 'Sorry.' He crooked one arm behind his head. 'I didn't mean to push you from your perch.'

'Your feet smell,' she said huffily. It was the first thing that came into her head and totally untrue. There was a knock at the door and she leapt to throw the bolt across, grateful for the distraction from the big masculine body sprawled behind her. Two servants stood in the corridor, carrying wooden pails of steaming hot water. Eva stood there, dumbly, her mind bereft of speech.

'Bring it in and pour it in the tub,' Bruin ordered from the bed. 'Who's going to be first? Me or you?' His metallic eyes fixed on Eva's wan face.

She was desperate for a bath. The rank smell of her hair permeated her nostrils, every pore on her skin imbued with the sweat and mud and exertion of the day. But what was Bruin going to do? Was he going to lie there, on the bed, and listen as she removed her clothes, as she sank into the deliciously scented hot water? How could she bear it? She eyed the flimsy screen that obscured the bathtub from the rest of the chamber: three panels set in a zigzag line, thick colourful tapestries stretched over the wooden frames.

'Eva, go on,' he urged. 'The water will be hot.'

Behind the screen she could hear the servants talking to one another, and then the gush of water hitting the wooden sides of the tub. She toed the floor, hesitating. 'Do you have to be in this chamber? Can't you go somewhere else?'

'No,' he said. 'I'm staying here. But I promise not to move from this bed.'

Eva chewed on her bottom lip, thinking of the wonderful scented water that awaited her. 'All right,' she agreed doubtfully. 'But you will stay there, won't you?' The lure of the bath was too great to ignore. Bruin nodded, an air of uninterest crossing his features, giving every indication that he would keep his word. She heaved a sigh of relief, shoving the bolt back across the door as the servants left the chamber.

Removing her cloak, she laid the heavy material across an oak coffer set against the wall, then kicked off her boots, bending down to set them straight, the leather tops folding down to one side in soft gathers. Suspecting Bruin's scrutiny, every movement she made felt contrived, awkward; but when she darted a look towards him on the bed, his eyes were closed. The tough line of his mouth had relaxed into a half-smile, making him look younger, more approachable somehow. She remembered those lips on hers, the heated promises made in his questing kiss. Her heart flipped, stupidly.

His eyes shot open, pewter chips, bright and sparkling. 'Get a move on, Eva. That water will be cold if you stand there any longer.'

She jumped like a scalded cat, hurrying behind the screen. A host of candles flickered from a floor-standing candelabra in the corner, wax dripping down from the wicks. Steam rose from the tub. A thick linen sheet had been laid on the inside to protect the skin from rogue splinters, the ends laid over the rough wood at the top. The water swirled in the glistening candlelight, the surface scattered with rose petals. Pulling off her circlet and veil, Eva plucked swiftly at her side lacings, loosening the gown; she dragged it over her head, throwing it to the floor. Her underdress followed, then her chemise, drawers and stockings. She was naked, goosebumps rippling her skin; she glanced at the screen once more to check that it was still in place.

She climbed in, sinking down into blissful liquid heat. The water rose to her neck, coalescing around her exhausted limbs, warming them, driving out the chill of the day. She suppressed a groan of utter delight, mindful of the man who lay on the bed. Closing her eyes, she rested her head against the side of the tub, pulling out the pins in her hair, dropping them to the floor one by one. Her hair straggled down, curling ebony tendrils, floating on the water like undulating seaweed. A lump of oatmeal soap had been left on a high stool next to the tub; she lathered it over her scalp and hair, digging her fingers in vigorously. Grains of oatmeal stuck to her skin as she rubbed the soap over the rest of her body, using the linen washcloth to rinse herself, skimming over the reddened scar on her leg. Her wound had almost healed.

Scrubbed clean, she tipped her head back, closing her eyes, her thoughts wandering. She ought to climb out now and let Bruin have a bath before the water cooled too much. But a few more moments wouldn't hurt, would they? She spread her palms out, flattening them across the water, scooping aside the rose petals, lifting them to her nose. The scent was heady, strong, reminding her of long, hot summer days. Summers with her family, when she was young and naïve, innocent to the uglier ways of the world. How could she have ever known what was going to happen? That she would lose her family and her fortune by the time she had seen twenty winters?

Hunching forward, she gripped her ankles, burying her face into her wet knees. The hot water cocooned her, made her feel safe; she was in no hurry to leave, despite Bruin waiting. Her heart gave a small, lopsided flip. What was he doing? Was he just lying there, listening to the slop and churn of the water as she bathed? Or had he fallen asleep? She peered hard at the crowded stitches in the tapestry screen, frowning, almost as if she suspected him to have crept up to spy on her through the gaps in the fabric.

'Bruin?' she called out tentatively.

'Hmmm?' His voice was a low comforting rumble, percolating through her like liquid silk.

Eva sank back into the water with relief. His voice was far enough away to reassure her that he had remained on the bed. 'What are you doing?' she asked.

'Nothing.'

'Were you asleep?' she ventured.

'Not really.'

The mattress rustled as he moved. 'You are on the bed, aren't you?' she asked hurriedly.

'Yes,' he replied, his answer languid and drawn out. 'Although I wouldn't mind having a bath some time today.'

Eva stared in dismay at the soap scum floating on the water around her. How could she have done such a thing? Even the rose petals had sunk down, faded shreds at the bottom. It was inconceivable, embarrassing, that he should have to climb into this water after she had made such a mess of it. 'Er… I think—I think you might have to send for some more water.'

'Why, have you drunk it all?'

Laughter bubbled within her, but she suppressed it, shaking her head ruefully. 'No, but the soap's made a mess and there's no rose petals left. The water looks awful.'

'Is that all you're worried about?' He laughed. 'That

I'll be upset about a bit of soap scum and a few missing rose petals? Do you think I'm bothered about things like that?'

'Well, yes,' she said, skirting her hand across the water. 'It looked so nice, so inviting when I got in...'

'Eva, I'm a soldier. We often don't bathe for weeks and then it's often only a muddy puddle. Just climb out and let me have a bath, will you?'

Standing up abruptly, Eva stepped out of the tub, sweeping a large linen towel around her shoulders. Water sluiced down her bare limbs, pooling on the wooden floorboards. The cool air puckered her skin, chilling her flesh. She shivered.

'Are you ready?' Bruin's voice boomed behind the screen.

'No!' she squeaked. 'Go away!'

'Let me move your clothes over to the bed and then you can dress while I have a bath,' he suggested.

'Bruin, I haven't got anything on!' Eva protested as he moved around the screen. She staggered back, almost knocking into the iron candelabra. Her mind hazed, shimmered breathlessly. Bruin wore only his braies: snug woollen leggings riding low on his hips, close-fitting around the bunched muscles of his legs. He had removed his surcoat, the chainmail hauberk and his shirt. His chest was bare, honed, massive plates of flat pectoral muscle rising up from the strong indent of his sternum. His skin held a polished sleekness, silk over stone. A line of bronze-coloured hair ran from his navel, downwards. Her blood thickened and slowed, a numb weight bolting her to the floor, preventing movement. Her throat was dry, belly melting like liquid fire. Igniting.

'What are you doing?' she whispered.

'I'm putting these on the bed for you,' Bruin explained. Without glancing in her direction, he scooped up her discarded clothes. He disappeared behind the screen, his spine a long powerful rope, shoulder muscles rippling and flexing.

Sweat prickled her hair line; she raised a shaking hand to wipe it away. How could she have known a man could be so beautiful? She had to move away from him, create some distance between them. But her befuddled mind refused to help her, refused to arrange her thoughts into any sort of order. He returned, the wide expanse of toned flesh dancing provocatively before her eyes, tormenting her.

'Eva!' he barked at her. 'What's the matter with you? Will you not go and dress?'

The raven-coloured satin of her hair was plastered in wet coils across the pristine white towel, water dripping from the curling ends, scattering dark spots across the floorboards. A droplet of water quivered like a diamond on her earlobe, before spinning down to track across the pearly expanse of her neck. It disappeared beneath the towel that she held in a firm, taut grip across her body.

Her naked body. Damp skin smelling of roses.

Nay, he could not think of that.

'Come on,' Bruin said briskly. 'Anyone would think you hadn't seen a man's bare chest before!'

At his jesting words, Eva flushed, a sudden flood of vivid colour suffusing her cheeks. Ducking her head, she made to move past him, jostling his arm. He caught her by the shoulder, pressing the flat of his hand to the fine bones beneath the towel.

'You haven't, have you?' he said. Surprise laced his words.

'What do you think?' She glared at him stonily, her

eyes sparking fire, brilliant orbs of turquoise. Her voice rose shrilly. 'What kind of woman do you take me for?'

'I thought—' He ruffled one hand through his hair. From his armpit, reddish-gold hairs sprouted vigorously. 'My God,' he whispered, 'you really are an innocent, aren't you?' Raising his hand, he trailed his fingers across the plush velvet of her cheek. Her lips parted, as if of their own volition; her breath kissed his knuckles. His groin tightened.

'What of it?' Eva whispered. 'Better to be an innocent than to be a whore.' Runnels of lightning fire burst beneath his touch, a dam breaking, looping around with such velocity she thought her heart would burst.

'I agree,' he murmured, smiling at the fire in her eyes. Her grip loosened fractionally on the towel. He glimpsed the tantalising curve of one round breast, shadowed by her knuckles. Below the snare of her hand the towel flowed downwards in loose gathers. What would it be like to dip his hand beneath, to lay his fingers across the warm, scented flesh of her belly?

His jaw tightened. Gripping her shoulder, he turned her violently around, pushing his fist into the sinuous indent of her spine. His voice was a low, grating command. 'Go! Get out of here.'

Chapter Twelve

Eva staggered to the four-poster bed, knees whippy as saplings, her muscles wrung out, barely supporting her. Delight scorched her slim frame: wild, pulsating waves of heat, relentless, turning her logical mind to mush. Clawed by a deep yearning, her belly hollowed out, jerky and volatile. The briefest touch. The skim of his fingers against her cheek. Her body had responded to him with such force that a tremble of fear rattled through her.

Flinging herself across the bed, she buried her hot forehead in cool linen. She wanted to shout aloud, to thump and bash at the plump pillow, to tear at the fragile cover; make the feathers fly. But she bit down hard on her bottom lip, reining in her careering frustration. For the man who had made her feel like this was also the man who sat in a bathtub a few feet away. She mustn't make a sound.

How dare Bruin have this power over her? This ability to turn her limbs to mush, a helpless pulp. To turn her into one of those simpering maidens in their filmy satin gowns, wafting about great halls, doing nothing all day but glance covertly at the handsome knights and hang upon their every word as if they were pearls of wisdom. She was not one of those women! She was Eva, practical, forthright Eva, the woman at whom people laughed because she could ride and run as well as any man. The woman who had fought for the right to run her own estate after the death of her family, only to have it stolen away from her by Lord Steffen's underhand methods.

She yanked the towel more securely against her back and hips, holding the edges closed within the hollow of her belly beneath her. The fur coverlet tickled her clenched hands. Desire stalked her: a treacherous lust that gripped her loins, made whispering promises. The way she reacted to him, his nearness, his touch; the way she looked on, an impotent observer, as her cheek rubbed against his knuckles. Self-restraint fled, a mocking banshee cackling into the wind, no help to her at all. She had never known anything like this before, this need, this craving to lie with a man, to delight in his flesh, to revel in it. Startled, she blinked against the pillow, eyelashes scratching against the linen. She wanted to weep at the shame of it. Her thoughts were that of a wanton, surely, not a respectable maid! And yet, for all her self-chastisement, the flame of devilment burned brightly, hugely, in her heart, refusing to be doused, refusing to be cowed by such outrageous thoughts. She wanted him. She wanted Bruin. She wanted to lie with him.

'Oh, I thought you'd be dressed by now.' Bruin's voice ripped through her scandalous thoughts, a knife through silk.

Startled by how quickly he had bathed, Eva rolled over, not thinking. The towel parted, falling aside to reveal slender legs, skin like gossamer satin, curving hips, her womanhood nestled beneath the slim indent of her stomach. Her wet, unbound hair, snaking across the furs in loose tendrils. A fleeting glimpse of devastating beauty. Her blue eyes rounded in horror and she wrenched the towel back into place, flushing angrily.

He drank her in. Devoured her. Shocked to the spot, stunned, his gaze galloped across those silky legs, the lustrous skin of her belly, her breasts a shadowy hint beneath the towel, cramming in all that he could see in that moment. The ethereal delicacy of her limbs. The sweet crook of her knees. All that feminine softness, plush and velvety. He wanted it all. Like a man starved, he thought, desperate to fall on her, to drive himself within her tender folds. Sweet Jesu. Heat pumped through him, sheer undiluted lust, rocking his big body. How easy it would be to take her, to take what he wanted, right now, her puny strength no match for his.

Dredging frantically for the scattered remnants of his self-control, he tore his eyes from her, turning to the door in absolute disgust at himself. He was not that sort of man, to rape and pillage without so much as a by-your-leave. He never had been. Not even when he had been at sea with the exiled Lord Despenser, plundering merchant ships in the Channel, with women waiting for them in every port. Not even then.

'Put your clothes on,' Bruin snapped. 'I will wait outside.' The iron latch rattled violently as he slammed the door behind him. Mortification washed over her, a swelling flood of defeat. For a moment, she lay there, winded by his harsh tone. Eyes filling with tears, she gathered up her clothes, pulling on her chemise and undergarments, then each gown, lacing the garments with rough, jerky movements. Bending down, she rolled her stockings up over her ankles, up to her thighs.

The damp towel lay in a crumpled ball on the floor, mocking her. How could she have been so stupid? Why had she not dressed as soon as she had finished her bath? Recalling Bruin's look of pure disgust as he turned from her, she squeezed her eyes shut, trying to eradicate his harsh expression. He had made it absolutely clear what he thought of her, what he thought of her body. Puny. Short. She had heard it all before. She was surprised he hadn't laughed in her face.

Securing the pink ribbons that threaded through each stocking top with tight, decisive knots, Eva stood up, skirts skimming the floor, glancing about for her leather boots. She sighed; maybe this was a good thing to happen, after all. His rigid scowl and terse commands had taught her a valuable lesson. She was a commodity to him, a bundle to be delivered; she was a fool if she thought she was anything more than that. It was imperative that she controlled her feelings around him. Knotting her hands across her belly, she nodded to herself to emphasise this decision, to confirm it. But her heart pleated with sadness.

Securing her hair into a loose knot, she clamped her veil and circlet on her head, then smoothed her hands down the front of her skirts. There was nothing left to do; now, she must face him. He would be waiting for her in the corridor. Her blood picked up speed, filling her cheeks with colour as she lifted the latch with tentative fingers.

Flickering torches had been slung into iron brackets along the corridor. Bruin stood beneath the nearest one, one massive shoulder propped against the plastered wall. Bunched muscle roped his forearms, sinews sleek and toned beneath his skin. His hair was wet from the bath, the gold-red colour darkened to copper, damp strands falling across his forehead. He had shaved the gold bristles from his chin and his jaw held a satiny gleam.

'Bruin—' She reached out, her fingers grazing his elbow.

Deep shadows etched the slashing lines of his face. 'I must dress,' he growled, pushing away from the wall. He strode past her, into the chamber, leaving the door ajar. 'Stay there where I can see you.'

Misery surged through her at his brusque manner. He was revolted by her, by what she had done. But it hadn't been intentional. She clapped a hand across her mouth, aghast. Mother of Mary, did he think she'd rolled over deliberately, offering her naked body to him? She wanted to sink to the floorboards in shame.

'Ready?' Bruin asked, appearing in the doorway. He barely glanced at her. His chainmail hauberk had been replaced by a shirt of white linen, long-sleeved, over which he wore his customary red surcoat. He wore the same fawn leggings and leather boots that he had worn with his chainmail. The civilian outfit should have made him more approachable, less warlike somehow, and yet one glimpse at his stony, blank expression made her almost want to run down the stairs without looking back. But no. She was made of sterner stuff; she had endured worse than this. Setting her shoulders back in a straight line, she tilted her chin up at him, blue eyes flaring.

'Shall we go?' A note of impatience entered his voice when Eva failed to move. She was blocking the doorway.

'Not yet,' she said. 'I want to say something first.' Her voice was a muted whisper, echoing around the confined space. She cleared her throat. 'I wanted to say that—that

I'm sorry about—in there.' She tilted her head towards the chamber. 'I should have dressed straight away.'

'I beg your pardon?' Incredulous, Bruin stared down at her, eyes glowing like coals in the half-light. 'Please tell me you're not apologising for what just happened in there?' He rested his hands lightly on her shoulders. 'Are you?'

'Yes, Bruin, I am!' Her voice rose shrilly. 'You have to know that I'm not the sort of woman to do something like that! As if I wanted you to—to—' Her words wobbled, then stalled in her throat; she couldn't say them. A raging flush rose up her neck, flooding her cheeks. 'I'm not that sort of woman,' she finished limply.

'Eva, I know.' Bruin's voice was gentle, the low melodic tones curling through her heart: a balm. A faint smile played over his mouth.

'Then why are you so angry?' she asked in a small voice.

'Angry?' He jerked his chin up. The smell of burning tallow filled the air; a ragged pall of smoke drifted above them. 'I'm only angry with myself, Eva. Not you.' He sighed. 'I am the one at fault. I should have checked you had something on before I came out from behind the screen.'

'I'm sorry you had to see what you did.'

He blinked down at her, stunned. She talked about her body as if she were ashamed of it, as if it were something ugly. Did she honestly not realise how beautiful she was? How entrancing? Sweat gathered across his chest, in his armpits. His hands shook as he lifted them carefully from her shoulders. 'It wasn't that bad, Eva,' he managed to croak out. 'Come on, let's go and eat.' Spinning on his toes, he walked off down the corridor, gold-tipped hair glinting beneath the torches, expecting her to follow.

He only stopped as they neared the entrance on to the high dais. From the other side, the merry sound of harp and pipes emerged, muffled, coupled with bursts of raucous laughter, shrill chatter. The steady, thumping beat of a drum. Bruin turned to her, seeking out Eva's bright face in the gloom, his eyes sparking like diamonds. 'Remember that we are supposed to be married.' He stuck his hand through the wet hair on his forehead, ruffling it. His words held a trace of reluctance, as if he regretted ever making such a suggestion in the first place.

'I will play my part,' Eva assured him, 'if you think it will protect me.'

A vision of Eva's naked body spread-eagled across the bed danced before his eyes. 'It will,' Bruin replied. Doubt swirled in his mind, the flicker of desire burning steadily. He could protect her from others, aye, but from himself? Of that, he was not so sure.

The top table was set for feasting: pewter plates, silver goblets, huge serving platters containing meats and cooked vegetables. The air was hot, hazy with woodsmoke, filled with the scent of food and candle wax. Knights and their ladies sat in ornate carved chairs, ranged along one side of the top table, chattering and laughing. They glanced behind them with interest as Bruin strode in, Eva at his side.

'Bruin, my good man, over here!' Goodric, his bulbous nose red and sweaty, lifted his fist up, pointing out the two empty places either side of him. 'Allow me to introduce my good lady, Margaret.' A tall, elegant woman rose up, her rose-silk gown glowing, a myriad of rainbow colours in the candlelight, and bowed towards Bruin and

Eva. Further along the table, Goodric's four daughters sat, inclining their heads in unison towards the visitors, brown eyes flaring with interest at the sight of Bruin.

'Come and sit beside me, my dear,' Margaret said to Eva. 'I'm anxious to hear all about you! We are starved of news, stuck away in this place!' Eva slipped gratefully into the chair beside Margaret. With the substantial, noisy character of Lord Goodric between her and Bruin, she had some small respite from him.

'Have some wine.' Margaret picked up the earthenware jug in front of her and sloshed the red liquid liberally into Eva's pewter goblet. Her hair had been rolled high on either side of her head; the arrangement poked out of her heavy linen veil in an odd fashion. A voluminous wimple obscured her neck and throat, the material falling in dense curving gathers beneath her chin. 'I hope you and your husband have been made comfortable in our guest chamber?'

Husband. The lie stabbed into her, sheening her spine with sweat. Eva wriggled awkwardly, her mind crowding with images: Bruin, his chest bare and gleaming, fingers stroking her cheek; Bruin, turning away because he couldn't bear to look at her. 'Aye, thank you, my lady.' She inclined her head respectfully. 'Everything has been done to make us feel welcome.'

'I haven't had the pleasure of meeting you before, have I?' Margaret jabbed a fork into a plate of chicken and lifted several pieces on to Eva's plate. The chicken skin was roasted, crisp, shiny with grease. 'Your family owns Striguil, I understand?'

'Owned it, yes,' Eva corrected. 'It belongs to Lord Steffen now.' She fought hard to keep the bitterness out of her voice, her stomach roiling at the sight of the meat flopping over the side of her plate.

'Ah, yes.' Lady Margaret waved her fork airily. 'This wretched civil war drags on and on. I heard there was some trouble—but then, we women don't normally involve ourselves in that sort of thing, do we?'

'We do when we happen to be right in the middle of it,' Eva said bluntly. Picking up her goblet, she sipped at her wine, wiping her mouth delicately with a napkin.

Lady Margaret cleared her throat. 'I know—I know things haven't been easy for you.' She was trying to be kind, Eva realised, even though she had so little knowledge of what had really happened. 'But tell me…,' Margaret lowered her voice conspiratorially '…how did you come to be married to Bruin?' Her eyes flicked down to Eva's bare fingers; she frowned.

Eva tucked her hands hurriedly beneath the table. Of course, she should be wearing a wedding ring! 'I left my rings upstairs; I forgot to put them on again after my bath,' she explained hurriedly, face flaming.

'Do be careful leaving them about, my dear. We trust our servants, but some have been known to pilfer.' Margaret patted her arm, smiling. 'Never mind. I'm anxious to hear how you met and how you came to be married to him. We never thought he would, after his last betrothal. After what happened.'

Eva jerked upright, startled. She choked slightly, grabbing at her wine to cover her confusion at Margaret's words. What in Heaven's name was this woman talking about? Bruin, betrothed?

Lady Margaret laid her wrinkled hand on Eva's, her weighty silver rings winking in the candlelight, sparking green fire. 'Oh, my poor dear, do not distress yourself.

What a time you must have had. He became a different man after what happened.'

Eva nodded. As Margaret removed her hand, she unfolded, then refolded her napkin carefully, slowly, her thumb digging along one edge to smooth out the creases. She felt like a traitor to Bruin, drinking in Margaret's words. But something pushed her on, made her want to find out more, to discover the man behind those enigmatic grey eyes. 'Aye, he did,' she whispered the lie, for she spoke of a time unknown to her, the time before she had met him.

'And all that time at sea, with the exiled Lord Despenser. Raiding and looting merchant ships with no thought to life or limb. The King was in despair. He thought he'd lost his best commander.'

Eva nodded, shock sparking through her. She had not realised the extent of Bruin's lawlessness. He was fortunate the King hadn't decided to clap him in irons for what he had done. Eva's heart was in her throat. Every revelation from Margaret seemed to plunge her further into ignorance, as if she were wandering around lost, abandoned, in a vast marsh, her foot about to plunge at any moment into an unseen hole, to sink without trace.

'But to look at him now, well, marriage seems to suit him. He's a changed man.'

'Is he?' Eva kept her tone deliberately neutral. If Bruin had changed so much then he must have been utterly terrifying before she had met him. This was the man who had scared her witless in the snowy forest, who had wrenched open the trap on her leg and boosted her on to his horse without a second thought. Who had pulled her, angry and spent, from the churning river water. But he was also the man who, with a single glance from his silver-gilt eyes, made her belly plummet with desire, made her long for his body next to hers. Eva flushed, her fingers skating across the tablecloth, setting her knife straight, fiddling with the ridged base of her goblet. Who was this man who could do such things to her? Obviously, she did not know him at all.

Margaret nudged her shoulder. 'Oh, you jest, Lady Eva! When I saw you walk in together, I thought to myself, now there's a couple who love each other.'

Eva flinched, reddening. How wrong Lady Margaret was. If only she could have seen what had happened in the bedchamber, earlier. Bruin's look of disgust as he turned away from her naked body. Her shame. Resting her arms on the table, she hitched her hips forward to glance past Goodric's expansive hand gestures. Bruin's grey eyes glowed over her; he raised his goblet slowly, a terse smile pinned on his lips, the mildest look of irritation.

Margaret was talking to her again, wine clinging to her fleshy lips, red flecks of spittle. 'And she was nothing like you. My husband has relatives at Count William's court, so we saw her when we travelled to Hainault. Fair hair.' A feverish look had entered the older lady's pale brown eyes; red blotches patched her cheeks. She slumped back in her chair, plucking irritably at her wimple.

'Sorry—who?' Eva switched her gaze to Margaret, forcing herself to concentrate.

'Why, Sophie le Nys, of course!' Pushing a chunk of cooked fish into her mouth, Margaret talked around her food, dabbing her lips every now and again with her napkin. 'What a beauty that maid was!' Her voice rose volubly above the general hubbub of the great hall, catching her husband's attention.

'What are you gabbling on about, Wife?' Goodric demanded. 'Have you allowed Lady Eva to speak at all?' His thick hair stood out in haphazard clumps from his scalp, grey and frizzy.

Sophie. Bruin heard the name drop from the older woman's lips. Like a flare in the darkness, a hook flying out on a flaxen line, snaring the sinew in his neck, digging deep. Hauling him back to those dark, awful days. He set his goblet down before him, slowly, deliberately; pushed his chair back, a violent grating sound. A clawing sickness rose in his throat; he pushed it down, forcibly. His heart seized up with memory, scrunching into a tiny, wasted ball in the middle of his chest.

Down on the lower floor, servants carried the trestle tables to the sides of the hall, in preparation for the dancing. Wooden legs scraped against the flagstones, discordant sounds. In one corner, a group of musicians settled themselves once more, making tentative sounds with their instruments, before breaking into a lively jig. Couples joined hands, smiling at each other, gathering into the jostling lines of a dance.

Bruin had no plan, only to move away from that woman, the woman who had spoken Sophie's name. His brain numb, ploughing through fog, he stepped towards Eva. She shone like a beacon, a salvation, the ebony beauty of her hair glowing beneath her veil. Her cheek held the downy patina of velvet as she inclined her heard towards Lady Margaret's endless wittering. His hand curled around her shoulder; Eva twisted around, turquoise eyes searching his face, her veil bundling in the crook of her neck.

'Come with me.' His voice was hoarse.

'What?' Eva replied abruptly, surprised by his sudden appearance.

'Oh, go on and dance; have a bit of fun! Don't mind me!' Margaret giggled, then hiccoughed loudly. She pressed her napkin to her mouth. 'Excuse me!'

'Come on.' Bruin reached for her hand where it lay on the table, pulling her out through the gap between the two chairs. His face was white, jaw rigid and strained.

'Are you all right?' Eva slid out beside him in a rustle of skirts. Concern laced her voice.

'No,' Bruin replied roughly, tucking her arm firmly beneath his. 'No, I am not.' His hip brushed hers, the point of his sword tangling in her gown as they walked from the high dais, down into the crowded noisy hall.

Eva paused at the bottom of the wooden steps. Her skirts flowed over Bruin's boots, fine blue wool over creased brown leather. 'You heard what she said.'

A pulse beat rapidly in his neck. 'I did.'

'Is it true?'

'Yes.' The calloused pads of his fingers kneaded her silk sleeve, paddling the skin beneath.

'That you were betrothed?' Eva's voice rose, amazed by his blunt confession.

'Yes.' His eyes hollowed out, bleak and piercing, as he stared over her head at the dancers. A rawness shifted across his expression, gouging into her heart.

'Oh, Bruin, what happened to you?' Eva asked softly. Unbidden, her hand rose to cup his face. The bristles on his jaw rasped against the fleshy pads of her palm.

His eyes roamed her face, her sweet appraisal. He hadn't expected her sympathy. Shock, disgust even, at Margaret's words, but not this, this look of care. Why, in Heaven's name, would she care about him? He was the man who had hauled her, against her will, across the country to meet a man she had no wish to meet. Who had made her life a living hell. And yet, despite all this, her huge blue eyes travelled across his face, worried for him, her hand embracing the chiselled roughness of his jaw.

The silence extended between them. Eva's hand dropped away. Her velvet eyelashes fluttered down across the pearly bloom of her cheeks. Her words had been too bold, too reckless. 'I'm sorry,' she continued quietly. 'I shouldn't have asked.' The line of dancers coiled across the floor; a thickset man jostled against Eva's back, throwing her forward against Bruin. He caught her elbow, steadied her.

Why had he gone to her? Why had his body moved towards her as if guided by an invisible hand, seeking her out, when it would have been simpler for him to leave the great hall alone, on some invented excuse? Seeking solace, he had stepped over to her without thought, the luminous beauty of her face lifting up to him like a flower opening in summer. In that moment of utter despair, he had thought only of Eva, of her support. Her quiet wisdom. With the utterance of Sophie's name unearthing the dark, horrible memories of the past, it was Eva he had wanted at his side.

And now he had her.

'Let's go,' he announced brusquely, tugging her hand. They skirted the hall, past the pushed-back tables, the whirling dancers, the musicians in the far corner. Parting the velvet curtain at the far end, Bruin plunged into the shadowed hallway, a cold empty space by the main doors. A single flame flickered from a rush torch; a vast shield displaying the coloured arms of Lord Goodric was secured to the wall, ornate swords crossed behind. Gemstones shone dully in the hilts.

'Why are we here?' she whispered, her breath a white cloud in the freezing hallway.

Because I want to tell you what has happened to me, Bruin thought. Because I know you will understand. 'Because I don't want you to hear things about me that aren't the truth,' he said, his voice a low growl. 'Lady Margaret,' he added disparagingly, 'is talking of things about which she knows nothing.'

'Then tell me what really happened,' Eva said softly.

Bruin crossed his arms over his chest, wrinkling the wool of his surcoat. 'Someone I was fond of, a woman, died,' he said.

'Someone you loved,' Eva whispered, dancing from one foot to the other. It was as if someone had reached into her heart and twisted hard, plucking her feelings out, to leave them exposed, scattered like small stones across the ground. She had to watch out; he would laugh in her face if he found out that she was starting to care for him.

An anguished look crossed his sculptured features. 'I thought I did.'

Eva bit down hard on her bottom lip, dispelling her own selfish, stupid thoughts. It was Bruin that mattered at the moment, Bruin whom she must look after. 'I am so sorry,' she said quietly.

'It was my fault that she died,' he spoke in a jolting tone, as if his words, untested, were having trouble finding their way out. His voice was clipped, brutal. 'While we were betrothed, Sophie fell pregnant, by another man. I was livid, mad when I found out. I told her it was over, that I never wanted to see her again.' His eyes bleak, red-rimmed. 'And I never did.'

'What happened?'

'She drowned herself.'

'Oh, my God.' Her heart flew to him. The pain of memory hunched his big body, despair a cruel blade driving through his expression. She gripped his forearms, thumbs rubbing against the powerful flex of sinew beneath his linen shirt.

He dropped his head. 'I don't deserve your sympathy, Eva. It's a horrible thing that I've done. You should be berating me, not comforting me.'

'It wasn't your fault. How can it be?'

Bruin glanced up, surprised. His silver eyes glittered. Outside the iron-riveted door, a guard shouted to someone in the bailey; the sound echoed around the lofty hallway. 'How can it not be? My anger drove her to do what she did. Surely this only confirms your lowly opinion of me: a barbarian and a thug, taking what I want, riding roughshod over people. What happened in my past proves that fact. You've been right all along, Eva. I just didn't tell you.' His tone was bitter, condemning.

'Whatever my opinion of you, Bruin,' she replied carefully, 'you are still not to blame for what happened.' He would never know what she truly felt about him, how her body yearned for him, for she could not risk the heartache of his rejection, the humiliation. Especially after what had happened in the chamber upstairs. Unconsciously, her thumbs circled across the solid flesh of his forearms. 'You shouted at her, you were angry, justifiably. But that didn't cause her death. She did that, all by herself.'

His eyes clung to her, his sense of dislocation easing. Was this what it felt like to have someone on his side? He had roamed so long in the wilderness of grief, he wasn't sure he could recognise such a feeling. The heat from her hands travelled up his arms. Her touch was a torment, stirring the blood in his veins. His muscles flexed, tightening with sweet awareness. 'God, I wish it were the truth,' he breathed unsteadily. In the shadows, her silky skin was translucent, supple, like liquid cream. Her plush mouth tilted up at the corners, the ghost of a smile, tender, compassionate. Lust shot through him, a dangerous wildfire, volatile, unstable. With a supreme effort of will, he pushed her arms away, clamping them firmly to her sides. 'We had better go back.' His voice was hoarse.

'Are you going to be all right?' Eva murmured.

'Yes,' he said.

If you are there, then I will be.

Chapter Thirteen

The remainder of the evening passed in a torpid blur. Piles of food continued to arrive from the kitchens, many more cups of mead and wine. Grease splatters, gobbets of spilled food littered the length of the tablecloth. Wax dripped down the candlesticks in weird contorted shapes. Servants wove around the tables, lifting dirty plates, hauling away empty serving platters. And the music and dancing went on and on: an endless whirling of colourful clothes, of waists gripped hard, of women spun around, laughing. Apart from a single ribald comment from Goodric as Bruin and Eva returned to the hall, nobody had directly questioned their temporary absence.

Bruin's words crowded through Eva's mind: the sadness chasing across his taut cheekbones, haunting the mineral glitter of his eyes. He had loved another: Sophie, a woman who had held his heart and, judging by his reaction when he heard the name, she still held it. Eva's heart plummeted with the sudden realisation. Jealousy reared up within her, rash and volatile, and she squashed it down, annoyed. It was ridiculous, to feel jealous of a dead woman. And yet, she hated her. Her heart curled with forlorn longing.

Margaret jogged her arm once more, telling her some endless story. Eva had lost track. Fatigue clouded her brain; her eyes drooped. As her spine sagged once more against the back of the chair, she made an effort to pull herself upright, forcing herself to listen, to keep her eyes pinned open. And then, finally, thankfully, Margaret stood, along with her daughters, indicating that it was time for bed. Eva wobbled to her feet, the overwhelming tiredness making her light-headed.

As she turned, Bruin was there, standing behind her. He crooked his arm, indicating with a faint tilt of his head that she should take it. Eva didn't even possess the energy to throw him a mocking smile, but took his arm gratefully, hung on to him as they climbed the stairs together.

'You're exhausted,' Bruin said, as they paused at the door to the bedchamber. A bluish tinge shadowed the hollows beneath her beautiful eyes. Her fingers were laced over his forearm.

'Yes, yes, I am,' Eva admitted, hanging her head.

He gave a short laugh. 'It's not a crime, you know. You are entitled.' He pushed the bronze-coloured locks back from his forehead. 'You've had an exceptional day, starting with throwing yourself into a river. I'm not surprised you're tired, after what you've been through.'

She raised her head slowly. He was acting as if nothing had been said between them, as if he hadn't uttered those damning words in the icy hallway: he loved another. Had he said those words to warn her away, to keep a distance between them? Had he peeled back the flesh around her heart and read the truth contained within? She chewed down hard on her bottom lip, staring at the front of his surcoat, where blue embroidery stitches met gold.

Bruin studied the top of her neat head, the silken veil settled lightly over her glossy hair; the silver circlet gleaming in the dimness of the corridor. 'You need sleep, Eva. We both do. I will wait out here, give you time to get into bed. I'll knock before I come in.' He placed one big palm flat on the wide elm boards of the door and pushed it open. The four-poster bed revealed itself: carved posts supporting the linen canopy above, a delicately wrought tapestry hanging at the back. Expensive fur pelts rippled across the bed; the pillows were sewn from pristine linen, bleached in the sun. The bed dominated the chamber.

The intimate scene startled Eva from her reverie. Dryness scraped at her throat, a hot flush sheening her neck. 'Look,' she said, adjusting her veil, nervously patting the fabric into place on her shoulder, 'I'm not sure about this—' Her eyes rounded on him, a deep luscious blue, faintly accusing.

'Nobody knows the truth but us,' Bruin explained calmly. 'Everyone downstairs believes us to be married.' His mouth twisted wryly.

She scowled, irritated by her feelings of uncertainty around him, glancing miserably at the bed. How could she lie next to him and actually sleep? It would be impossible, an endless torture, trying to keep her limbs from touching him, holding her body aloof, at a distance. Every nerve taut, straining, hour after dark hour. She would probably have a better night's sleep if she stretched out on the floor and wrapped herself in one of the rugs. 'Bruin, we can't share that bed together,' she whispered unhappily.

'I know,' he replied cheerfully, bracing one massive shoulder against the door frame.

His stance was so nonchalant, so relaxed, that she glanced up at him in surprise, frowning. 'What are you saying? Are you going to sleep in another chamber?'

He laughed at the lilting hope in her voice. 'No, but there is a truckle bed that I can sleep in. It's tucked under the big bed. I checked earlier.'

'Fine,' Eva snapped at him. 'I'll go and get ready then.' By withholding the information about the second bed, he had forced her to reveal her worries; she felt foolish now, cloth-headed. She swept into the bedchamber, head held high, spine rigidly straight, and shoved the door closed. Why could she not act normally around him? The way she used to be? It was if he had taken every aspect of her previous character and instructed it to behave differently. She didn't know who she was any more. She didn't trust herself.

The chamber was blissfully warm. The screen had been pushed back around the wooden tub; the water had been emptied. The smell of wax polish permeated the air. An earthenware jug full of water stood next to a bowl on an oak coffer. Eva moved over to it, removing her circlet and veil as she went, folding them neatly. Her cloak lay where she had placed it earlier, the dark blue pleats gathered on the oak coffer; she put her veil and circlet on top.

Unpinning her hair, she scattered the hairpins beside the jug. Her braids looped down over her shoulders, the curling ends brushing her hips. She sloshed some water into the bowl and scrubbed her face and hands, so vigorously that she made her skin tingle. This journey with Bruin was torturous; how could this man come to matter so much to her, after such a short time in his company?

His simple confession downstairs had only made it worse: he had suffered so much. She bit her lip; her answer was there, hovering in the outer recesses of her mind, but she refused to acknowledge such a thought, because it was so impossible, so inconceivable.

Clasping her hands before her, Eva made a decision. She would wear her gowns to bed. Even with Bruin lying in the truckle bed, she wanted to remain fully covered. She could not risk exposing herself to him, as she had earlier. The shame of it! Her face flamed with the memory; stifling a swift gasp of dismay, she covered her mouth with her hand.

'Eva? Are you ready?' His low voice was muffled, insistent, through the door.

'Yes!' Fully clothed, she scuttled over to the big bed, threw back the covers and jumped in, dragging the linens up to her neck. Her braided hair rustled against the pillow. She had no wish to start a debate with him on why she was wearing all her clothes in bed.

Bruin prowled into the chamber on silent feet. His glimmering glance sought and found her in the bed; he gave a small nod of approval, striding over to the jug of water, the earthenware bowl.

Eva turned away from him on to her side, closing her eyes. She heard the sounds of washing, and then, of garments being removed. A boiling heat coursed out from the very centre of her, flooding her whole body, and she closed her eyes, blood thrumming in her ears, willing him to climb into bed very soon.

'Don't worry, Eva, it's not as bad as you think.' Bruin chuckled as he rounded the bed, saw the fierce set of her face. 'I still have my braies and shirt on.'

She peered at him. Bruin bent down, pulling out the

truckle bed. The simple wooden frame had a rudimentary wheel attached to each leg which made the task much easier. He dragged it out into the middle of the room, a significant distance from the four-poster bed she was relieved to see. Throwing back the meagre covers, he lay down on it. His body was too big: his feet and legs overhung the end of the bed up to his knees.

Consternation rattled through her. She was much shorter than him; she could fit in that bed easily. Bruin hunched himself into a ball, tucking his knees and feet up. The frame creaked and strained beneath him. The muscled rope of his spine rippled beneath the gauzy bleached linen of his shirt. He would be so uncomfortable.

'Bruin, that bed is far too small for you,' Eva announced, levering herself up on to her elbow. 'Let me sleep there.'

'I've slept in far worse places.' He turned his head, glittering eyes regarded her calmly. Against the whiteness of his pillow, his hair appeared darker, more coppery; beech leaves in autumn.

'I'm sure you have,' Eva replied. 'But I can fit into that bed, whereas you cannot. You'll never sleep properly like that. It makes no difference to me.' *Because you are still here, in this chamber, with me.*

'Why so considerate about my welfare?' Bruin asked. Suspicion traced his voice. 'I hope you're not feeling sorry for me, after what I told you downstairs?' His mouth hardened. 'Because believe me, I am not worth the worry.'

You are! she wanted to scream at him. 'No, no! Nothing like that,' she responded immediately. 'I'm thinking only of myself. You'll be tossing and turning all night in that rickety bed; you'll keep me awake.' Despite the faint blush of colour touching her cheeks, she managed to keep her tone brusque, practical; he must never guess her true thoughts.

'Well, if you are sure—' his eyes sparkled as he sprang up from the low bed '—I won't turn down your offer. Thank you.'

Eva threw back the covers, her stockinged feet touching the floorboards. Her skirts rumpled messily around her.

'I thought you said you were ready for bed.' His withering look took in her gown, the stocking-covered feet. Her ebony-coloured braids swung down past her waist. His heart lurched; the long plaits made her look younger, more vulnerable, if that were possible.

'I am.' She wound her arms across her chest, a defensive barrier. 'I prefer to sleep like this. I feel—' Her speech faltered to silence beneath his piercing gaze. What had she been about to say, that she felt safer like this? But he would question her logic, because he had told her to trust him. An immense foolishness rolled over her. It probably wouldn't have mattered if she had appeared stark naked in front of him; he was immune to her; he had made that perfectly clear, even before he had told her about Sophie. 'I thought, I thought I would be warmer like this,' she explained lamely. 'And I have no nightgown.'

Bruin moved over to the bigger bed. 'It's up to you, of course,' he said, 'but I think you will be too hot.'

Through the gauzy linen of his shirt, the honed slabs of his chest flexed as he came towards her. Towered over her. She dropped her gaze. His large feet were bare, a strangely intimate sight against the burnished floorboards.

'As you say, it is my choice,' Eva croaked out, pushing past him. She lurched for the safety of the small truckle bed, diving beneath the thin covers, turning her back towards him. She could hear him climbing beneath the furs, a small sigh of satisfaction escaping his lips, and her belly melted at the sound, liquefied. She scowled at the plastered wall, horribly awake, senses acutely aware of the man in the bed, of his limbs stretching across the feather mattress, his coppery hair curling wildly across the pillow. A faint headache creased her brow. Sleep was a long time in coming.

Eva heard the shouts behind her, louder now. The guards were climbing the spiral staircase towards the ramparts. Knees buckling, she forced herself to run harder, faster. Up the spiral steps, out into the midnight air, on to the walkway that skirted the inner castle walls. Nerves bouncing wildly, her knuckles scraped against the rough stone wall, drawing blood. Doubt plagued her heart, for what she was about to do seemed utter madness. But it was the only way. The only way she could escape from him.

Setting her slippered foot on a gap in the crenellated wall, she placed a hand either side on the stone work, balancing herself. Her fingers ground into the gritty stone. Down below, the water in the moat glittered in the moonlight. She hoped, prayed that it would be deep enough to break her fall. She jumped out into the dark air, skirts flapping, stifling a scream as she hit the chill, dark water. Then a hand grabbed her, dragging her on to the bank, and she hit out at the faceless assailant, tears coursing down her cheeks—no, no, this couldn't happen!

'Eva—stop this!' A cool firm voice penetrated the

swirling fog of her brain, the nightmare that consumed her, chasing the fragments of horror back into the dark recesses of her mind. 'Eva, wake up now! You're dreaming.'

Her eyes popped open. Bruin knelt on the floor, looming over her. Firm hands lifted her upright. Sweat sheened her skin. She pressed a shaking hand to her forehead; her hairline was wet. Her gowns stuck uncomfortably to her body, hems bunching around her hips beneath the linen sheet. She must have thrown off the blanket and furs in her sleep, for they lay in a discarded heap on the floor.

Bruin sat back on his haunches, his shirt glowing white in the dimness of the chamber. Moonlight slanted through the window, pooling to the floor with pale luminescence. His eyes moved over her. Wisps of hair had escaped her braids, clinging to her cheeks in a net of damp fronds; her face burned with a bright, fiery colour. 'Eva, you're too hot. You need to take your gowns off.'

Embarrassment washed over her; she hung her head, fingers pleating the edge of the sheet. 'I'm fine,' she replied bluntly. 'I'm sorry I woke you.'

'You cried out.' Her screams had ripped through his deep sleep, hauling him awake in a moment; snapping back the sheets, he had vaulted over to her. Writhing around on the sparsely stuffed mattress, Eva had seemed impossibly wrapped in fabric: her clothes, the sheet, the blankets and furs, all trussing her body like a cocoon. He had torn them away, shaking her awake.

Eva drew up her knees, encircling them with her arms. 'It happens sometimes.' Her voice was a whisper. Fear chased across her face.

'What was it about?'

Bruin's question hung in the air between them. The dying embers from the charcoal brazier cast a flickering glow across his lean features, accentuating the tough line of his jaw, the shadows beneath his cheekbones. Eva's fingers clutched at the sheet, creasing the fabric. 'It's always the same,' she replied in a small voice. 'My escape from—' she met his eyes squarely '—your brother.'

His hand reached out, pushing back a damp strand of hair from her cheek. The rough pads of his fingers trailed down from her ear, savouring the silken caress of her skin, lingering.

'No.' She gripped his forearm, delicate fingers surprisingly strong. 'I don't want your pity,' she said, misinterpreting his gesture.

His hand slid down, cupping her chin. 'I don't pity you,' Bruin said. 'But I hate the fact that this haunts you; that the memory of what happened to you is always there, lurking in the back of your mind.' He could have been speaking about himself, he thought suddenly.

'You feel sorry for me.' Eva twisted her face away: a halting gesture. His hand fell away. 'Why would you care, anyway? If you did, then you wouldn't keep insisting on taking me to your brother.'

'But those nightmares are never going to go away unless you confront your demons,' he said.

'Like you have faced yours?' Eva flung back at him immediately. A faint sarcasm laced her voice; she folded her arms across her chest as if bracing herself for the onslaught of his anger.

He rocked back on his heels, stunned by her perspicacity. 'This has nothing to do with me.'

'It has everything to do with you,' she replied tartly. 'You are forcing me to confront my demons, in this case, your brother. I suggest you do the same. Let go of your guilt about Sophie.'

He stared at her for a long moment, waiting for his anger to rise, waiting for the guilt and hurt and desperation to flood over him. But it never came. Eva's eyes sparkled over him, huge blue pools that challenged him; he clung to them, drinking in their beauty. No one had ever said anything like this to him before, no one had ever dared to speak to him about Sophie's death. But here she was, this enchanting woman whom he'd found in the snow, blundering into the subject, forcing him to think, to question. The tight bands around his heart eased a little, fiercely knotted ribbons loosening.

'Careful, Eva. You know little about what you speak.' Despite the warning, tenderness edged his voice.

'You had nothing to do with her death,' she insisted. 'I know that, at least, even if I hardly know you.'

But the people who should know him well, his mother and his father, his friends and comrades back in Flanders, all of them had been too frightened of his reaction to say anything at all. So he had fled, guilt-ridden, to bury his self-hatred in a life of lawlessness. It hadn't worked. These last few days with Eva had done more to change his opinion of himself than his year at sea.

'Sometimes the clearest perspective comes from people who know you the least,' Bruin replied enigmatically. He rose to his feet. His toes were numb, the nerve endings squashed, prickling; he had been kneeling for too long. 'Do you think you will dream again?'

'I hope not.'

'Take those gowns off,' he said again.

She pursed her lips stubbornly. 'Then go back to bed and close your eyes.'

He chuckled, turning away. She watched as he climbed back into the big bed, sliding his long limbs down beneath the covers, his back towards her. Her breath released slowly, by degrees; beneath the covers, she proceeded to wriggle out of her cumbersome garments.

Eva awoke again in the early hours, light peeking through the wobbly, hand-blown glass in the casement windows. Rays of sun touched her face, but there was no heat in the light. Bruin snored faintly. Rolling over, Eva felt her heart skip stupidly. He lay sprawled on his back, the sheets crushed down around his waist, one arm flung out, over the edge of the mattress. Strong tapered fingers hung suspended in the air, the roped sinew of his wrist lacing up his tanned forearm.

Her gaze prowled across him, tentatively at first, half-expecting those shuttered eyes to spark open and catch her watching him. He had removed his shirt, after all. She traced the blue line of a vein up to the crook of his arm, then higher, to the bulging muscle of his shoulder. A pulse beat in the corded strength of his neck; coppery hairs brindled his bare chest. Her eyes tiptoed across his body, feasting on the dips and hollows: the shadowed line of his collarbone, the flat rippled plane of his stomach. Her mind consumed him, delighted in exploring this unknown masculine territory. He would never know how much she desired him, how much she had come to care for him, but at least she could have this secret, hidden moment, this precious parcel of time to study him.

What would happen if she went over to him now and slid her body next to his? Would he turn towards her and take her in his arms? Kiss her like before, his firm lips capturing hers? Her flesh shivered in lustful anticipation. Her silken limbs pushing against that hard, roped flesh; chest against chest, thigh against thigh. She knew how a man and a woman lay together; she was not naïve. Her belly quivered, racked with longing, plunging down into a morass of unrequited pleasure. She gasped at her own wantonness, wrenching her gaze away.

Sadness stumbled through her and she threw her covers off, stepping carefully towards the window. What was the matter with her? No other man had consumed her thoughts like this; she had considered most to be arrogant buffoons, or imbeciles, at best. Leaning her forehead against the cool panes of the window, she searched her mind for sanity, for some remnants of the woman she used to be: sensible, resilient—a woman who could survive alone. Where was that woman now?

Bruin opened his eyes. Sunlight spilled across the bed furs, sheening the pelts with a velvet caste. His breath misted the chill air; the flames in the charcoal brazier had died out long ago. And Eva's bed was empty; the sheets rumpled, a colourful pile of gowns heaped on the floor. A movement by the window snared his eye; she was there.

Light seeped traitorously through the diaphanous material of Eva's chemise. Beneath the gauzy fabric, she was naked, the glorious silhouette of her body outlined in sunlight. Desire punched him, hard in the solar plexus, a blow from nowhere. The fine hairs on his body stood up in ripe anticipation. Lust churned in his belly, a dangerous wildness, kindling swiftly to a raging, unstoppable blaze. His logical mind admonished him, told him to look away, to close his eyes. But his flesh was weak, defenceless, stalked by desire, entranced by the woman at the window, the magic of her body.

Oblivious to his perusal, Eva leaned against the windowsill, resting her stomach against the cold stone, peering out. Her chemise shifted forward, clinging lovingly to her hips, the slim column of her legs. The rounded lines of her rump pushed out the lightweight fabric. His self-control fled, defeated, chased away by a hot savage lust. Very slowly, Bruin lifted the sheet back, settling his bare feet against the floor. Caught in her own thoughts, her silent reverie, Eva did not hear his step. He crept towards her, quietly as a cat, flesh taut with desire.

'Eva.'

She gasped at his closeness, but didn't turn around. Her chemise was transparent; she had left her bed without any form of cover. If she stayed with her back to him, it would protect her from his knowing gaze. She jumped as he placed his big hands squarely on her hips, thumbs rasping the fabric. The heat from his body flared into her. Her breath seized; although his touch was light, she could not move, or pull away, as if a single thread held her suspended, dangling, stretching slowly, slowly until surely it would break and she would fall.

A sigh escaped her lips, a breath of longing. She prayed silently: God forgive me.

She leaned back. Into him.

Bruin groaned, hands sliding forward, around her neat waist, yanking her roughly against him. His groin pressed against her backside; her body melted, liquefying, sinking down and down into a whirlpool of quivering need. His hands splayed possessively across her belly, sliding up the sinuous indent of her waist, cupping her full breasts, thumbs scuffing her nipples. Shock sliced through her, volatile and edgy; her blood raced at his intimate touch, fringed with fear. Where was he taking her? She wanted to lie with him; every bone, every sinew in her body cried out for that delight, but then what? He would take what he wanted and discard her; she recalled the look of disgust on his face as he turned away from the glimpse of her naked body. She couldn't risk that again, the sneer of mockery on his face.

She grabbed his wrists, pulled his hands from her body, trembling. 'Nay,' she croaked out. 'I cannot.'

The quiet sadness in her voice ripped through his roaring blood, tore at his heart. Stopped him, even though the voice in his head bawled at him to continue. Go on! Claim her for your own! The shrill tone of a petulant child; his mouth twisted with self-disgust at the direction of his thoughts. His chest was a hair's breadth from her spine. A delicious scent of roses lifted from the back of her neck, at the point where her hair divided into her two plaits. Delicate wisps of hair formed little curls at her nape. She held his wrists out to the each side of her, as if unsure what to do with them, hanging her head. Vulnerable. Innocent.

What did he think he was doing? Trampling over her feelings as he rediscovered the man he used to be? It never would have happened if he hadn't met Eva. His spirit, brittle, bludgeoned into passivity by Sophie's death, had started to unfurl again, sparking into life. Eva had done this. And this was how he repaid her, by treating her like a whore. She deserved more respect than that, much more.

The neckline of her chemise rode low around her shoulders, a white ribbon gathering the material into tiny pleats. Above, her bare skin was smooth, creamy, like marble, blotched by the rose-coloured birthmark. If he hadn't stepped on her trailing hem that night, then he would never have seen it, would never have realised who she was. Would that have been better for both of them?

'I'm sorry,' he said. Blood thumped disconsolately through his veins, thwarted, unsatisfied, the speed dwindling.

Her small hands manacled his wrists, the press of her fingers like silk. She released him and he stepped back, away. The glass before her eyes blurred with tears; heart closing up with misery as she fought for equilibrium. She cursed the fear that had made her stop; why had she not let him continue, why had she not seized the moment to be with him, to lie with him? She hugged her body with her arms; could she really let a man who had no feelings for her take her innocence? Was she so mesmerised by his sheer beauty that she would let such a thing happen? Inwardly she groaned, for she knew the answer and hated herself for it. If she had possessed the courage, the bravery, then it would have happened.

Dipping down to the truckle bed, Bruin grabbed a blanket. He laid it carefully around her shoulders. Eva was shivering; his hands rested on her shoulders. 'Forgive me.' His voice was low, unusually hesitant, speaking to her bowed head. 'I promised that you could trust me and I broke that promise.' His pupils were wide, dark, obliterating all colour in his eyes.

Amazed by the tenderness in his voice, she turned in his loose hold. Her eyes shimmered, a magnificent periwinkle blue. 'It wasn't your fault, Bruin.' She hesitated—could she risk telling him the truth? 'I stopped because I was afraid.' The words blurted out on a whisper.

Bruin's diamond gaze roamed across her face. His blood hurtled, an unstoppable force. What was she saying? That she would have lain with him, would have given him her innocence if she had been brave enough?

The rigid walls around his heart weakened and crumbled, as if made of dust, blown away on a stiff breeze.

'Afraid of me?' he asked gently.

'No,' she replied quietly. 'But afraid of…what would happen.' A hectic colour flushed her cheeks. She jammed one fist against her mouth, aghast at the words emerging from her mouth, her thoughts spilling out before him like unwashed laundry. He didn't want to know about her feelings, for God's sake, he didn't even care about her! She had never talked like this before, to anyone, let alone a man!

'I wouldn't have let it go that far,' Bruin murmured. He hoped his words would reassure her; he wanted her to believe that she was safe with him, that she could trust him, but as he focused moodily on a crack in the stone work behind her head, he knew he was lying to himself. He had been moments away from carrying her on to the bed, moments away from bedding her.

His words sloshed over her like ice-cold water. Eva stumbled back with a faltering step, shocked and embarrassed. Shame flooded over her, an ugly red tide of discomfort. So he had been playing with her all along, completely in control of the situation, whilst beneath his questing fingers, her own body had betrayed her! He had never intended to take things any further, whilst she had assumed… Oh, God! She pressed her fist to her mouth. She had assumed that he would lie with her. And here she was, trying to reassure him that it wasn't his fault!

Eva scrabbled for something to say. 'I'm glad to hear it!' Her voice dripped disapproval, the discordant tones cracking through the shimmering desire between them, trampling roughshod, a spooked horse running amok. Yanking the blanket firmly around her shoulders, she straightened her spine. 'I must dress,' she said coldly, her speech jerking out, high-pitched, unnatural sounding. Her pupils were tiny, pinpricks of black in huge irises of aquamarine. She had to be strong, resolute and fight to keep her distance from him. Head held high, she stalked over to the messy pile of her gowns on the floor. 'Please leave.'

His words, supposed to absolve them both, had angered her instead. Bruin wondered why. He knew he deserved her chill dismissal: he had taken advantage of her innocence and she was aggrieved. He had failed to keep his promise. But the way she had nestled back into him—his heart flared wildly at the memory—had been the behaviour of a woman who desired him. But he told himself it was better this way, better that she viewed him with disgust, for that disgust would protect her. His damaged soul would blight her brightness, drag her down. And yet, it was her very brightness that lifted him up from the depths of his despair.

Chapter Fourteen

By the time they were nearing Deorham, solid white clouds had covered the sky in a thick ribbed mass, obliterating the sun; it was snowing heavily. Large feathery flakes cascaded down at an angle, driving relentlessly into Eva's face; she huddled down further into her cloak, shivering. She had pulled up her hood, tightening the drawstrings, so that only her face and hands were exposed to the cold air. The tip of her nose burned in the freezing air. They had been riding for so long without a break that her feet were numb, blocks of ice dangling uselessly at the end of her legs. The scar on her shin ached slightly, the damaged skin puckering with the cold beneath her woollen stockings.

Bruin never stopped. From the moment they had left Goodric Castle, he had ridden up front, tapping his heels into his horse's flank to pick up speed, expecting her to follow without question. His pace was relentless. He hadn't even attached the leading rein to her horse. The temptation to yank on her reins and kick her horse to freedom had occurred to her, but they both knew that such a foolhardy act was completely futile: he would catch her in a moment. In the few hours that they had been travelling, he had scarce said a dozen words to her and those words had consisted of barked orders, as if she were some common foot soldier.

But she wasn't surprised. She hadn't expected anything else, after the humiliating episode in the bedchamber at Goodric Castle. 'I wouldn't have let it go that far.' His words fixed in her mind as if burned in place by an iron brand, trampling her heart to a miserable pulp. He was experienced, no doubt having spent many nights in the company of women; she was not and had made the mistake of revealing her pathetic eagerness to lie with him. A wave of heat passed through her; she tightened her elbows into her sides, slumping down in the saddle. What a mess. No doubt he was desperate to be rid of her, anxious to complete this business with his brother before moving north to serve with the King once more. As soon as she had met with Lord Steffen, their time together would be over. Bruin would have done his duty, done what his brother had asked of him. A kernel of sadness fluttered deep within her gut, but she squashed it down violently, annoyed with herself. Self-pity would not help her now; she had to face reality: that Bruin would leave and she would be alone once more.

They followed the path south along the river now, the track passing beneath bare-leafed ash, oak; snow mixing with mud to form a treacherous slush which forced the horses to slow their pace. Up ahead, a heavy iron chain was strung taut across a narrow part of the river, black links bobbing against the grey colour of the rushing water. A wooden raft bumped gently in the shallows on their side of the river: a flat-bottomed vessel that would carry them across to Deorham. Through the whirling snowflakes, Eva tipped her gaze up to the castle on the other side, balanced on a promontory of land, turrets peeking above the bare-boned trees. Fear, a freshly sharpened scythe, flipped through her. Nausea roiled in her belly. Up there, in one of those chambers, Lord Steffen awaited her. Even now, he might be peering down at them, watching their arrival. She shuddered.

The ferryman sat on a rock beside the raft, partially obscured by a thick, felted cloak, hood pulled low over coarse grimy features. Snowflakes settled across his shoulders. As they picked their way along the path towards him, he stood slowly, as if all his joints were aching. Bruin dismounted, murmuring a few words to him, placing gold coins in the man's hand. A stiff breeze rippled the surface of the river, sending a rush of frothy wavelets to the gravelly shore.

'He will take us across.' Bruin turned and grabbed Eva's reins. As a concession to the freezing weather, he had dragged his cloak out from his saddlebags at the beginning of the journey: a calf-length blue garment, sadly creased from being packed away for so long. The tip of his sword angled out from beneath the hemline. 'Almost there,' he said, leading her horse and his own on to the raft, tying both sets of reins to the low rail that encircled the vessel. The animals' hooves made a hollow clopping sound on the single wooden planks. 'Do you want to dismount?'

The stitching on one of his gloves was coming apart; his tanned flesh, the sinewy curve of his thumb, were visible beneath. She twitched her gaze away. Muscles sluggish with cold, she jerked her head in assent, allowing him to grab her by the waist and set her on her feet. There was no point in attempting any maidenly resistance with him, of insisting that she dismount without his help: he was immune to her. He had made that point perfectly clear. She stamped her feet, trying to warm them, and twisted her icy fingers together. Already they were in motion, the ferryman gripping the thick chain, hand over hand, hauling the vessel through the churning current. Perspiration glistened across his florid cheeks.

'I should be doing that,' Eva said. 'It would help to warm me up.'

Bruin smiled down at her, her bright cheeks patched with red, wide eyes reflecting the pale grey of the water. Her earlier aloofness seemed to have dissipated with the journey, and for that, he was glad. Snow festooned the top of her hood; he resisted the urge to brush it away. 'We'll soon be in the warm.'

'How can you be so certain?' Eva tilted her head up to him, worry tracing her features. 'Lord Steffen will probably throw me in the deepest dungeon the moment he sets eyes upon me.'

His eyes glittered, silver discs of light. 'No, I told you, he's bedbound, incapacitated. He would not be able to do such a thing.'

'He can speak, can't he?' she replied grumpily as the raft bumped the muddy bank on the other side of the river. 'He can still give orders.'

'I won't let it happen.' Bruin's mouth settled into a firm line. And yet a small trickle of doubt niggled at the back of his brain. Everything Eva had told him tallied with the brother he had known back in Flanders. The sick fear he had experienced when he first brought Sophie to meet his parents, Steffen's avid gaze upon his fiancée's fair beauty. The sense that his brother always wanted to ruin, to destroy things.

'I wish I had your confidence,' Eva replied grimly.

The ferryman secured the raft with a fraying rope around a post, indicating with a deliberate nod of his head that they could disembark. Bruin bent down, cupped his hands. Bracing herself on his shoulders, Eva placed her foot in the makeshift cradle of his fingers and he boosted her slight weight up into the saddle. She settled herself gracefully, every inch the noble woman, adjusting the back of her cloak around so that it lay in neat folds across the horse's rump.

'Is that giving you any trouble?' Bruin asked, nodded towards the leg that she had injured in the trap. 'Is it healing all right?'

'It's fine, thank you.' Gathering the reins, she patted the side of the horse's neck.

'No swelling around the wound?' Bruin stuck his booted foot into the shining stirrup, swinging easily into the saddle. The large horse sidled in irritation beneath his weight, scraping one hoof across the wooden planks of the raft in mild protest.

Comfort stole through her at his concern. She shifted awkwardly in the saddle. He was making it difficult for her to keep her distance when he asked such personal questions. It would be better if he ignored her completely. 'Bruin, it's fine, I promise you.' The wound had healed well, the torn edges of flesh knitting back together with no problems.

He ignored her terseness. 'I'm just making sure that you're taking care of yourself.'

Her heart twisted stupidly at the mild possessiveness in his tone; she told herself to ignore it. 'Why?' she replied acerbically. 'Are you worried I'm going to drop dead before I meet your precious brother?'

'I do hope not,' he replied, his voice laced with amusement. A wave of protectiveness rattled through him, but he was not surprised. Eva had no idea how he had, over these past few days, come to care for her, wanting to keep her safe. Now, he felt as if he were about to betray her, leading her into the lion's den.

'And are we still supposed to be married?' Eva asked, leaning forward to adjust the bridle around her horse's ear. 'It would be helpful to know before we arrive.' Her tone was faintly mocking.

What would it be like, he thought, to spend the rest of his life with her? In the past, any reference to marriage had conjured up images of Sophie, of what had happened to her: his culpability. But being with Eva was different. She was a good companion: feisty, intelligent—aye, she was his equal. But she was more than that: beautiful and entrancing, with a body like silk. After what had happened with Sophie, he had ruled out the chance of ever spending the rest of his life with someone. But now?

'It would keep you safe,' he murmured. He chucked the image away: two people hand in hand, tied by the Church. It was a stupid hopeless dream, and one he would do well to forget. His black-hearted soul would devour her goodness and he had no wish to do such a thing to her. She could do far better than marry the likes of him.

'Would it?' She flicked her gaze up to him, openly challenging. 'I doubt anything could keep me safe up there,' she pronounced with a deadly finality. 'Not even you.'

'Who does this castle belong to?' Eva's voice echoed around the gloomy shadows of the gatehouse as they clattered through, their horses' hooves sliding and scraping across the cobbles. The guard at the drawbridge had waved them on, recognising Bruin immediately. They emerged into a deserted inner bailey, surrounded by high curtain walls. Clumps of snow, inches thick in places, lined the tops of the battlements, settled in the deep creases between the cobbles.

'Lord Hugh Fitzosbern,' Bruin replied, jumping down from the saddle, passing his reins over the horse's head so that they hung down below the animal's neck. A stable lad darted out from a dark archway, his expression serious, eager, as he snatched up Bruin's reins. 'But he's not here, he's fighting further north with the King.'

'Another of Edward's favourites,' Eva replied bitterly, handing her own reins to the stable lad. 'This castle used to belong to Gilbert de Clare, did it not?'

Bruin came over to her, his cloak swirling out in the breeze. 'I have no idea,' he replied, reaching up for her. His chainmail sleeves glinted dully, the links flexing, creasing at the elbows, as he lifted Eva down in one swift movement. 'I haven't been in the country long enough to know everything that has been going on. But Fitzosbern has given my brother sanctuary in his last days, and for that I am grateful.'

She flicked her eyes up at him, scowling. 'The King takes the land and castles of anyone who opposes his rule. And yet the opposition is justified; the King is behaving like a tyrant, allowing his barons to do as they please, to take what they want—'

'Eva, hush, you cannot speak like this, not here.' Bruin cupped her elbow, leading her towards a flight of steps. At the top was the entrance to the castle: a huge door, vertical wooden planks made stronger with diagonal wooden cross-pieces, riveted into place with great iron bolts. 'We can argue about the state of England later, but right now, we need to see Steffen.'

He led her through a quilted curtain into an empty great hall, then through an archway that opened on to a spiral staircase. Eva's terror grew as she and Bruin climbed the stairs to the upper floors, a fear that filled her lungs with a sense of utter desperation, of entrapment. She wanted to close her eyes, to sag against the damp gritty wall and refuse to move. But Bruin held her hand firmly, tugging her along. He wouldn't let her drag behind, or stop.

'Shouldn't we find a servant?' Eva asked breathlessly as his long legs spanned two steps at a time. Her hood slipped back over her silken veil as she tipped her head up to him, pulling on his hand to halt their fierce progress. 'We can't just barge into a bedchamber, unannounced. No one knows we are here.'

'There's nobody here to know,' Bruin replied. 'Only my brother is here with a few servants attending on him. Everyone else is with the King.'

'Even the ladies?'

Bruin paused in the stairwell. An arrow slit spilled a pallid light down across his scuffed boots. 'Hugh Fitzosbern never married. There are no ladies at Deorham.' His gloved fingers squeezed her hand, coarse leather ridging against her palm. 'Look, I know how you feel about this, but the sooner we visit my brother, the sooner you are free.' He gave a short laugh. 'And free of me. Surely that is something to look forward to?'

Sadness shifted through her; a dark coating of loss. Lifting her skirts, she allowed him to pull her up the stairs once more and on to the long corridor where the bedchambers were situated. Bruin rapped sharply on the first door—no answer. Eva's heartbeat filled her throat, bumping erratically; there was a roaring in her ears and she wondered if she were about to faint.

'Maybe—' she said tentatively.

'This is Steffen's chamber.' Bruin cut off her speech abruptly. He thumped again, louder this time. The door swung loosely inwards on oiled hinges, creaking slightly.

Inside, a small room. The bed made up neatly, sheets tucked beneath the single mattress; the pillow smooth: no creases, no dent made by a sleeping head. A window stood ajar, stray snowflakes settling on the sill, allowing fresh air to sift through the room. The coals in the charcoal burner were cold, white-grey ashes. An elm coffer, decorated with intricate carvings, stood against one wall, an earthenware jug and bowl placed on top. The chamber was empty.

'We're too late.' Bruin stuck one hand through his hair, sending the bright strands wayward. Releasing Eva's fingers, he strode into the room, then stopped, as if at a loss. 'He's gone,' he bit out, tight-lipped. Eva sagged against the door frame, her slight frame wilting beneath the impact of Bruin's words. A sense of relief. Steffen was dead. She was silent; there was no point in telling Bruin how sorry she was, for she would be lying and he would know it.

A movement at her back; she turned. A manservant hovered in the shadows, bowing deferentially to her, hopping from one foot to another. His skin was shiny and very white with florid pink cheeks; his bald pate gleamed like an eggshell. 'My l-lady—?' he stuttered out in question. 'Can I help you in any way?'

'Oh!' she said, startled, bracing her feet either side of the threshold. She hadn't heard him approach. 'I came with Lord Bruin—' She gestured into the chamber with an outstretched hand. 'His brother—' she whispered.

'When did it happen?' Bruin demanded, recognising the man as Steffen's servant. His chest bumped against Eva's shoulder, the heft of him filling the doorway, hulking over her. She was trapped, caught between him and the servant. She resisted the urge to lean back into the solid muscle of Bruin's body, a delicious lightness stealing across her body, a sense of renewal, of moving forward. Steffen was dead. The shackles of her past unleashed, tight knots unravelling, falling away.

The servant bowed to Bruin, a look of consternation crossing his face. 'I beg your pardon, my lord?'

'When did it happen? When did Steffen die?' Bruin's voice was calm; a muscle flexed beneath the rigid line of his cheekbone.

'Goodness, Lord Steffen isn't dead, my lord. He's very much alive and down in the archery field, firing off arrows in the snow.'

The words drove into Eva, stabbed into her like knives. Her mind scrabbled for logic, for anything that would make sense of this awful situation. Alive? Steffen was alive? A red mist rolled before her eyes, her knees buckled and she swayed, her head knocking back against the door frame. 'No, it can't be—' she muttered. Bruin slid an arm around her waist, steadying her. 'I thought you said he was dying,' she whispered. His chin was inches from her forehead; the stubble across his jaw glinted, gold hairs mixed with bronze. Doubt, a huge wave steadily gaining strength, engulfed her. 'How could you do this to me? How could you?' Wrenching violently from Bruin's hold, Eva staggered back into the corridor. 'How can you stand there and *pretend*?' she bit out. 'All this time, I believed you about your brother! "Trust me, Eva", you said. "I will look after you." What a fool I've been!'

Bruin caught her flailing arms, pushed them gently back against her sides. 'Eva, calm down. I'm telling you the truth. Steffen was ill, injured with a head wound. I saw him myself, lying in this bed.'

'Aye, it's the truth, mistress,' the manservant chipped in, keen to help, to dispel any element of doubt. 'Lord Steffen was wounded at the Battle of Burton Bridge, but his injury was not as bad as everyone first thought.'

Bile rose in her throat, thick and coruscating. 'Then he tricked you,' Eva spluttered out, her gaze holding tight to Bruin's eyes, steel blades of light. 'He made out his injury was worse than it actually was. He wanted you to pity him, so you would do his bidding. So you would fetch me.' Eva shook her head, a listless, defeated movement. Every joint, every muscle in her body ached, stretched thin with tension, as if someone had taken a hammer and mashed her into a useless pulp. 'I'm done for,' she murmured.

'Don't you think I would have seen through such an act?' Bruin asked, hating the defeated hunch of her small frame, the hunted desperation lurking in her turquoise eyes. But even as he spoke the words, doubt flooded through him. It was entirely possible that Steffen might have done such a thing and he had been too caught up in his own selfish grief to notice.

She shrugged her shoulders. 'He's clever, Bruin. Unpredictable. You told me so yourself.' Beneath his forearm, her spine was stiff, a tense rope of vertebrae, fragile yet strong.

Bruin sighed. 'Let's go and see him, Eva, let's sort this out.'

'If Lord Steffen is better, then he won't need to beg me for forgiveness,' she said hastily. 'I can leave.' Her toes curled down in her boots, a gesture of resistance.

'Do you want to run scared for the rest of your life? I think you need to see him.' His arm tightened around her waist, an indication that they should move from the doorway, but Eva placed her hand against his chest, stalling him.

'Bruin, there's something I haven't told you.'

He raised his eyebrows. 'I'm listening.'

'I still have something that Lord Steffen wants. And it's not my forgiveness.'

Bruin's eyes drifted over to the manservant waiting respectfully in the corridor. 'Eva, if this is another of your stalling tactics, then—'

'It's not, I promise you. Your brother held me prisoner in order to claim all my land and wealth. But there was one item of value I thought Steffen knew nothing about. So that even after I had signed over everything he wanted, I would still have enough to live on.'

'What was it?' The foreign lilt was prominent in the hushed, urgent tones of Bruin's voice.

A noise at the far end of the corridor made them both turn in unison. The servant's head whipped around, an obsequious look passing over his face as he bowed low. A tall, broad-shouldered man was walking down the corridor, bronze-coloured hair, cheeks flushed ruddy with cold, pulling off his leather gloves as he approached. A man who looked exactly like Bruin.

Lord Steffen.

Chapter Fifteen

'Ah, you have returned, I see!' Striding forward, Steffen thumped Bruin's shoulder, glancing down at Eva. She shrank back against Bruin's broad frame. 'You did well, Brother, in bringing this little lady back to me.' His eyes swept over Eva's petrified features, a triumphant smile flickering across his mouth. 'Where did he find you?'

Eva was silent, eyelashes fluttering down to avoid her tormentor's piercing gaze, Bruin's arm supporting her. Hot and cold shivers tracked up and down her spine. Lord Steffen's manner was jovial and benign, completely contrary to the man who had imprisoned her. This was not the true Lord Steffen; he was playing a role for Bruin's sake. Bile rose in her throat; she swallowed hastily. The urge to turn and plead with Bruin, to beg him not to be fooled by his brother's behaviour, rose within her, but a paralysing terror restricted her; it was all she could do to remain upright.

To her dismay, Bruin clapped one hand on Steffen's shoulder. His forearm brushed her veil lightly. 'Good to see you up and about, Brother; I thought you were truly done for the last time we met.' Eva's stomach coiled inwards on a tide of fear; was she about to lose Bruin to his brother's charm? Or had she ever had him at all?

'So did I, so did I.' Steffen nodded. 'So...' he clapped his hands together, his gaze switching from Bruin to Eva, then back again '...will you join me in the hall for something to eat? I am eager to talk to you, my lady, and that's best done over a glass of mead and some food, rather than standing in a doorway.'

'We'll be there in a few moments,' Bruin said. 'I also need to discuss something with Eva.'

Irritation creased Steffen's brow, quickly clearing. 'As you wish,' he replied. 'Please, use my chamber.' He flicked his wrist powerfully at the empty made-up bed. 'Make yourselves comfortable. But don't tarry too long; I want to go outside again before the light fades.' He smiled, fixing Eva with a blank stare, then marched off down the corridor, his manservant in scurried pursuit.

Bruin pulled Eva into the chamber, shutting the door. His arm fell away as he turned to her, searching the pale, anxious lines of her face, the rapid pulse in her neck, partially obscured by the sweep of her veil. 'What was it, Eva? What were you about to tell me about, before Steffen came up the stairs?'

Her eyes were huge, shimmering pools of turquoise light, shot through with darts of gold. A sense of betrayal swept through her, a tide of desertion. In the spot where his arm had lain her back was cold, bereft of his touch. 'You greet that man, that monster, like a long-lost friend. You keep saying that you're on my side...' Her voice trailed away miserably.

Bruin folded his arms across his chest, wrinkling the embroidered crest. 'I am on your side, Eva. I don't trust him any more than you do. But I think we should give him a chance to make amends.'

She laced her fingers, pale skin stretched taut across her knuckles. Her neck muscles ached from exhaustion. 'How do I know that you are not in league with your brother, that you are not lying?'

He thought of the number of times his brother had cut his girth straps and hidden his armour when they were younger; how once Bruin had become stronger and better than him in the field, how much Steffen had resented it and wanted Bruin to fail, to make a fool of himself in battle or at a tournament. 'You don't. You have never been in a position to choose. It would have either been me or someone else who would have dragged you, one way or the other, back to Steffen.' His eyes gleamed over her, iridescent chips of pewter.

Her eyes snared his; held. *Then I'm glad it was you,* she thought.

'Besides, I have nothing to gain from upholding this promise to my brother. I thought he was dying and I wanted to fulfil his last wish. But now I know what he did, I will protect you from him. I'm on your side, Eva, but we need to sort this out, otherwise he might plague you for ever.'

She pushed her hand against her forehead, closing her eyes momentarily. 'I know. I know,' she whispered. Her fingers shook. 'But seeing him again—my God—'

'He can't touch you with me here.'

She wavered, a willow bending in the wind. Filling her lungs with air, she fought to retrieve some sense of balance, to find her inner strength. 'What your brother wants,' she iterated the words slowly, carefully, 'is a ruby.'

Bruin tilted his head to one side, listening patiently. Waiting for her to explain.

'It's a gemstone that has been in my mother's family for generations' She lifted her eyes towards Bruin. 'The only thing I have left to call my own.'

His fingers tangled with hers, squeezed tight. 'Then we will have to make sure that he doesn't get it,' he said, a slow determination colouring his voice.

Soup slopped over the edges of Eva's pewter bowl. Across the surface, a skim of fat globules congealed slowly. Steffen had not been jesting when he said their food would be cold. And not only cold, but stale as well. The bread rolls, piled on a chipped pottery plate, held flecks of blue mould; the meat, although cooked, smelled rancid. But Eva didn't care about the food, for, although Steffen sat beside her, Bruin's final words in the chamber had given her renewed strength and hope. He was on her side.

'I do apologise for the food,' Steffen announced. 'Hugh Fitsosbern took all his servants into battle, including the cook. To our detriment, unfortunately. Cooking has never been Simon's strong point.' Simon was no doubt the manservant whom they had first met and now moved between them, pouring mead from a large jug into their goblets. They were the only people in the great hall; the fire was unlit, the air chill and damp against her skin. A bland light hunkered down outside the vast arched windows; outside it must still be snowing.

Steffen's eyes swept over Eva. 'Forgive my manners, my lady. Would you like me to take your cloak?'

'I think I'll wear it for a little longer,' she replied tersely.

His eyes roamed over her, a darker grey than Bruin's, almost black, coals in the raw whiteness of his skin. Compared to his twin, Bruin's face was tanned, chiselled angles of muscle beneath taut skin, whereas Steffen's face showed signs of ageing, the hint of a fleshy roll beneath his chin. Her fear of him began to drop away, ebbing back like a slow tide.

Steffen sniffed, biting enthusiastically into a piece of bread, then chewing with obvious displeasure. 'Aye, you're making the right decision; it's freezing in here.' Crumbs of bread spilled from his mouth as he spoke, scattering across his tunic. He cleared his throat. 'Do you know why I asked Bruin to fetch you?'

Eva nodded, her gaze fixed on the grimy tablecloth. An old wine stain had formed a rusty-coloured blotch to one side of her plate. Despite her uneasiness, this encounter with Steffen had not been as bad as she had predicted. She drew strength, courage, from Bruin's quiet, calm presence. And although it was because of him that she sat here now, facing up to her enemy, she knew that Bruin had been right: she needed to stand up to her fear of this man and face her demons.

Steffen glanced at Bruin, making sure that he had his attention, before turning back to Eva. 'I was so ill, I thought I was going to die,' he explained, a simpering expression crossing his face. 'And all that time the only thing I could think of was what I had done to you. The awful way in which I treated you. I had to ask Bruin to find you, so that I could ask for your forgiveness.'

Eva tilted her chin up, facing Steffen squarely. Her arm lay across the tablecloth, fingers playing idly with the stem of her goblet. The tiny pearl buttons on her sleeve glowed in the flickering candlelight. 'And how are you going to do that?' Her tone was scathing, dismissive. She didn't believe a word of what he was saying and she had to make Bruin realise the falseness of Steffen's behaviour. She wanted to reveal his brother's true colours.

A puzzled look crossed Steffen's face. 'Well, I'll ask you, of course. For your forgiveness.' He cleared his throat noisily.

'So, you'll give everything back, then.'

'Why, you little—' Scowling darkly, Steffen caught Bruin's eye and swallowed a mouthful of wine hurriedly, spluttering. He wiped his lips with the back of his sleeve.

'The castles that belonged to my father, the lands. My mother's manor house.' She folded her arms across her chest, wanting to goad him. 'I think that was it, wasn't it?'

The smile dropped from Steffen's face, his lips tightening to a harsh, grim line. He glanced up at Bruin. 'It seems Mistress Striguil and I have much to talk about,' he said, a dangerous edge to his voice. 'It would surely bore you to death to hear it all; you might want to leave us for a while. There's a fire in the kitchens.'

'I'll stay,' Bruin said easily, adjusting his sprawling frame to the carved wooden chair. He stretched his legs out beneath the table.

'It's all very dull, Brother. Lady Striguil and I have unfinished business. It would be better if you left us.'

'And I want to stay,' Bruin said again. 'This lady has no secrets from me.'

Apart from one, thought Eva, shifting uncomfortably. That she loved him. A secret never to be revealed.

'Who appointed you the lady's protector all of a sudden?' Steffen snorted angrily. 'Very well, stay if you must. What you hear might change your opinion of her, mind you.' He turned to Eva. 'Now hear me, my lady.

Your father and brother were rebels against the Crown; I took your castles and lands on the direct orders of the King, and only he can decide to give them back to you. I had nothing for myself, you understand? I am only sorry that you had to be the one caught up in all this.'

'Do you really expect me to believe that?' she responded, anger welling up within her, making her voice shrill. 'That you're sorry for what you have done? That you're sorry that you held my arm over a blazing charcoal burner until I agreed to sign your documents? That you locked me in a chamber for days on end, with no food?'

Steffen sat back in his chair, a smug satisfied smile on his face. 'The woman's clearly raving, Bruin. Surely you can see that? She's completely mad; all that she says is a lie. Lie upon lie.'

'I believe her.' Bruin leant forward in his chair.

Eva flicked a grateful glance towards him, but his attention was focused on Steffen, the lines in his tanned face stern and hard. 'It is you who have lied to me, Brother. You pretended that you were dying so I would bring Eva back to you. And you clearly have no intention of apologising for what you have done…'

Steffen stood up abruptly; his chair legs scraping back with a vicious sound against the floorboards. 'That's enough!' he yelled, his index finger jabbing the air. 'You have no idea what you are talking about—this woman—she's made a fool out of you, just like Sophie did!'

'We're leaving,' Bruin said quietly, tight-lipped. He rose, pulling Eva up out of her chair. The manservant, Simon, appearing from the kitchens, stopped suddenly, his eyes wide, sensing the tension in the hall. A coil of steam rose slowly from the platter he was holding: baked fish, several days old.

'You're going nowhere,' Steffen threatened coldly. 'Mistress Striguil has something of mine and I intend to have it.'

'Just like you took everything of mine when we were boys, Steffen?' Bruin's eyes darkened dangerously. 'You haven't changed at all, have you? You can't bear for anyone to have more than you, or to be better than you.'

'I was always better than you!' Steffen shouted, his face adopting a mottled hue. 'You could scarcely hold a sword on the level—why, it was laughable! What a joke.'

Bruin ignored him, tucking one arm casually through Eva's, turning his back on his brother. 'Keep walking,' he muttered.

The blow to Bruin's head was sudden: an earthenware jug propelling through the air, smashing down brutally on to his skull. His great weight sagged against Eva, falling like a great oak, sprawling back unconscious across the floor. His head hit the floorboards with a ragged thump. Behind him, Steffen stood, a broken jug handle dangling from his fingers. 'That'll teach you to turn your back on me,' he announced triumphantly. Tipping his chin up, he yelled for the castle guards.

'Oh, my God, what have you done?' Eva cried, dropping to her knees beside Bruin. A shard of broken earthenware drove through her gowns into her shin. Bruin's eyes were closed, blood seeping from the wound, matting his golden-red hair. Through a haze of panic, Eva fought for sanity, for how to help Bruin. Stop the bleeding, she told herself, stop the bleeding now.

Grabbing the edge of the tablecloth, she yanked it viciously. Goblets and dishes clattered down, a discordant, jangling sound tearing the air. Chunks of food bounced across the floorboards; wine flicked up in a rose-red arc of liquid. She ripped at the cloth, wadding it into a ball, pressing the material hard against Bruin's head to staunch the bleeding. The air from his lungs dabbled her wrists as she worked. Thank God.

Steffen smiled, revealing rickety yellow teeth. 'My, my, how touching,' he said, his eyes widening with realisation. Then his expression stiffened, flicking over to the two guards who had come running at his shout. 'Take him away, will you?' Folding his arms over his pot belly, he cocked his head on one side. 'Now, my dear,' he said, in an odd, sibilant tone. 'Let's see how you fare without your protector.'

Tears gathered in the corner of Eva's eyes; she dashed them away angrily, watching in despair as Bruin was carried away, one guard clutching his shoulders, the other at his feet. The tablecloth, stained with his blood, hung between her hands. They bumped and jostled him against the door-frame as they made their way through. Then he was gone.

'Let me go to him!' Eva cried. 'You can't just fling him in a corner somewhere; his wound needs to be washed, tended.' She flung the stained material on to the table.

'All in good time, my lady,' Steffen replied. 'Why don't you sit back down, so we can talk? I'm sure we can both be reasonable about this.'

'Reasonable?' she flared at him. 'Since when have you ever been reasonable?'

Steffen's eyes flicked over her coolly. 'You would do well to watch your mouth, my lady. I think we can both agree that I have the upper hand here.'

Her shoulders sagged forward, defeated. 'Just let me go to him,' she whispered. 'You cannot let your own brother bleed to death.'

Steffen raised his eyebrows, as if he were considering the option. He slumped down into his chair, legs sprawling outwards. 'There's only one way I would let you do that,' he said finally; his tone holding the sneer of insolence.

'Tell me!' she cried out desperately, darting a glance towards the doorway through which Bruin had been carried.

'Give me the ruby.' Steffen crossed his legs, clasping his upper knee with both hands. 'Ah, yes, you were very clever, my lady, to conceal such a gemstone from me, but I found out eventually. I found out what you were hiding from me.' His voice sharpened. 'Where is it?'

'Will you let me see Bruin if I tell you?'

'Yes,' he replied.

She had no choice but to trust him. 'It's in the castle at Striguil.' She would do anything to be able to see Bruin, to care for him, even if it meant giving up the last valuable thing she owned: her security in these troubled times. 'In the chapel, there's an alcove containing a statue of the Virgin Mary. If you lift up that statue, there is a hollow in the base of the stone, and the ruby is wedged up into that hollow.'

'My God.' Steffen rocked back in his seat. 'I can't believe it; the ruby was there all along and yet we searched and searched for it.' His hand floated across his forehead, touched the side of his hair briefly, almost in disbelief. 'Why would you give such a thing away so easily, after keeping it safe all this time? Why would you do it?'

Eva raised her head listlessly, glared at him. 'Let me go to Bruin.' She balled her hands into fists beneath the folds of her gown.

Steffen frowned hard at her, as if trying to decipher

the workings of her mind. He laughed, a hoarse, croaking sound. 'Oh, Lord, I see it now; you've fallen in love with him, haven't you? Just like all those pretty ladies before you, falling at his feet. Unbearable to watch.'

Eva was silent. She heard the resentment in Steffen's voice, the hatred of his own brother. She thought of Bruin as a child, the weaker sibling, enduring the years of insults, the petty jealousies, and she bit her lip, tears gathering slowly. Steffen lurched out of his chair, striding towards her. She held her ground, curling her toes inside her leather boots, stiffening her resolve against the approaching enemy. He brought his face close to hers in a waft of foetid breath. 'No good will come of it, mark my words, my lady. No doubt you've heard what happened to his fiancée; aren't you worried he might do the same to you?'

She struggled to speak through the clenched, frozen muscles in her throat. 'He isn't a murderer.'

'As good as,' Steffen replied. 'He drove the poor girl to suicide, or at least he thinks he did.'

'What do you mean?' Eva drew her fine arched brows together. Steffen's manner unnerved her.

'I fooled him good and proper.' He threw the last dregs of his wine down his throat, chucking his empty goblet back on to the table. The detritus of previous meals lay scattered around the chair legs and under the table: slices of meat, upturned platters, spilled wine and soup.

Eva dismissed Steffen's words. There would be time later to wonder at his meaning. Right now all she wanted to do was find Bruin. 'You have what you want.' She tried to flatten out the tremble in her voice. 'I want to see Bruin.'

'But how do I know that you're not lying to me?' Steffen folded his arms across his tunic. 'You're a slippery fish, Mistress Striguil, and we both know that. What if we ride to Striguil and find nothing, eh?'

'If you don't trust me, then lock me in with Bruin and keep me there until you return with the ruby. Then you can let both of us go, because you will have what you want.'

Steffen's gaze travelled down her body, an insolent leer pinned to his face. 'You're playing with fire, Mistress Striguil, you do know that, don't you? My brother is a ruined man and he will surely ruin you.' He tapped his fingers idly along the back of a chair, then cocked his head, suddenly. 'All right, I agree. Simon will take you to him and I will travel to Striguil.'

Eva stumbled back with relief. It was done; she had traded her precious ruby in order to help Bruin. And he would never, ever know.

Chapter Sixteen

A couple of burly guards, grim and unsmiling, flanked Eva as she walked from the great hall. Along the plastered wall, candles had been stuck haphazardly into iron holders; the soldiers' hauberks rippled in the pale light, sword belts strapped around their hips. They wore no helmets and their tunics bore the crest of Hugh Fitzosbern, the owner of the castle. A ram's head was embroidered on to the woollen cloth, a black splotch in the middle of blue. Gold thread picked out the animal's horns. A queasy vulnerability swept through Eva; the tall soldiers made her diminutive figure even more apparent. Lord Steffen's eyes were upon her, tracking her neat, graceful progress across the hall, her gown trailing across the flagstones behind her; her spine prickled with awareness. One guard drew back the unwieldy curtain from the doorway, indicating with a sharp jerk of his head that she should pass through.

The entrance hall was cold, shadowy, moisture cloying the air. The same guard wrestled with the iron bolt, rusty in places, on the main door.

'Where is Lord Bruin?' Eva asked. Her voice trembled with worry. 'Where have you put him?'

'He's out in one of the stables, mistress,' the younger guard said, touching the leather hilt of his sword like a talisman. His face was white, shining like a greasy moon; strands of black hair splayed out across his forehead.

'My God, he'll freeze out there!' Eva clutched at her throat, hopping from one foot to the other, blue eyes wide with anxiety. Blood rattled through her veins, thready and rapid with fear; she hoped she would reach him in time, before—nay, she couldn't think like that. The blood spreading across the floorboards beneath his head—she sucked in her breath, heart puckering. She sent up a silent prayer to the heavens: please, please let him be all right.

The underside of the main door scraped across the flagstones as the soldier opened it, a small stone catching beneath the weighty planks. Outside, in the darkness, the inner bailey was deserted, the occasional flake of snow falling, trailing a lazy, diagonal path through the icy air. Then, on the far side, a door opened, light blazing out from the interior, spilling across the cobbles. Two figures emerged: a tall woman, a woollen shawl crossed tightly over her upper body, carrying a flaming torch, and a child, huddled close into her side.

Eva peered closely at the child. A boy. He looked familiar, with his hair of flaming bronze, shining out clearly beneath the woman's torch. His hair was the exact colour as Bruin's. Eva's mind scrabbled for comprehension. Was it possible? Did Bruin have a son? Dismay rippled through her and she frowned suddenly, dismissing the odd feeling. If Bruin did have a son, how could it be possible for his son to be here, in England? But curiosity, jealousy, she knew not what, made her reach forward for the soldier's arm, clutching at his elbow, stalling him.

'That child,' she blurted out, jabbing the air with a pointing finger, 'who is that child?' She watched the figures descend a flight of steps across the bailey and disappear through a shadowed archway.

The soldier shook off her arm, his face a dark scowl. 'That's Lord Steffen's son,' he replied curtly. 'Young Arwin.'

A jittery relief flooded through her. Of course. Lord Steffen was Bruin's twin; he had the same hair colour. It made perfect sense that the boy should be in the image of both of them.

'And the woman?' she asked. 'Is she Lord Steffen's wife?'

'Aye, she is,' the guard confirmed with a nod. 'That is the Lady Sophie.'

The raised hayloft was at the end of the stable, accessed by rickety, open-tread stairs, almost a ladder. A wide door at the top, bolted securely, led off from a small landing bounded by a wooden rail. The construction of the rail and steps was crude, uneven, both made up of roughly planed branches. Standing at the bottom, Eva's thoughts floundered, riven by conflicting emotions. Sophie. The lady crossing the yard had the same name as the woman who Bruin thought was dead and buried. Could that tall, willowy woman be the same person? The girl whom he had intended to marry?

'Come on, mistress! We haven't got all night!' The young soldier glared down at her from the top of the stairs. Eva shook her head, bunching her weighty skirts in one hand. Now was not the time to be thinking of such things. She needed to tend to Bruin. Setting her small foot on the first wobbly step, she climbed steadily and fast; the guard leaned down, giving her his hand to pull her up on to the wooden landing.

'Well done, my lady.' He smirked briefly, a hint of praise.

'Open the door, please,' Eva ordered. Her chest and throat prickled with emotion, as if she were about to cry. Blood filled her ears; her heart bumped unsteadily. Grinding her teeth into her bottom lip, she dug her nails into her palms, willing herself to remain in control, to ignore the giant hollow in her chest. Bruin will be all right, she kept saying to herself. He will be all right.

Thick iron bolts held the door firmly shut; the guard shot them both back swiftly. Grabbing Eva's shoulder, he shoved her into the darkness, closing the door behind her with a slam. The bolts rasped on the outside of the door. 'Have fun in there, mistress!' he guffawed.

At first it was impossible to see anything; the hayloft was pitch-black, shadowy, and yet, as her eyes adjusted, she discerned the outline of a square window, high on the opposite wall. Stars shone through the open space, twinkling against the midnight blue of the night sky. The snow had stopped completely now, the low cloud shifting away. A slick of fear passed through her like a blade. 'Bruin?' she whispered. 'Where are you? Speak to me, please!' Urgency lifted her voice, making the pitch shrill, terrified.

A muffled curse emanated from the corner of the chamber, then a groan. Dropping to her knees in the bundled hay, Eva groped her way forward to the source of the sound. A quivering hysteria rose in her chest. Her fingers bumped against cloth, a rounded arm muscle;

Bruin was sitting up, his back propped against the stone wall. 'Bruin, is that you?' Her voice jerked out with sobbing release. Tears ran down her cheeks, luminous pearls of light, falling across her wrists and into the hay. Relief surged through her. She touched his hair, the side of his cheek, as if in wonderment that he was there at all. Her hands fluttered along the corded sinew of his neck, a butterfly touch.

'Aye, it's me, Eva,' he said softly.

'Oh, thank God!' Winding slim arms around his enormous shoulders, she hugged him tightly, sparkling tears creating dark spots across his red surcoat. 'Thank God!' Her cheek nuzzled against his jawline, her veil drifting over his bright gold locks, the diaphanous silk floating down across his back. 'I thought he had killed you!' She sobbed against his ear, a ragged sound, muffled.

Her breasts pressed into his chest. The scent of her skin, rose petals in rain, filled his nostrils. His groin tightened. 'It would take more than a blow to the head to kill me, Eva,' he managed to croak out. The sudden onslaught of sensation struck his mind and body like a whirlwind, battered him: the cool silk of her cheek, her arm cradling his shoulders; the delicious flex of her body against his. Excitement flickered deep within his belly, sparking into life, amassing with a slow, heavy power.

'There was so much blood,' Eva choked out, on a whisper, her face buried in his neck. She blinked against his skin, velvety eyelashes skimming the bronzed bristle of his jawline, inhaling his musky scent. 'It was spreading across the floor.'

'You've had a shock,' he said, his arms lacing her waist to comfort her, spanning her slender frame. 'I have a small lump on my head, nothing more.' His thumbs splayed upwards, along the delicate rope of her spine.

She sighed against his cheek, a small gasp of relief, shifting against him. The pleated fall of her cloak draped across his legs, rich velvet rippling across his fawn braies. He closed his eyes, forcing himself to stifle the fresh surge of delight pulsing through him. Her knees nudged his hip. He should push her away now, unwind those fragrant arms from his neck and set her back in the hay with a stern word of caution.

He should.

He told himself he was in complete control; he could stop this all in a moment, break free from the trap of her enchanting beauty. He knew he was taking advantage of her, luxuriating in her beauty, when her only intention was to offer kindness towards him. But the Devil was on his shoulder, urging him forward with persuasive whispers, burrowing beneath his swiftly diminishing self-control. She was so utterly beautiful, so desirable and yet completely innocent to the lust raging within him: the savage tightrope, wobbling and unsteady, on which he balanced.

'Let me look at it for you,' Eva mumbled against his neck. Reluctantly, she began to pull away, turning her head. The corner of her mouth brushed his. She stopped, her heart stalling. Blood pounded in her ears. Time hung between them, the moment drawn out, caught in a bubble of air. His lips tasted of salt, the faintest hint of soap. Her belly plummeted, stabbed by a sudden, intense longing. All concern for him fled from her mind, chased away by a snapping, incoherent yearning. As if poised on the edge of a whirlpool, her body seemed unable to move forward or back, teetering on the brink of unspent desire, waiting for him to push her away.

But he did nothing.

Her breath punched out, unsteady, erratic. She should draw back from him now, stand up and back away, instead of behaving appallingly like this, like a wanton. Was this sort of behaviour even normal? To want a man like this? To crave him so much as to drive all common sense from her mind? She had no idea. All she could do was follow her instincts, her gut feeling. But as her mind commanded her to retreat, her heart and belly drove her on, like a hand at her back, nudging her onwards into the unknown. She had nothing to lose and fully expected him to reject her, but she would hate herself for ever if she did not at least try.

She covered his mouth with her own. A tentative, delicate manoeuvre, for she was an innocent and had little idea of what she was doing, of how to kiss a man. His lips were firm and cool. Bruin groaned, his hands sweeping around to cradle the sides of her face, to lift her mouth closer to his. Her lips were like the first cherries of summer: lush, plump and delicious. Warm. He ground his mouth against hers, taking charge, riding roughshod over her halting virtue. Lust burst through him, a blistering rush of sensation. All self-restraint fled, utterly destroyed, trampled to dust beneath the solid weight of his desire. His tongue flirted inquisitively along the closed crease of her mouth, intimate, sensuous.

Eva gasped; his tongue slid deep into the sweet cavern of her mouth. Her body liquefied, melting into his muscled warmth. His powerful kiss sapped her strength, making her weak, pliable; the ligaments in her knees and shins refused to hold her up any more and she sagged against him, unable to support herself. Bundling her in his arms, Bruin rolled her down into the hay, his lean, rangy frame sprawled across her, the links of his chainmail glinting in the faint starlight cast through the window.

The clamours of restraint grew fainter and fainter, the doubting whispers that sat in judgement on the threshold of his heart. With a supreme effort, he slid his mouth from hers, feasting on the glossy pink curves of her lips, the pulse beating hard and fast in the pearly hollow of her neck, and the way she watched him, midnight eyes gleaming with delicious anticipation. Desire etched her expression and his heart leapt. Was it possible? That she wanted him as much as he wanted her?

Holding himself up on propped arms, his sculptured cheekbones wavering above hers in the dark, his lungs fought for breath, for the energy to speak. 'Eva, for God's sake if you value your innocence, push me away now!' His voice was throaty and raw, silver eyes glittering in the half-light.

The low rumble of his voice thrilled along her veins. Her lips burned with the searing impact of his kiss, cheeks scuffed red by the bristles on his chin. She shook her head from side to side in the hay, a violent movement. *Don't stop. Please don't stop now.* Her eyes pleaded with him, enormous pools of blue light, and her rumpled veil flowed out beneath her like the white wing of an angel. How could she tell him that her innocence mattered not, that nothing mattered other than this moment in time, this moment in his arms, so precious and beautiful, that she wanted to continue, for ever and ever.

'No,' she whispered. 'I am not going to do that.'

'Eva, do you know what will happen?' His voice caressed her flesh.

'Aye, I do.' She smiled up at him shakily. The hard contours of his thighs pressed through her gown into the cushiony pillow of her hips; the nub of desire in her belly rippled out, concentric circles of pleasure, a stone thrown on to the surface of a quiet pond.

In response, he fell upon her, wedging his brawny build against her slender frame, hip to hip, thigh to thigh. His booted feet knocked against her ankles, and she welcomed it, welcomed the feel of him against her, rocked by one newborn sensation after another. He dipped his head, slanting his mouth against hers, prowling steadily, roaming. Curving her arms upwards, she wound her arms around his back, smoothing one hand down the powerful cord of his spine, wanting him closer, wanting more of him.

Raising to his knees above her, Bruin gripped the hem of his surcoat, tearing it over his head. His glittering hauberk was chucked into the corner, followed by his linen shirt. His bare chest gleamed: bulky slabs of pectoral muscle above the rigid planes of his flat, honed stomach. The waistband of his braies, held up by a knotted leather tie, dipped below his belly button, riding low on slim hips.

Eva gazed up at him in awe as he rose above her like a god of old, a golden Adonis. She lifted her fingers, knuckles sketching against the sheen of his skin, the ruts of muscle packed across his stomach. He sucked in his breath at the tentative contact, then grabbed her wrists to pull her upright, plucking swiftly at the side-laces of her gown, his movements feverish, expansive. She should have felt shy, but instead, a feeling of an innate safety spread through her, a trust that he would treat her properly, with care, and she laughed out loud as he tried to yank both her gowns over her head at the same time, muffling her in yards of cloth.

'Too many clothes,' she said, her cheeks bright with effort, as he finally managed to pull them away from her and throw them into the corner.

'I agree,' Bruin said, his eyes trawling across her gauzy white shift, the push of her bosom against the filmy fabric, the rosy tip-tilt of her nipples. In response, she lifted the shift over her head, clinging to his eyes as she did so, revealing her nakedness in that one swift movement. His lungs emptied of air; he struggled to breathe, his mind battling to comprehend, to make sense of the beauty before him. Her skin was pure satin, gleaming with a pearl-like lustre. Her ripe breasts were firm and luscious, her waist indented in a neat elongated curve before flaring out over her hips. Sweet Jesu, she was perfect.

And in this very moment she was his.

'My God,' Bruin stuttered. His arm wound around her bare back and he crushed her against him, skin to skin. His blood looped dangerously, boiling, surging with a barely uncontrollable force. He hadn't lain with a woman in some time, yet he knew he must be careful. Eva was—she was special. He didn't want to ruin this for her by rushing things, and yet, by God, he would need every ounce of his experience to hold back, to stop himself ploughing roughly into her sleek lustrous body.

They fell back into the hay, Bruin's eyes darkening, silver-gilt caverns of desire, scorching, intent, as he crushed her against him, hip to hip, belly to belly, hard muscle packed against pliable curves. Air twisted heavily in her lungs as the lean, naked length of him wrapped around her, powerful and aroused. Tracing his lips against her delicate collarbone, he moved his mouth lower, then lower again, to the shadowy cleft between her breasts. Her insides squeezed with pleasure and she cried out, thinking she would die beneath the tumult of sensation ricocheting through her. 'Bruin...?' Something gathered, deep within her, a spiralling sensation, a flowering of need. As if a distant, secret place within her drifted to the surface and unfolded bit by bit before him, laying itself bare before his silver eyes. Revealing her innermost desires, exposed to his knowing gaze. Her stomach contracted, vibrating with sweet awareness, excitement bubbling like scalding liquid.

He moved his big body over hers. His skin was cool, the hairs on his legs tickling her satiny calves. A flick of fear pierced her stomach, coupled with a burgeoning anticipation; the blistering heat of his desire was hard against her thigh. His mouth seized hers once more, before she had any time to think, or question, his lips roaming across hers, deepening the kiss. She arched up against the sculptured planes of his chest and, in that moment, he moved into her, slowly, easing into her tender folds. Her arms flew outwards like startled birds, shocked at the sudden onslaught, at the bewildering sensations pummelling her within, searching for a hold, for some stability, a rock to which she could anchor. Her hands found his face and she clung to him, tying herself fast to the savage gleam of his eyes, bracing herself against the inevitable storm.

Unable to hold himself back, he surged into her then, his body consumed by a desire that took him completely by surprise. The fragile barrier of her virginity made him pause for a moment, before he pushed into her completely, utterly. Blood pounding in her chest, Eva's head knocked back against the hay, stunned by the force of his possession, her flesh consumed by him, aching from him. And yet, when he moved again, it was with such gentleness that the mild pain dissipated, to be replaced by a soft, eddying fullness. She began to match his movements, slowly at first, but soon, with a delighted eagerness of her own. Her eyelids dipped, the conscious part of her brain folding away, ripples of desire lapping deep within her belly, her groin. Her breath emerged in short little pants. She thrust her hands into Bruin's hair, gripping tightly, holding on for dear life, rocking against the man she longed to call her own. A boiling, surging wave broke through the very innards of her flesh, shooting white-hot flashes of light across the darkness of her mind, a storm of scattering stars.

She cried out then, her body shattering into a thousand brilliant pieces, as Bruin pounded into her, deeper and deeper, sweat dropping from his chin, his hands tangling in her hair. The taut straining skin that stretched and stretched between them split with sudden violence; waves of undiluted pleasure surged through her body, again and again, leaving her gasping. Above her, Bruin shouted his own release, shuddering with her, then collapsing on top of her, heavy, replete and, for the first time in a long while, blissfully alive.

Chapter Seventeen

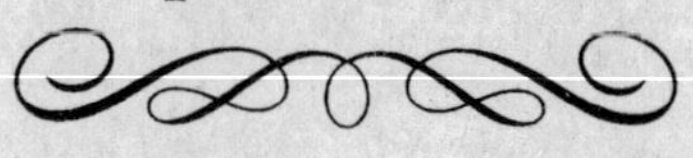

Blood slowing, Eva lay against Bruin's chest, the sinewy rope of his arm clamping her naked flesh with a fierce possession. His chest hair tickled her ear; she listened to the slackening thud of his heart. Her palm spread over his belly, the sweat drying on his cooling flesh. My God, how could she have known how wonderful lying with a man could be? Her knowledge had been scant; nothing could have prepared her for what had just happened. Her body ached, quivered with the memory of him, but it was the sweetest hurt she had ever known: as if every muscle and sinew in her body had been stretched and slightly altered, reset into a new and better place.

Bruin said nothing and she was glad. His hand fumbled across the hay, searching for something to cover them, and pulled the voluminous folds of her cloak over their cooling bodies. Now was not the time for apologies, or recriminations. She wanted nothing to spoil the beauty of the experience; tomorrow was soon enough to face any doubts. And there was no question that it was she, Eva, who had made this happen. Bruin had given her the option to stop; she had been fully aware of what was happening.

She snuggled against Bruin's heated flank, her eyelids drooping. Her lashes fluttered down, sweeping across her flushed cheeks. Bruin heard the small sigh, the shift of her body relaxing against him, her slowing breath as she fell asleep. His chin rested on her glossy crown, the satin ropes of her hair still pinned to her head. In their haste, he hadn't even bothered to loosen her hair. A rawness twisted his expression, his eyes bleak, riven with guilt. How could he have done such a thing to her? How was it possible that he had lost control like that, especially with her, Eva, the woman so different from any other woman he had met, the woman who—he might have dared to love?

He had allowed Eva to sleep for a few hours, wrapped in his arms, as he watched snowflakes blow sporadically through the opening above their heads, tracking their dancing journey through the dim light. He had relished the feel of her: her bare flesh like plush velvet against his flank, the spill of her hair across his chest. A hollowness gnawed at him, a wretchedness: he had betrayed her trust and hated himself for it. He had told her time and time again that she could trust him, that he would protect her from his brother, and he had reneged on both those things. As the first fingers of dawn light filtered bleakly down on to the hay, he shifted his position, jostling her out of sleep. 'Eva, you need to wake up now.'

Reverberating beneath her ear, his speech rumbled in his chest, which rose suddenly, tipping her sideways into the hay. Rolling away, her befuddled mind registered the sound of Bruin pulling on his clothes: the slither of braies and surcoat, the heavy chinking of his chainmail falling into place across his brawny thighs. His sword sliding into the leather scabbard.

'Here.' His tone was brisk, matter of fact, as he bent down to pick up her chemise, her gowns. Eva sat up hazily, pushing back an errant curl of ebony hair behind her ear. A hairpin dug into her scalp and she raised one arm, poking it savagely back into place. Bruin's heart lurched, heat jolting through his belly. Bare-breasted, she looked like a mermaid in a sea of hay, propping herself on one arm with her legs bent behind her, the magnificent sheen of her skin adopting the pure translucency of a pearl, the glimmer of satin. And last night, he had devoured her, consumed that beauty with all the rutting instincts of a boar on heat.

A dull redness covered his cheeks. 'Cover yourself, will you?' he said, exasperated with himself, annoyed that he could not control his feelings, his desire for her. He turned away, kicking irritably at the swathes of hay, searching for his boots.

Shivering in the chill air, Eva crossed her arms over her chest, heart plummeting with sadness, hurt pride. Sticking her chin out at a mutinous angle, she picked up her creased chemise and pulled it over her head, her chest caving with despair at his sharp tone, the scowling expression on his face. She clamped her lips together, fiercely, telling herself she wouldn't cry, nay, she couldn't! She had lain with this man willingly, with her eyes wide open, and had been fully aware of the consequences. So why did the blunt edge of disappointment hammer clumsily at her spirit, making her movements leaden, defeated?

Anger would be her best defence now, not this crushed,

miserable attitude. The hurt coiled with her, solidifying, hardening, shot through with a flare of anger. Show him that you're not affected by what happened and act with courage, a shrugging nonchalance, Eva told herself sternly. Standing up, she tugged the cumbersome gowns over her head. 'There,' she said, fumbling to tighten the side-lacings of the gowns, 'are you happy now?' Sarcasm laced her tone; she welcomed it.

Bruin glowered at her, buckling his sword belt. 'No, I'm not happy.' He stuffed his big feet into his leather boots. 'I took advantage of you last night and for that I am truly sorry.' He stuck his hand into his hair, sending the vigorous bronze-coloured strands awry.

'Don't be,' she bit out. 'Don't be sorry. It doesn't matter.'

'It does matter, Eva. You should hate me for what I have done. I've dragged you here, against your will, forced you to lie with me—'

'No. You didn't force me, Bruin. You gave me the chance to push you away—' She placed her hands on her hips, the stance lending her strength. Her heartbeat accelerated as she remembered the muscled hardness of his thighs against hers, his big hands roaming across her flesh.

'But you had no idea what you were letting yourself in for.' A lone muscle jumped high in his cheek. 'I took what was not mine to have.'

Eva ducked her head, embarrassed by the bluntness of his speech, shamed. How could she tell him that it had all been worth it, to lie with him, to savour his touch against her body, to feel him move against her? Her innocence was something she had been prepared to give freely. She would never forget this night; the memory would rest in her heart for ever. He had to know, even if it meant she would drive him further away.

'I wanted you to have it.'

'Eva—?' His eyes widened, stunned by her simple admission. 'Oh, my God, why? Why would you give yourself away so arbitrarily, to me of all people?' He scooped up her cloak, shaking out the heavy folds, brushing bits of hay from the cloth. 'Me, the ruffian who dragged you here. Remember?' His metallic eyes met hers, shot through with anguish.

Because I love you, she thought. Streams of hopelessness lapped her heart; she bit down hard on her bottom lip, reminding herself how to behave: to be strong, resolute in the face of his rejection.

Bruin sighed, scuffing the loose hay with his boot, shaking his head ruefully. 'I am not a good person, Eva.' His voice was low, the foreign inflection more pronounced. 'I have killed people—men. After Sophie's death, I went to pieces, lost control, and there was no limit to what I wouldn't do. I was given orders and I followed them, blindly, without question. I gave no thought to what I did. That is the sort of man I am.'

Eva took her cloak from him. A chill wobbled through her at the mention of Sophie's name. The image of the women striding across the bailey, the boy at her side, loomed across her vision; at some point she would tell Bruin about her and her own suspicions: that the lady was the same Sophie he thought was dead. But now was not the time. Now, she realised, she was fighting for the man she loved. Snow crystals blew in through the opening above her head, speckling the dark blue wool over her arm. 'That's the sort of man you *were*,' she responded quietly, emphasising the past tense. 'You're different now.' Her voice was clipped; she would not plead for him to change his mind, but a small voice whispered at her, nay, begged her, not to give up on him, just yet.

His eyelashes dipped fractionally, hooding his brilliant eyes. 'No, I'm not. The things I have done, Eva, they live up here—' he tapped the side of his skull '—and they will never, ever go away. You're a fool, if you think I can give you anything.'

A horrible sense of desolation chewed into her. Flags of colour patched her cheeks. She tipped her head to one side, her bright eyes challenging him. 'I don't want anything from you, Bruin. Let's be clear about that.' Beneath her cloak, her nails dug cruelly into her palms. 'But please don't ruin what we shared together. You owe me that at least. But if you want to forget about it, then that's fine. Forget it, forget it ever happened and never speak of it again.'

Shocked by the bluntness of her speech, the unexpectedness of it, his chin shot up. He frowned at her, brindled eyebrows drawn close together. 'You—I beg your pardon?'

'You heard me,' Eva responded brutally. 'Forget it ever happened.' Reaching down for her veil, she jammed the fragile cloth savagely into place with her silver circlet, mouth set in a terse, rigid line.

Bruin peered at her, then touched her shoulder, lightly. She flinched away, resenting the contact. He had expected tears and lamentations, not this bullish stance, tight-lipped and stony-faced. But he had underestimated her, he realised that now. He had forgotten how she had fought him in the forest, how she had battled for her freedom. 'You don't have to be like this.' He saw the turbulent mixture of fire and false bravado, the hurt in her eyes. She was like a wild cat, he thought, fractious and diffident, on the edge of running away to lick her wounds in private.

Oh, yes, I do, she thought. *Otherwise I will sink to my knees and weep at your feet, and that is the very last thing I want to happen. I will not plead with you to love me, or honour me, after what you have done.* 'How else should I be?' she responded waspishly. 'I'm not going to cry about it, if that's what you're expecting. I have no regrets, even if you do.'

Her eyes shimmered with unspent tears. Her stance was tense, poised tightly, as if she balanced on a thin ledge, peering with trepidation into the chasm below. Her arms maintained a fierce grip on her cloak. She clutched it to her stomach like some sort of buffer; a cloth wall between the two of them. But then, what had he been expecting? He had pushed her away before she had even time to fully surface from sleep, erecting his well-worn barriers, his impenetrable defences. He had caused all this: her terse, strained demeanour, the sadness floating in the huge blue pools of her eyes.

A wave of guilt jolted through him. 'Why are you even here, Eva?' Walking over to the door, he rattled the iron latch with impatience. 'Why would Steffen lock you up with me? I thought he would at least have given you a bedchamber to sleep in.'

Eva let out a long surreptitious breath. Bruin was convinced, she was certain, convinced that she was unaffected by what had happened, that she didn't blame him in any way. It was a good thing he couldn't see her heart, or the tattered remains of it, for then he would realise her behaviour was a sham. 'Steffen doesn't trust me. I've already escaped from him once; I suspect he thought I would try it again.'

Her explanation made sense. Bending down, Bruin plucked his cloak from the hay, his hair glinting a dull bronze in the stark dawn light. And on the side of his head, a web of matted hair, clotted with dark red blood.

'Oh, God, Bruin, your head!' Eva cried out when she saw it. All her reasons for maintaining an aloof distance from this man vanished in that moment. Shame flooded over her, guilt that she had forgotten what had happened to him, that she had neglected him. 'Oh, Bruin, I'm so sorry, your wound looks nasty and I forgot to look at it!' The tough unnatural lines slid from her face. Tears welled in her eyes before she could stop them.

Straightening up, he swung the cloak around his broad shoulders, a practised, efficient manoeuvre. He read the concern in her expression, the glimmer of tears, and wondered at them. His breath hitched in his chest. Why would she still care for him, after all that he had done to her? They both knew why she hadn't looked at his wound; in the heat of their passion, the reason they were in the chamber had been forgotten, slipping away, lost in their clamouring need for each other. 'It's fine,' he said, firmly.

'But it's bleeding!' she protested, stepping forward. 'I need to clean it, to bind it with something before it becomes infected!'

'It will have to wait, Eva,' Bruin replied. He touched her elbow, lightly, in acknowledgement of her worry. 'We must leave this place, as soon as possible, before Steffen starts trying to find out where your ruby is.'

Too late, she thought dully. I traded the whereabouts of the ruby to be by your side. Her mouth twisted down slightly, mocking her own stupidity.

Bruin's silver eyes darted around the grey-lit chamber, alighting on the opening high up in the wall. 'I don't suppose you remember if the door is locked or bolted on the outside?'

'Bolted,' Eva replied immediately, recalling the stiff, grating noise as the guard had pulled the bolts back. A lifetime ago. She had been a different woman then.

He raised one eyebrow at her, questioning. 'In that case, do you think you can fit through that window?'

'I can try,' she replied.

Dropping her cloak to the ground, Eva tucked her foot into the cup of his hands, bracing herself on his shoulders. He hoisted her light frame easily and she pushed her arms through the window to grip the ledge on the outside. The cold air numbed her fingers as she wiggled her body up and through, the fine embroidery on her gown rasping on the coarse stone. Palms balanced on the soles of her slippers, Bruin hoisted her up until his arms were at full stretch, then he released her.

'Hold on!' he said suddenly, snagging one of her swinging ankles, fine-boned beneath silk stockings. He worried he might crush her ankle bone beneath his grip. 'Eva, can you see how far the drop is to the ground out there?'

Sides squeezed by the opening, she peered down into a thicket of shrubs and brambles, only a few feet away: the height of a man. Trees clustered alongside the shrubs, close enough for her to grab hold. The temperature had dropped below freezing, too cold for snow; everything was covered with a thick, hard layer of glittering ice. Beyond the shrubs, a forest of deciduous trees stretched back into the distance. An eerie light, watery, slowly dissipated as the sun rose, flickering through the bare branches The winter forest turned into a mass of delicate sparkles.

'Not far.' She turned her head, keeping her voice low. This back wall of the stables formed part of the bigger curtain wall circling the castle, but the trees on this side had been allowed to grow too close to the wall: a weak point in its structure. She could slither down, right now, and run, run away from all this, from Bruin and her night of shame, leaving him locked in the barn to await his brother's return. She closed her eyes, the long-held tears finally falling, streaming down her cheeks, dropping through the icy air, crystal droplets. No. She couldn't leave him.

'Eva, can you hear me?' His voice was muffled.

'Yes,' she managed to reply. 'I can jump down easily and I'll come around.'

'Be careful,' she heard him say.

She looped her arm around a branch and swung out from the window. Lichen smeared a green stain on her sleeve. The chill air flowed beneath her skirts, piercing the fine wool of her stockings. Teeth chattering, she plunged into the thicket of brambles, ice bouncing up around her, thorns scratching her legs and arms, tearing at her gown. Her gaze darting this way and that, she checked to see if anyone was around on the ramparts behind her, in the forest. The place was deserted.

Silently, she extricated herself from the brambles, lifting the whippy, snagging tendrils up and away with careful fingers, intending to walk along the curtain wall until she found an opening. Her boots crunched over the frozen earth as she followed the mossy stones, flecked with ice crystals. An undulating path, fairly well-trodden, mirrored the line of the wall. With a sinking heart, she realised that the only way back into the castle was through the gatehouse itself, where Steffen would have guards posted. Rounding a corner, the stone structure rose before her and she stumbled on a protruding stone, her step hesitant, wondering what she could do.

Eva stopped. Inside the gatehouse, someone was shouting. A male voice, harsh and booming, coupled with the clash of swords. Then, amidst a cacophony of warning shouts, Bruin sprang out from beneath the archway on his horse, no saddle or bridle, his reddish-gold hair like a flame against the drab stone. Chainmail glinting, his brawny thighs urged the animal forward, flicking a flaxen rope around the horse's neck, controlling the animal. He spotted Eva immediately, crouching in the shadows next to the wall. He waved his arm in a wide arc, grinning triumphantly, indicating that she climb up to the path that led down from the gatehouse.

Heart flaring with relief, Eva scrambled up the slope, frost lacing her skirts. As her toe hit the rubble of the track, Bruin came towards her, the horse at a fast trot, mane flaring out like a sun ray. Leaning low in the saddle, he braced his arm around her waist and swept her up before him in a flurry of skirts, wedging her back against his stomach. Secure. Safe. As her back thumped hard against his chest, an arrow whistled through the air towards them, bouncing off the iron-hard ground. Breathless, smiling, she shifted around, inhaling the musky scent of him, catching at the collar of his surcoat for balance, questions tumbling from her mouth.

'Later,' Bruin said. 'Let's get out of here first.'

Chapter Eighteen

Racing through the frost-spangled trees, Bruin urged his horse on, the pace relentless, his arm braced like a vice across Eva's stomach. Despite their speed, the lack of a saddle, a sense of security stole over her; she knew, instinctively, that he would not let her fall. He controlled his horse with expert precision: a twitch on the makeshift rope bridle, a nudge of his knees; man and animal working together. Errant flakes of snow, floating through the air, whispered against her cheeks, dabs of cold. Around them, everything was white: the rolling fields, stone walls, hedgerows, all covered in a hazy coating of frost. Icicles, blasted by the wind during the night, hung from branches in weird, contorted shapes. As the sun rose, the sky lightened to a translucent blue, grey-streaked, and the sound of creaking ice permeated the woodland.

Pulling gently on the rope around the horse's neck, Bruin slowed the animal to a walk. The solid muscles in his chest flexed against her spine, sturdy and comforting. 'Let's walk for a bit,' he said, his breath stirring the top of her veil. 'I think we're far away enough now.'

Her fingers pleated the coarse hairs of the horse's

mane. Her hands were freezing, her gloves left on the table at Deorham. She should tell Bruin there was no need to run, or to hide; Steffen wasn't even at the castle. But that would reveal how she had traded the ruby in order to see him, to be with him. Humiliation chafed her innards. 'How did you escape?' she asked instead. 'It was only after I had jumped that I realised the only way back into the castle was through the gatehouse. I wasn't sure what to do.'

'I realised it, too.' Bruin laughed, a confident sound ringing around the silent, serried trees. Trunks ridged and calloused like old man's skin. 'But luckily for me that poor unfortunate manservant arrived with food to break our fasts, and I was ready for him.'

'What did you do?'

'Knocked him over the head with my sword hilt, then bolted him in. My horse was in the stables below, so I untied the rope and made for the gatehouse.'

'With no saddle and no bridle,' she murmured with admiration. 'You make it sound so easy.'

His laughter rumbled against her back. 'That's because it was, Eva. The guards on the gate were half-asleep anyway.' Lifting his arm, he pushed back a low, overhanging branch so they could ride beneath it. 'I'm surprised you waited for me, though. This was your chance, Eva. You could have run away and had your freedom from both me and my brother.'

She twisted her head around, appalled that he should think such a thing. 'The idea never crossed my mind!' Blue fire shone in her eyes, ferocious, flecked with outrage.

'Why not?' He lifted his shaggy eyebrows. 'After everything that has happened, Eva? After what I did?' His reference to their night together was obvious, blunt, and she blushed, eyelashes dipping fractionally towards her red cheeks.

'Because I'm not the sort of person to leave you locked up.' A loose thread, silken and fragile, poked up from the neck seam of his surcoat; she concentrated hard on it, avoiding his gaze. 'And I don't go back on my word.'

The granite of his eyes lightened to iridescent silver, streaked with blue. 'But I, of all people, don't deserve your loyalty, Eva,' he murmured, the cleft above his top lip deepening, as if some invisible person pressed their thumb into the space, shadowing his skin. 'Why did you not run?'

Stupidity, hot and breathless, swept over her; he made her feel foolish for not taking the chance. Had she made the biggest mistake of her life? In the glorious aftermath of their lovemaking, that effervescent bubble of limitless time, her mind had flirted with the thought of a life with Bruin. An insane, madcap dream, a chimera. She knew that now. Of course, he was desperate to be rid of her and was astounded, probably annoyed that she hadn't taken herself away. It was time for her to leave him, before her heart withered away with sadness.

'Oh, I don't know,' she replied, her words miserable, flat. 'I wasn't thinking.'

The odd, off-key note of her voice jarred through him. Bruin peered down at her. Her head was tilted regally, stony gaze fixed straight ahead. A breeze sifted between them, blowing her flimsy veil to one side, exposing the downy skin of her neck, the lustrous coil of hair. Alternate threads of blue and green wool made up the warp and weft of her over-gown. Gilt embroidery embellished her collar: a neat chain stitch, worked by an expert hand, intricate lines and whorls.

His heart lurched. His upper arms grazed her slim shoulders. He remembered the goose-down perfection of her skin sprawled against him. So fragile. And yet her physical appearance belied an inner strength that surpassed the courage of even the very best of his men. He was glad she hadn't disappeared. That she had stayed. His blood had soared with unexpected joy when he had spotted her as he rode out from the gatehouse, pursued by angry shouts. He was in no doubt now that she would have worked out some way to free him, if he hadn't managed to extricate himself. But why would she do such a thing—for him? A glimmer of hope laced his heart.

It was market day in Ranscombe, a sprawling, untidy village lying to the north of the forest. Laden carts, glossy rumped horses, ponies with heavy packs tied to their backs; all jostled for space in the central square. Stalls lined the cobbled area; people crowded into the middle, muffled up against the cold in heavy fur cloaks, woollen felt hats. Merchants shouted out their wares, each trying to raise their voice above that of their neighbour, vying for trade. Dogs sniffed at leather-bound legs, lurking around for scraps, then scooted off suddenly, shouted away by some indignant trader, some dogs so thin that the outline of their ribs poked through their coarse-haired pelts.

'We can stop here and find something to eat,' Bruin announced, as he steered the horse towards a wooden rail. His chest grazed Eva's back as he dismounted and secured the horse's rope with a loose knot around the rail. He clasped Eva's waist, sweeping her down from the horse's back.

'You're very quiet,' he said, as soon as her feet were steady on the ground. His silver eyes narrowed, gimlet-sharp, shrewd. Was she reflecting on her robbed innocence? A knife of guilt twisted in his gut; he cleared his throat. 'Are you thinking about—?'

'No, I'm not!' She thrust her chin up, cheeks flaring red. She knew what he had been about to say; she had no wish to listen to his apologies, his regrets. A huge lump lodged in her throat. Her chest fluttered, dangerously. Don't, don't cry, she told herself firmly. She drew her spine up straight, his large frame shadowing her from the bright noon sun, and cleared her throat. 'Bruin—' she said, her speech emerging awkwardly. She smoothed her veil against one shoulder, fingers fretting the material, patting nervously. 'The thing is—I think it would be best for both of us if you leave me here now.'

'Leave you—?' Horror creased his lean features. Of course, she couldn't wait to get away from him after last night. After what he had done.

'Yes, Bruin. Leave me here. You need to go back to your own life—with the King, I suppose…' she waved her hand in the air distractedly, as if indicating the spot where she believed the King to be '…and I—I need to find Katherine, make sure she's settled into her new life.' Yes, yes, that was what she should do; the idea came to her in a moment: find Katherine, for her friend would help her as she had helped in the past.

A man pushed past them, carrying a large, flat board of currant buns, fragrant, just cooked, followed by a drift of steam. His scrawny shoulder knocked against Eva, making her stagger. Bruin scowled darkly at the man, catching at Eva's wrist to balance her. His brain scrambled to understand her words. Surely she needed to stay with him for longer? His thumb played along the cuff of her gown, rubbing unconsciously against the raised embroidery, slipping over the silken flesh of her wrist. Her pulse throbbed beneath his touch. Hopelessness, a sense of desolation, swept over him; he didn't want her to go. His mind searched for reasons to keep her with him, all the time studying her tight-lipped expression, her hunched shoulders. Guilt scoured his chest; he had done this to her; no doubt it would be better for both of them if they parted ways. But he couldn't let her go. Not just yet.

'You can't be on your own, Eva.'

His hand lingered on her wrist. She scarce heard his words. Eyes blurring, she stared as if mesmerised, his strong tanned fingers stroking her white skin, the trace of blue veins. Her belly fluttered, sensation coiling, remembering. His hands on her naked body, rough and questing, no boundaries. Her resistance began to fray, a fragile rope stretched taut, weakening. She shook her head so forcibly that her tears flew out, darting spangles. 'Don't,' she breathed. 'Please don't.'

He snatched his hand away. 'Sorry,' he muttered, mouth settling into a grim line. She must resent even the smallest touch after what had happened. Entranced by the sleekness of her wrist, he hadn't been thinking. 'Eva, it's not safe for me to leave you on your own. Steffen will still come after you. You know that.'

She lowered her head. Her boots poked out from her skirts, muddy, stained with dew. 'No, he won't.' Her voice was quiet, threaded with sadness.

'But Steffen wants to know where your ruby is.' He clung to the excuse like a lifeline, a rope that linked them together; this had to be the reason why she must stay at his side. He would protect her from his brother; he owed her that, at the very least.

'He already knows.'

His breath seizing, he recoiled as if she had stabbed him in the chest, his mind tacking back to the evening before, the meal with his brother. 'What happened after Steffen hit me over the head, Eva?' A ruddy colour rose in his cheeks. His eyes darkened, forbidding, unsteady. 'What did he do to you?' Sweet Jesu, why had he not thought to ask her earlier when she had come to him in the stables? But earlier had never happened, had it? He had fallen on her like an eager puppy, never giving her the chance to speak, or explain. 'What happened?' A searing wretchedness ripped through him.

'Nothing happened, Bruin. Your head was bleeding so much, and I wanted—' Eva's voice drifted off, unsure how to explain her need to care for him, without revealing her true feelings.

'You wanted—? What did you want, Eva?' he rapped out sternly.

'To tend your wound,' she whispered tremulously. Tears brimmed against her eyelids. 'Stop shouting, Bruin, please...' Her voice wobbled.

Guilt flooded his stern expression. Contrite, he cupped her shoulders. 'I'm sorry.' His voice was muted. 'So the only way Steffen would let you come to me was if you told him the whereabouts of the ruby!' Had she truly done this? For him? He could scarce believe it. 'You traded the only thing you had left in the world for me,' he acknowledged quietly. A dancing lightness wheeled around his heart. A bubbling effervescence, gaining momentum.

She nodded, hanging her head, waiting for roar of his

anger, his condemnation. He would tell her how stupid she was, what a fool she had been to give away the last drop of her security and waste it on him. Only it hadn't been a waste. Not for her, anyway.

To her surprise, he seized her chin, tilting her tear-streaked face upwards, compelling her to meet his eyes. 'You did that for me,' he murmured, amazement colouring his low tone.

'Yes,' she replied simply. Her breath puffed out, white smoke in the chill air.

'But why?'

Because I love you. The words ricocheted against her heart, unspoken. 'I couldn't leave you like that, Bruin,' she said instead, trying to imbue her tone with a sense of brusque practicality. 'No one would have. You were injured.' She clasped her hands together, flicking nervously at her thumbnail with her index finger.

'I would have been all right.'

'I didn't know that then. Anyway, I knew I would feel safer with you than in a bedchamber with Lord Steffen lurking about.'

'Did you?' His tone was husky, eyes alight with scintillating flecks, darts of molten silver.

The tip of his thumb grazed the bottom curve of her lip. In her mind's eye, she watched their bodies rolling naked in the hay, the hushed whispers of their fevered breath. The muscles in her chest contracted, her brain sweeping hot with the memory of their desire. She closed her eyes. This would not do, this thinning of her self-imposed resolve.

She turned her head, trying to wash her mind of its sensual thoughts; his hand fell away. 'Steffen is not a threat to me any more. He has everything he wants now. You can let me go.'

No! I don't want to let you go.

The words banged in his brain, insistent, clamouring. He thought quickly, eyes like iron flints, charged with liquid light. 'But Steffen has stolen something that was not his to take. Are you going to allow him to do that?'

'I have to. This way I am free of him, free of the worry that he will always try to come after me.' She laid a hand on Bruin's chainmail-covered forearm. The links lay flat, chill beneath her skin. 'Do you understand that?'

'Aye, I do,' he replied. He folded his arms across his surcoat, expression openly challenging. The pallid morning light fired the short bristles on his jaw. 'But I still think you need to take back what is rightfully yours. Where has the woman gone who fought me in the forest just a few days ago? The woman who battered my chest with her fists? Who called me a thug, a barbarian; who wouldn't even deign to ride the same horse as me? My brother is in the wrong and if anyone can fight to win back what belongs to them, then it's you, Eva.'

She heard the note of praise in his voice, wondered at it. Did he really have that amount of faith in her capabilities? 'I can't. How can I do that, a woman alone?' Her eyes widened, sparkling lakes of turquoise, the shimmer of sea at daybreak. Her voice dropped to a whisper. 'It's inconceivable.'

He nudged the toe of her boot with his own, a companionable gesture, catching her attention. 'Not when you have someone to help you.' His eyes gleamed, silver fire.

'But, Bruin…' she spread her arms out, fingers splaying out, a gesture of futility '…I have no one.'

'On the contrary,' he replied, a generous smile consuming his features, overjoyed that he had found a reason to keep her by his side. 'You have me.'

They ate hungrily, devouring hot meat pies from a market seller, Bruin handing over the coin for payment. Standing side by side, Eva watched him eat, licking his lips with obvious pleasure as he consumed the last morsel, giving the merchant more coin in exchange for more. 'Do you want another?' he asked, inclining his head towards her in question.

Eva laughed. 'No, thank you. I have enough.' She held up the half-eaten pie in her hand, pleasure suffusing her heart, happy that they would be together, in each other's company, for a little while longer. He was doing it out of a sense of duty; he felt guilty for what he had done to her, but she didn't mind. But doubt niggled at her, worried at the fringes of her brain; she was the weak point in this plan. Was her resolve strong enough to protect her heart when she was with him? Or would his continued presence, and the memory of what they had done, carve the nub of her soul into tiny little pieces, leaving her wretched? It was a risk she was willing to take. The ruby was just an excuse. She wasn't agreeing to this plan to retrieve what was owed to her; she was agreeing because she wanted to stay with Bruin. Just for a little while longer.

The pie had been wrapped in a muslin napkin; she wiped her hands on the cloth, dabbing discreetly at her mouth. She shivered; although the inside of her body was warm, nourished from the pie, they stood in the shadow of the buildings, where the air was chill. Ice slicked the cobbles, a treacherous surface; a merchant walking past, slipped, then stumbled, uttering a foul string of curses as he managed to right himself.

'Bruin, thank you for helping me. It's very kind of you.'

Kind. The word grated on his conscience. How could he tell her that he had an ulterior motive? He wanted to be with her. He shrugged his shoulders. 'Steffen is out of control,' he said. 'Someone needs to make him account for all he's done.' His eye alighted on a horse and rider crossing the square; the animal was misbehaving, tossing its head, hitching to the right unexpectedly. The crowd parted like a sea, not wanting to be kicked by an errant hoof. 'I should have been prepared for him to try something.'

'Why?' she asked. 'Steffen is your brother; you didn't think he was going to attack you.'

Bruin smiled ruefully. 'He's never been physically violent before. His attacks were always more underhand, more devious when we are children, fuelled mostly by jealousy. He was clever and our parents suspected nothing. And then, when Sophie died, I thought he had changed—for the better. He helped me, you see—' His voice trailed away, beset with unwanted memories. A gust of wind snagged the swinging sign outside the inn; the gilded angel on the wooden board creaked to and fro, squeaking incessantly.

Eva clutched his fingers, a gesture of support. She thought of the woman in the bailey and the boy who was Steffen's son. And she thought of Steffen himself, the way he acted around Bruin. *'I fooled him, good and proper,'* he had said in the great hall. She stiffened, awareness prickling along her spine.

'How did Steffen help you?' she asked suddenly. Her voice was sharper than usual. 'How?'

'It was he who brought me the clothes Sophie had been wearing when she died; he who comforted me after she had gone.' His firm mouth tightened. 'Without him, I don't know what I would have done.'

'Did you see her body?' Eva blurted out. A painful dryness scraped her throat, sweat sheening her palms. Sadness cleaved her heart; she had to tell him and yet to tell him would take him away from her for ever. For he would go back for Sophie and claim her for his own.

'What—?' Bruin growled at her, astounded. His head reeled back in shock. 'She drowned herself, Eva, how can you say such a thing? She's at the bottom of the sea for all we know.'

She toed the ground, her foot frozen within her boot. A numbness crept across her flesh. How to tell him about the woman she had seen; her suspicions about his brother, about what he might have done? 'Bruin—' Her voice was tentative. 'I think Steffen might have done something awful to you, I think he might have lied—'

'Well, that wouldn't surprise me,' he said mildly, sticking his thumbs into his sword belt. He frowned at the intense expression on Eva's face. 'What is it, what are you thinking?'

'When the guards brought me over to the hay barn I saw a woman and a child,' she explained slowly. 'The guard told me that the boy was Steffen's son.' Bruin's eyes burned into her, glimmering dangerously. Her breath wobbled in her lungs; she forced herself to continue. 'He also told me that the woman was Steffen's wife and that her name was Sophie.'

Her words lingered in the air. All around them, the

whirling bustle of the market continued: the shouting of the hawkers, the smells of the produce, meat, fish and bread, mingling in the air. Dogs barking, the clop of hooves scraping across the cobbles, water sloshing down from an upstairs window, followed by a snarl of disgust from below.

Eva held his gaze. 'If we are going back to Deorham, Bruin, then you need to know. A lady called Sophie is married to Steffen and I think she is the same person as the one whom you thought you had lost.'

Chapter Nineteen

His eyes bored into hers, brilliant chips of mineral light. Seized in a taut, suspended bubble, the silence stretched between them, Bruin's face twisted in confusion. 'Are you telling me the truth?' Thrusting his hand through his hair, he winced as his fingers brushed against the wound. His cloak pulled apart with the movement, revealing his red tunic beneath, the wink of gold embroidery.

'Why would I lie to you?'

Bruin's broad shoulders slumped. 'No.' His gaze prowled over her, eyes gimlet-sharp. He knew her now. 'But—I can't make sense of what you are saying—you think you saw—Sophie? What did she look like, this woman?'

Misery flooded through her, a surge of unspent longing, coupled with regret. 'She was tall and slim; her hair was blonde.' Even to her own ears, her description seemed woefully lacking.

'Which describes about half of the ladies in England,' he replied drily.

'Her name is also Sophie and she is married to your

brother,' Eva insisted. 'It's more than a coincidence, don't you think?'

'Possibly.' A hint of reluctance stained his tone. 'But if this is true, why was she not in attendance when he was ill? The child wasn't there either.'

His reticence was puzzling. A questioning look crossed her face. 'What's the matter?' she whispered.

Bruin wiped his hands on the linen cloth that had held his meat pie. 'I'm sorry, Eva. You're sweet and kind and I know you want it to be her, but it just cannot be her. Sophie is dead and that part of my life is over. You must have been mistaken.' It was strange that he could speak Sophie's name and not feel the shadow of loss drive into him. The sadness was still there, aye, and grief, too, but it was a blunted sensation, muted. He knew why. The woman standing before him lit up his heart and drove the unsettling memories away, like a bright sun burning away cloud.

'I wanted you to know what I had seen,' Eva said quietly. 'Otherwise it might be a shock for you. When we go back, I mean.'

Her protective tone made him smile. Speaking as if she were his knight in armour, as opposed to the other way around. His saviour. And in a way, she was. His prowess with a sword and fists could only keep her safe physically. She was the one who had made his heart feel whole again, patching up the crude lacerations that had harried him since Sophie's death, knitting together the torn ragged pieces with her gentle ways, and soft voice. Her beauty.

With a few gold coins, Bruin procured a palfrey for Eva, a docile grey with white markings, splotches across her rump. He bought saddles and bridles for both of them, tacking up both horses with skilful proficiency, drawing up the girth straps, adjusting the stirrups for Eva.

'Here,' he said, pressing some coins into Eva's palm. 'Buy some food for our return journey, while I finish this off. I am not sure how welcome we will be when we show our faces at Deorham again. It might be best to eat something beforehand.'

The sun was higher now, flooding the whole market square with brilliant light. Squinting, Eva walked amongst the colourful stalls, eyeing the tempting piles of bread, the great wheels of cheese. At a stall selling all manner of dried herbs, foul-smelling tinctures in glass bottles, she bought an earthenware pot of salve for Bruin's head. She procured a few bread rolls from a wizened old woman, whose back seemed permanently bent forward, and a square block of cheese.

'Long journey, my lady?' the woman at the cheese stall enquired.

'No, no, just to Deorham,' she replied, placing the money in the woman's outstretched palm, gnarled fingers bent in like a claw.

'That husband of yours is a handsome devil,' the woman cackled, nodding over to the spot where Bruin tacked up the horses. She must have watched Eva walk over from that direction. 'Make sure you keep a firm hand on him.'

'Oh, but he's—' Eva spluttered to a stop, a warm sensation stealing across her heart. She savoured the feeling, revelled in it. Was this what it could be like? To be married, bound by the Church to a man she loved, and wander amongst the market stalls, knowing that she was safe, protected; that someone would always look after her? She gritted her teeth. Do not become accustomed to this, she told herself sternly. It is fleeting, ephemeral, and will be blown away when he sets eyes on Sophie again.

Bruin had finished with the horses by the time she returned, arms laden with provisions. He picked them out of her arms, one by one, packing them into his leather saddlebags strapped to the rump of his horse, until she was left with the pot of salve.

'What's that?' He raised his eyebrows in question.

'For your wound,' Eva explained. 'I know I haven't had time to clean it, but if you let me put this on, it will help to stave off any infection.'

'What—you want to put it on now?' He smoothed his palm down his horse's nose. His chainmail sleeve pulled back with the movement, exposing his broad wrist, corded veins splaying out across his hand. His animal snorted loudly, scraping one hoof against the cobbles.

'I do.' Her reply was emphatic. 'The wound has been left too long already! I should have looked at it the moment I came into the barn…' Her voice trailed off, halted by memory.

'I didn't give you a chance, did I?' he murmured below the hubbub of the marketplace. A wave of chagrin catapulted through him.

Eva raised her shoulders listlessly, not wanting to dwell on his obvious regret. 'You gave me the chance to say "no", Bruin.' She tamped down on the hurt, the sadness that wreathed her heart. 'Please forget about it.' Wrinkling her nose, she fixed him with what she hoped was a haughty, confident stare. 'Let me look at your wound.'

Dutifully, he bent his head, allowing her to part the matted hair and inspect his split, bruised skin. How could he forget? Her fragrant body furling around his, the delicious scent rising from her neck, her hair, slippery satin. Why had she not pulled away from him when he had given her the option? Had she been hoping that he might turn out to be a better man than he was? That he would *marry* her? The thought did not stun him as much as he thought it would.

Eva rubbed a grainy ointment along the puckered lines of his wound, a thick paste that covered the broken flesh. The smell of the salve rose to his nostrils, pungent and acrid. 'What is that made of?' he asked, flinching at the overwhelming stink.

Eva stepped back, replacing the cork stopper on the earthenware pot. 'I'm not entirely certain,' she admitted, 'but the woman assured me that it was an excellent treatment for wounds.' The breeze caught the mud-splattered hem of her gown, blowing the material across his legs.

He smiled at her. 'Thank you, Eva, for taking care of me.' He couldn't remember a time when such a considerate gesture had meant so much to him. Holding out his hand for the pot, he stowed it in his saddlebag. He turned back, mouth quirking in a half-grin. 'Now, are you ready to claim what is rightfully yours?'

The grey walls of Deorham rose up forbiddingly, towering blocks of stone. Eva glanced furtively up at the castle, half-expecting a hail of arrows to come arcing down towards them. Intense fear gripped her solar plexus. A blade slicing across her flesh. 'I can't believe I'm coming back here,' she said. 'I must have been mad to agree to this!'

With the sun sliding down towards evening, she had followed Bruin back through the forest, her gentle-footed mare matching the pace of his stronger horse, and now they rode side by side up the stony track to the castle gates. The low evening light struck the tower windows at an angle, a white-orange flash that forced Eva to screw up her eyes. She saw the spot where she had crouched by the walls, from where she had watched Bruin spring out through the gates. Her teeth bit her bottom lip, worried at the sensitive flesh. 'What is to stop Steffen and his men locking us back in the stables and keeping us there for ever?' Her voice trembled and she shivered, the evening chill beginning to take hold of her body.

'Me,' Bruin replied. 'He caught me unawares before, but I'm ready for him now.' He touched the jewelled hilt of his sword like a talisman.

'I wish I had your confidence,' Eva replied, as they steered their horses towards the closed gates. Iron rivets studded the thick wooden planks in a criss-cross pattern. Bruin thumped on the wood with his large fist, the sound reverberating inwards, around the gatehouse.

A voice emanated from the inside. 'Who goes there?'

'It is I, Lord Bruin, brother of Lord Steffen. Open up, I must speak with him.'

A narrow door, the outline barely perceptible as it was set within the larger gate, opened. A head poked out: the manservant, Simon, face as pale as eggshell, skin covered with a greasy sheen. 'Lord Bruin,' he stuttered out, his hand fluttering across his chin. 'Oh, God, something awful has happened. Lord Steffen is—he's dead!'

'What the—?' Jumping down from his horse, Bruin grabbed the servant by his collar, dragging him up from the ground, so that the man's arms dangled uselessly against his sides. 'What are you saying? How?' The man trembled in Bruin's grip, pale eyes rolling wildly, his lips opening and closing, making no sound.

'Speak!' Bruin demanded, giving him a little shake.

'His own man,' Simon managed to stutter out. 'They have only this moment returned from Striguil—' he flicked his gaze over to Eva, apologetic '—and one of his knights ran him through, took the ruby. It all happened so fast—there was nothing I could do—'

'Where is he? Where is Steffen?'

'In the bailey.'

Bruin helped Eva to dismount and together they led their horses beneath the carved arch and into the dank, shadowed space, the horses' hooves echoing loudly within the confines of the gatehouse. Green mould streaked the walls. A smell of something rotten permeated the air. Eva's upper arm nudged against Bruin's as they walked side by side. Emerging into the light of the inner bailey, her eyes rounded in horror at the scene before her. She gasped, stopping suddenly, fingers clawing at her throat.

Steffen was lying near the middle of the bailey, where the cobbles dipped down to a circular drain. His arms were stretched out either side of him, his legs together and bent over to one side with his knees drawn up. His eyes were open, staring and sightless. Blood seeped across the ground, leaking steadily out from his chest, soaking the pale blue fabric of his surcoat. A red stain. Beside him, another man, a knight, his body sprawled at an unnatural angle, was also dead.

Eva struggled to comprehend the horrific scene before her, to make sense of it. Shock eroded the strength in her knees; legs buckling, she collapsed against her palfrey, gripping the mane. Bruin turned to her, his big shoulders blocking out the sight of Steffen's body, and caught her by the elbow. 'Go back,' he urged, disentangling her numb grip on the reins and pushing her gently into the shadowed confines of the gatehouse. 'I don't want you to see this.'

He pressed her against the damp wall, squeezing her fingers: a swift gesture of reassurance. 'Stay here.' His silver gaze locked with hers. 'I will deal with this.' The cord fastening of her cloak had come undone; the heavy fabric slipped off her shoulder. Bruin hefted the sides together, knuckles skimming her chin, tying the cord with deft efficiency.

Eva placed her hand on his chest. 'It might be a trap, Bruin,' she whispered. Densely packed muscle rippled beneath her fingers. 'Be careful, you know what Steffen is capable of.'

He nodded briefly, then was gone.

Resting her head back against the stone, Eva stayed completely still, fighting the roiling nausea in her belly, forcing herself to quell the reckless pace of her heart. As her blood slowed, her breath quietened and she opened her eyes, curious now as to what was happening. She peeked around the corner of the gatehouse. Bruin crouched over Steffen's prone figure, Simon hovering beside him. Eva heard Bruin's low, oddly inflected tone rap out a question and the manservant answered, too muffled for her to hear, jabbing the air with his fingers, making a point.

And then, cutting across this whole, surreal scene, a woman screamed. An animal sound, hoarse and shrill, echoing out from inside the castle. A door slammed back on its hinges and Eva saw her again, the tall blonde-haired woman she had seen yester eve, now running, stumbling across the bailey with her skirts held up, white veil flowing out behind her. Her beautiful face was twisted up, as if in pain, mouth gaping open in horror. 'What has happened?' She flung her hands out before her, skidding to a halt, gesturing at Steffen's fallen body. Her movements were jerky, awkward, as if she had lost partial control of her muscles. 'Sweet Jesu, what has happened?' Sliding to her knees, her loose over-gown pillowing about her, the woman laid her head on Steffen's chest, then grabbed his tunic, patting at his ashen face. An engraved golden circlet secured her veil; beneath the flimsy silk, her blonde hair was coiled into two plaits on either side of her head. 'Steffen, speak to me! Steffen!' Her eyes were glazed, unseeing to all around her except for the dead man.

As she dropped beside Steffen, Bruin sprang to his feet, lurching backwards, staring hard at the woman on her knees. 'Sophie?' he managed to croak out. He closed his eyes briefly, hand touching his forehead, in disbelief.

The woman's movements stalled, her hands resting on Steffen's chest. Blood stained her fingers. Her head bounced back on her shoulders as she peered up at the knight who addressed her. 'Bruin? Is that you?' she whispered, hazel eyes wide with shock.

'How are you alive?' he blasted out, anger streaking his voice. His jaw was rigid; a muscle jumped high in his cheekbones. 'My God, how can this be? I saw your wet clothes—all these years I thought you were dead!'

The woman swayed. 'I don't understand—' she whispered faintly. 'Oh—what is happening?' Her eyes widened dramatically, hazel-coloured irises rolling back in their sockets as she slipped over into a dead faint, her arms draping slackly across Steffen's portly chest.

'Oh, dear, no. Come on, my lady!' Simon bent down

to Sophie, hands fluttering ineffectively around her as if he wanted to help, but didn't know how.

Bruin's expression was hard, immutable. Cast in shadow by the low angle of the sun, his cheekbones appeared as if carved, sculptured from a block of stone. He towered over the unconscious woman, his dead brother, brawny legs braced apart. 'What in hell's name is she doing here?'

'Why, she lives here! She's Steffen's wife.'

From the gatehouse, Eva had watched the blood drain from Bruin's face, the shock and fury, the utter incredulity that crossed his features at the sight of Sophie again. She darted forward.

'Bruin.' She touched his chainmail sleeve. The metal was cool beneath her fingers.

His head whipped around and down, regarding her fiercely, his raw expression easing fractionally as he acknowledged the woman at his side. Eva. He took a long, shaky breath, drawing comfort from her nearness, the fragrant smell of her hair wafting up to him. The scent of roses, reminding him of summer.

'You've had a shock.' Her voice was gentle.

'You could say that,' he replied through gritted teeth. Nothing could have prepared him for this; it seemed inconceivable, as if he had stepped into a nightmare. This was the woman he had loved. *Had* loved. He had no wish to hold Sophie, or to comfort her. An unusual hollowness clawed at his innards. His heart was numb. He felt nothing for this woman—absolutely nothing.

'I should help her,' Eva said.

'I'm not sure she deserves your help,' he said roughly. 'Or anyone's help for that matter.'

'I will tend to her. Can you carry her to a bedchamber?'

Bruin's jaw set in a grim, fixed line. His dark lashes stuck out from his brilliant eyes, velvet spikes. One hand hovered above his sword hilt, his lean frame held taut, as if he were about to challenge someone to a fight.

'She is Sophie, isn't she?' Eva confirmed tentatively, flinching beneath his scowling gaze. 'The same woman—?'

'Yes,' he growled out. 'The same woman to whom I was betrothed. The same woman whom I thought was dead. What is she doing with my brother? Married to him?'

'Now is not the time for questions, Bruin,' Eva said quietly. 'This lady has just lost her husband. If we can move her inside, I will tend to her. And then, when she recovers, I'm sure she will be able to explain things.'

Through the rocking sea of confusion in his brain, he cleaved towards Eva's voice, clinging to it like a lifeline, pulling himself up out of the troubled mire of his emotions, hand over hand, towards her. He relaxed slightly, his hand grazing Eva's shoulder. 'You were right,' he said woodenly, shaking his head. 'How did you even know it was her?'

'It was something your brother said, before they locked me up in the barn with you,' Eva replied. 'He said that he had "fooled you, good and proper". They were such perplexing words, Bruin; they made me suspicious.'

'You were right to be,' he replied, his voice steadier now. 'God, he must have planned the whole thing, wanting me to believe that she was dead, when in fact, he wanted her for himself! And then there's the child—? She must have been pregnant by my brother when I broke off our betrothal!' He stuck his hand through his hair, sending the bronze-coloured strands awry.

Simon was struggling to lift Sophie into a seated position, but her unconscious body refused to co-operate. Her head lolled against the manservant's shoulder; her arms flailed uselessly, palms turned up on her lap. With a hiss of exasperation, Bruin stepped over his dead brother's feet and lifted Sophie's limp form effortlessly into his arms. 'Lead the way to her chamber,' he ordered Simon.

Eva followed the small group, jealousy knifing through her, a dark beat of blood. Sophie's head rested against Bruin's muscular arm, a loose strand of blonde hair straggling across his chainmail, snagging against the silver links. She bit her lip, trying to quash the ugly feeling rising within her. She had no claim on Bruin; who did she think she was? She had given him her innocence, but something like that would mean little to him. Of no consequence. And now the woman he had loved all those years ago had reappeared, a widow with a small child. Eva had no chance.

An oak coffer sat beneath the window in Sophie's bedchamber. The wooden surface was cracked and damaged, dried over the years by streaming sunlight. Eva sloshed water from a pottery jug into a shallow bowl, dipping a linen cloth into the chilly liquid. She wrung out the cloth and moved over to the woman on the bed.

Sophie was still unconscious, but her eyelids, pale and blue-veined, moved rapidly, as if she were coming out of a deep sleep. She lay where Bruin had placed her, not gently, on the edge of a fur coverlet, head sunk into a feather pillow. Her golden circlet sat slightly askew, her veil rumpled untidily behind her head. Bruin had left the bedchamber as quickly as he had arrived, muttering something about Steffen, insisting that the hapless manservant accompany him.

Hitching on to the bed, Eva lifted the heavy circlet carefully from Sophie's head, then unpinned the veil, laying both on the stool beside the bed. She dabbed the damp cloth around Sophie's hairline, across her temples. Wisps of hair, pale gold, curled out across the woman's white forehead. Her skin held a parchment-thin translucency.

'Sophie?' Eva spoke her name gently, and then again, louder this time. 'You need to wake up now.'

The blonde eyelashes parted, then pulled fully open to reveal shimmering eyes of pale brown, shot through with golden streaks. Oh, Lord, she was truly a beauty, thought Eva, heart plummeting.

'I—' Sophie stuttered out. Her hand sketched the air, searching for something: a vague, dislocated gesture. 'What happened—?'

'You've had a dreadful shock,' Eva said carefully. She thought of Steffen's body, the blood. Bruin's fierce expression.

Groping for Eva's hand, Sophie held it fast. 'Is—is my husband, Steffen, is he dead?' She squeezed Eva's knuckles, her grip surprisingly strong.

'I'm so sorry,' replied Eva, resisting the temptation to pull away from the pincer-like grip. Be kind, she told herself sternly. This woman had done nothing to you.

'Where is my son?' whispered Sophie. 'Have you seen him?'

'No.' Eva thought of the chattering red-haired child, his freckled round face laughing as he crossed the bailey in the snow with his mother. Now without a father.

'His chamber is through there,' Sophie said limply, indicating a smaller door in the wall opposite the bed. 'Can you tell his nursemaid to keep him there until I can go to him? I don't want him to see—' A strangled whimper choked off the end of her sentence, tears leaking down across her cheeks.

'Of course.' Disentangling her hand, Eva slid thankfully from the bed. She rubbed her hand surreptitiously; if she looked down now, she would see bruises across her knuckles. Pushing open the door, she peered into the adjoining chamber. On the floor, the red-haired boy was playing with a wooden cart, trundling it up and down the floorboards. He looked so much like Bruin, the similarity was uncanny. He glanced up when the door opened, then almost immediately dropped his eyes, more interested in his game than the unknown woman at the door. Sitting alongside him was a smiling, red-cheeked nurse, herself a young girl. Her gaze moved swiftly over Eva's expensive gown and silver circlet; she started to scramble to her feet, her manner deferential.

'Nay, please don't get up.' Eva made a frantic pressing motion with her hand, indicating that the nursemaid should stay where she was. 'Lady Sophie wanted me to check on the boy. She asks that you keep him here for the nonce.'

The girl nodded. 'Has something happened, my lady? I thought I heard—'

Eva frowned hard at her, jerking her head abruptly towards the child. 'Just keep him here, will you, please?' she replied curtly. 'The mistress is unwell and I will stay with her.'

'As you wish, my lady,' the nursemaid said. Worry lurked in her eyes.

Closing the door, Eva moved back to the bed. 'Is there

anything I can get for you?' she asked Sophie. 'A hot drink, maybe? Or some food?'

Sophie's head rustled against the pillow as she turned towards Eva. The golden embroidery on her green-velvet over-grown twinkled in the fading light from the window. Beneath the loose tunic-style gown, she wore a more fitted dress of light blue wool, the sleeves buttoned from wrist to elbow. 'No, no, nothing, thank you,' she said, reaching again for Eva's hand, forcing her to sit on the bed once more. 'You are so kind and yet I don't even know your name,' she whispered.

'My name is Lady Eva of Striguil,' Eva replied.

'Striguil,' Sophie echoed faintly. 'That's over to the west, is it not? I'm sure my husband…' She trailed off, her head twisting weakly on the linen pillow.

'Please don't distress yourself,' Eva said. 'You need to rest.'

'I am sorry not to have met you before,' Sophie continued. She screwed her features up, as if trying to make sense of something. 'Am I right in thinking that you came with—with Lord Bruin?' Her voice was so faint that Eva had to tilt her upper body closer, in order to hear her words.

'Aye, that's right.'

'You are married to him?' Sophie asked.

'No, no, I'm not,' Eva said hurriedly. Now that Lord Steffen was dead, there was no need to pretend she was Bruin's wife. She had no need of his protection any more. The thought made her oddly bereft.

'Then why are you here with him?'

'We came because…' Her voice ebbed away, reluctant to say anything that would cause further hurt or distress to Sophie in her present state. 'Bruin was helping me to track down something that I had lost.'

Sophie closed her eyes; tears crept out from beneath her lashes, streaking down her pale cheeks. 'I knew him once,' she whispered, the air hitching in her throat. 'Some years ago now, in Flanders.' Her tapered fingers lifted to her brow; she kneaded the spot between her eyes. 'I am so ashamed. I treated him very badly. But Steffen—' Her voice limped to a stop, halted by uncontrollable weeping. 'Oh, Steffen,' she cried out, half-rising from the pillow, clutching at the dusty curtain hanging against the bedpost, 'why have you left me in this mess? What have you done to me?'

What have you done to Bruin? Eva thought as she helped Sophie settle back on the mattress. *You have cruelly tricked the man who loved you, ruining his life, and almost destroyed him.* Turning away from the bed, she headed for the door. 'I will fetch something to light the brazier,' she said, briskly. 'The air grows chill in here.'

Sophie was staring up at the canopy above her, her eyes wide, wretched. The huge four-poster bed swamped her willowy frame. 'Fetch Bruin to me now, please. I must speak with him.'

Chapter Twenty

With Sophie's command echoing in her ears, niggling at her, Eva left the chamber, closing the door quietly. Her fingers lingered on the iron latch after it had clicked into place; she stared blankly at the planks that made up the chamber door. The knots and dents in the wood, the worn, polished patina. A rank smell of mildew filled the hallway, the stone walls slicked with damp, a sheen of yellow-spotted fungus at the point where the wall met the floorboards. What would Sophie say to Bruin after all these years? Presumably she wanted to apologise, to beg his forgiveness. And Bruin would forgive her, because he had never stopped loving Sophie, even when he thought she was dead. His rejection of Eva after they had lain together had merely confirmed the fact. Sadness gouged her heart, scouring the fragile flesh.

Gathering her breath, Eva gave a deep, shuddering sigh. Arranging her veil in straight folds across her shoulders, she walked purposefully towards the staircase, angled steps spiralling out from a central stone column and down to the ground floor. There was no reason for her to stay any longer. Now the ruby had been stolen she lacked a pretext behind which to hide; surely Bruin would question her continued presence as unnecessary. Her true reason for staying, to be with Bruin, had vanished the moment Sophie had appeared. She would go to Katherine and tuck herself away in the busy chaos of domestic life, nurse her hurt in private. But a glance out of the thin arrow-slit window showed her a sky streaked with a myriad of blues and golds: twilight was descending, a hazy shroud across the sky. Stars popped out, brilliant diamonds against the darkening blue. She would have to spend one night here at Deorham and leave on the morrow.

Attending to practical details would carry her through the remaining hours, and stop her mind constantly darting back to the painful thought of Bruin sitting on Sophie's bed, holding her hand, talking in low accented tones. His silver eyes twinkling, holding nothing but love. Better to keep busy than dwell on what she had lost. Fires needed to be lit and food prepared; she could do those things at least, before she slipped away. She recalled Lord Steffen's words from the night before: the servants, the cook, all had gone with the lord of the castle into battle. There would no one to help her.

The kitchens lay beyond the great hall. Here, at least, a fire smoked fitfully in the hearth. She found a stack of dry logs in the corner and built up a cage of wood around the lacklustre flames, kneeling back on her heels to make sure the fire took hold on the new wood. The stone flagstones were cold, hard against her knees.

Lighting a wooden taper, she carried the flame around the kitchen, touching candles stuck into iron sconces. Soon the high chamber blazed with light. Removing her cloak, she laid it across a carved chair by the door, and undid the tiny buttons that secured her sleeves, shoving the fabric up to her elbows. Manoeuvring a burning log from the grate into a heavy iron pot, she carried it with a cloth back to Sophie's chamber.

Using her shoulder to lift the latch, Eva managed to open the door. The woman on the bed made no movement. She appeared to be asleep, her face pale, skin waxy in repose, like a marble effigy lying upon the white sheets. Eva's rival for Bruin's heart, caught in the light from the burning log. She should hate her. But all she felt was an overwhelming sorrow; the fact that she had allowed her own imagination to conjure up a future with Bruin that would never happen, obscuring the plain reality that sat squarely in front of her: that she loved a man who did not love her back. Tipping the log into the brazier, she piled the loose charcoal pieces over it haphazardly. Soot smudged her hands.

She jumped as the door from the next-door chamber sprang open and the nursemaid poked her head into Sophie's room. 'Oh, mistress, forgive me,' she stuttered. 'I thought you had gone. I was going to check on Lady Sophie.'

'She's still sleeping,' Eva replied in hushed tones, grateful for the distraction from her desolate thoughts. 'How is the boy?'

'Hungry, I'm afraid. He normally goes to his mother while I cook for everyone. The rest of the servants—'

Eva waved her explanation away. 'Yes, I know, there's no one here. Stay with the child; I will go and prepare some food. Take some light from the fire here; light all the tapers.' She chewed on her bottom lip. 'You must know—' her voice lowered '—that Lord Steffen is dead. By one of his own knights.' She waited for the gasp of astonishment, the clap of the nursemaid's hand across her mouth. But the young girl regarded her steadily, calmly. Eva frowned. Was it her imagination or did the nursemaid breath a silent sigh of relief?

'He's been killed,' she repeated with greater emphasis, thinking that the girl hadn't heard her properly.

'Yes, I know, my lady. I saw Lord Steffen—in the bailey. God rest his soul.' The nursemaid made a sign of the cross over her chest, but her words sounded false, stilted. Eva had the strongest suspicion that the news had brought the nursemaid a certain amount of comfort.

She slipped back down to the kitchens. The manservant, Simon, was crouched on his haunches by the fire, poking at the flames. He looked up as Eva clicked the door shut, his face pallid with tiredness. The pouches beneath his eyes seemed composed of many folds, stacked one on top of the other.

Bruin stood at the table, tearing pieces from a stale hunk of bread, chewing hungrily. Her heart leapt, then plummeted at the sight of him. He had removed his cloak, the blue fabric hanging over the bench that ran the length of the table. Chainmail glistening, his tall, muscular body filled the space with a dancing vitality, constantly snagging her gaze, his physical presence too big for the chamber. Icy air rolled off him, the pungent smell of the stables. His cheeks were dusted with red. Her body cleaved towards him, towards his beauty, his strength. She wanted to go to him, wrap him in her arms and never let him go. Instead, she faltered in the doorway, battling the weak resistance that sliced through her, shards of pain.

With a faint groan of effort, the manservant rose from the hearth and came towards her. 'How is the mistress?'

'Fine. She's exhausted. Sleeping. The boy—' Eva stuttered to a halt, thinking of the red-headed child who looked so much like Bruin, absorbed in his wooden animals upstairs. 'The boy doesn't know yet. Is Lord Steffen—?'

'We've moved his body,' Bruin said gruffly. His eyes sketched her wan face, molten silver. 'We carried him to the chapel; some women from the village are with him. Laying him out. They will keep vigil.' He threw the last piece of bread back on the table, his midnight gaze fastening to hers. His head moved down, an acknowledgement. 'Thank you for helping her, for staying with her. It was kind of you.'

Eva shrugged aside his compliment. 'She is distraught.'

'Understandably.' His response was cropped, stripped of emotion. 'Will you be all right here? I must see to the horses.'

'Bruin—please, wait.' An enormous lump grew in her throat, filling the gap where her breath should be. Dryness scraped her larynx; she swallowed rapidly. 'Before you go—Sophie wants to see you.' She strove to keep the wobble from tearing up her voice. Fumbling blindly for the door frame, she grasped at the solid wood, steadying herself. Do not cry, she told herself sternly. Do not cry.

A dark shadow crossed his face. 'I will see to the horses first.' Turning abruptly on his heel, he marched out of the kitchens, ducking his brindled head beneath the low wooden lintel, before Eva could think of anything further to say.

She gaped after him, surprised. His behaviour made

no sense: why would he not want to go and see Sophie immediately? The horses could have waited. Hope burst, a hesitant, flickering flame, in a secret spot close to her heart, but she clamped down on it rapidly, extinguishing the sentiment. Her heart had lied to her before; she could not trust her instinct. Stop reading hope into actions that meant nothing. Stop trying to make him love you, for it will never happen with that woman lying on the bed upstairs. Levering herself away from the door, she took several unsteady steps into the kitchen, forcing herself to shake off the desolation that cloaked her shoulders. Plastering a bright, false smile across her face, she turned towards the manservant. 'Simon, we must make some food for everyone. Can you show me what provisions you have?'

With a fearsome-looking kitchen knife, Eva chopped up some old onions on a wooden board and threw them into a cooking pot suspended over the fire. She added a few handfuls of oats and some diced pieces of heavily salted bacon that she had found in a sealed pot. It wasn't the food of kings, but the oats were plentiful and would fill hungry bellies. The bacon would add flavour to the bland-tasting gruel, together with some dusty sage leaves discovered at the back of a pantry shelf.

'Smells good,' Simon said, coming in with another armful of logs and stacking them neatly on to the pile in the corner of the room. Flakes of snow glistened on his tunic, melting quickly to dark spots against the fawn-coloured fabric. Eva pushed back her hair from her eyes, her face damp, flushed red from the steam. She stirred the mixture with a long-handled wooden spoon, frowning. Bruin had been ages. Sophie would be waiting for him upstairs, anxious to talk to him.

'Did you see Lord Bruin when you were out collecting the wood?'

'No.' The manservant tilted his head to one side, considering. 'I suppose he could have gone to talk to the soldiers in the gatehouse, tried to find out what happened to Lord Steffen.'

'Maybe.' Eva stared down into the simmering pottage. Flakes of sage rose to the surface of the bubbling liquid. Extracting the spoon, she laid it down on the table. 'Could you find bowls and take some of this up to Lady Sophie and her child? The nursemaid, too, please.' She pressed her hands down the front of her skirts. 'I will go and find him.'

Outside, the temperature had risen by a few notches. A blanket of cloud had moved across the sky, obscuring the moon and stars, and it was snowing again, large lazy flakes spinning across the bailey. Her eyes flew to the spot where Steffen had been slain, the cobbles stained dark with his blood. So much had happened in such a short time, her mind could scarce comprehend the speed of events. Last night, she had given her body to Bruin, roped safely in his muscular arms, foolishly believing that whatever happened, she would be able to cope with the consequences of such a foolhardy action. Now, as she stumbled towards the stables through the snow, she was not so sure.

The stables were empty. A rush torch, slung into an iron bracket, burned by the wide-arched doorway, spitting occasionally as wayward snowflakes blew in and touched the flames. Bruin's destrier was there, tethered loosely in his stall, dragging out hay from the manger with its big teeth, chomping contentedly. Her palfrey stood in the stall alongside, turning her head and nickering quietly as Eva appeared. The saddles and bridles had been removed and hung over the wooden gates of the empty stalls. So, Bruin had dealt with the horses. Where could he have gone?

Placing her hands on the edge of the stall, Eva bent her head, stretching her arms to their full length. Her neck muscles knotted painfully, tense and strained. Her head pounded, an incessant ache scything across her forehead. Releasing her hands, she balanced her elbows on the gate, pushing her face into her hands. Her eyelashes rasped gently against the creases in her palms; the sound like a spider's touch. What was she doing here? Her heart was almost broken, finished. Why witness Bruin heading up to see Sophie, or risk seeing them together? He might even be up in her chamber at this very moment. It would be better to go now.

Tears marring her vision, she blundered towards the hanging bridles, unlooping the leather straps, the jangling fastenings, from the iron hook. Letting herself into the stall, she squeezed along her palfrey's flank, standing on tiptoe to place the bridle around the animal's head. The smell of horses filled the air, pungent, earthy. Her fingers fumbled with the stiff, awkward buckles and she frowned, a crease appearing between her finely drawn eyebrows as she concentrated on securing them. The horse whinnied, nibbling companionably at Eva's flapping sleeves. She had forgotten to button them again when she had left the kitchens. It didn't matter now. Nothing really mattered any more.

Her saddle was slung over the wall dividing the stalls;

shoving her hands beneath the unwieldy leather, she hauled it down against her chest. Staggering beneath the unexpected weight, she balanced herself quickly so as not to drop it. Tears ran down her cheeks, dropping from her chin, liquid crystals falling in the jittery light of the torch.

'Going somewhere?'

Eva gasped, eyes widening in surprise. A debilitating weakness ripped at the strength in her knees. Bruin stood beneath the stone arch, his massive frame silhouetted by the blustery snow. Flakes covered his bronze hair, diamond flecks brushing down over his chainmail sleeves, settling on the red wool of his surcoat.

She hugged the saddle to her chest, shielding herself against his intrusion, the huge weight dragging against her forearms and shoulders, yanking at the muscles and making them sore. She squinted up at him. Pain thumped across her forehead. 'I thought it would be best.' A rawness invaded her speech.

'Why?' he said lightly, coming forward, lifting the saddle easily from her grasp, slinging it back over the wall. His eyes, silver-bright, drilled into her.

Desire stabbed through her. Would this torment never end? Dropping her eyes, she toed at the greasy cobbles. Her hem was wet, stained with spots of mud, errant bits of straw, her leather boots filthy from riding. The miles of countryside she had covered with Bruin. 'Isn't it obvious?' The words clogged her larynx. The cobbled floor blurred before her vision.

'Not to me.' Bruin took a step closer, snaring her rose-scented fragrance. His heart contracted in memory: the gossamer patina of her skin sealed against him, the sleekness of her flank. His knee knocked against hers; the folds of her gown whispered in response.

Eva raised her sodden, tear-stained face. 'Sophie wants to see you, Bruin. You must go to her.' She folded her shaking arms, pleating the blue fabric across her chest.

Ignoring her words, his hand cradled her chin, big thumb sketching across the tears on her cheek. 'Why are you crying?' His husky voice enveloped her, sensual, concerned.

'I'm not. The cold air makes my eyes water.' Her pathetic excuse hung between them, as desolation rocked her voice. 'Go to Sophie,' she urged again, her voice rising. 'She's upset, she wants to see you!'

She wants you.

The thought pierced her brain like shards of glass. The harsh reality of her situation burst through her, making her sag back against the stall. Why did he not go now, away from her, and run to Sophie? 'Please go, Bruin.' *Before I make a complete and utter fool of myself.* Wrenching from his touch, she turned her back on him, a gust of fresh tears welling in her chest, a great shuddering block of despair. Pressing her thumb and forefinger to the bridge of her nose, she closed her eyes, waiting for him to walk away.

Frowning at the defeated tilt of her head, Bruin settled his hands on her shoulders. 'Why are you so upset?' His voice resonated through the hushed stables, the occasional nicker of the horses. The rustle of straw. He thought he knew the reason why. Happiness, a chink of sunshine, cracked the mantle of his consciousness. Could it be true? He wanted to hear her say the words. He wanted to be certain.

Eva whirled around, dislodging his light hold, crying openly now. Her long eyelashes sparkled with tears. 'Oh, my God, Bruin, don't you see?' She drove her hands against her cheeks, covering her eyes; tears slipped over her knuckles, dripping off her wrists. 'I hate that woman lying up there.,' She jabbed up at the castle windows, her arms flinging out jerkily. 'I hate what she has done to you! She doesn't deserve you, yet she holds your heart! She has always held your heart, even when you thought she was dead! And now you have discovered her alive again, well, it's obvious what's going to happen!' A wildness tore at her voice as it gained momentum, raw and wretched. 'Let me go, please, for I can't bear to see the two of you together! My heart can't take it any more!' She turned away, stunned by the truth of her unguarded outburst, waiting for the look of scorn to cross his face, the disapproval.

It never came.

'Oh, my God,' he whispered. Joy burst in his chest, a shower of blazing stars. Catching her wrists, he levelled his gaze with hers, jewel-bright. 'Eva—'

She shrank away from him, shoulders wilting with defeat. The burst of anger, the wild speech had been replaced by shame. Humiliation pulsed through her. 'Let me go now, Bruin.'

'I will do no such thing,' he murmured. 'I will never let you go again.'

Caught up in her own mortification, Eva failed to hear him. 'I can't stay,' she pleaded with him. 'You will marry her and take on the child, and—and—' Her chest closed up around her fragile speech; she squeezed her eyes shut, unwilling to look at his face.

'No, Eva, you are wrong,' he said resolutely. 'I am not going to marry her. Another woman holds my heart and has done from the first day I met her.'

Her head spun on a wave of dizziness, heart teetering with uncertainty. As if she walked on quicksand, every step beset with danger. She clung to his fingers, the ridged sinews on the back of his hand prominent in the shadowy light. 'I—I'm not sure I understand…' Her voice drifted to a miserable whisper. 'Who—? Where is this woman?'

'Standing right in front of me.'

The deep, resonant pitch of his voice sank slowly down into the whirling chaos of her brain. 'Standing—?' she repeated, stupidly. She wasn't sure if she had heard him correctly.

'It's you, Eva. For God's sake, I love you!' Gripping her elbows, he steadied her, a huge grin splitting his lean, sculptured features. 'Do you hear me?' He leaned against her, chest pressing against her breasts, his mouth touching her ear. 'I love you.'

He loved her. She closed her eyes, inhaling his musky, masculine fragrance. The smell of him. Rough stubble pricked her cheek. 'I can't believe—I can't believe what you're saying.' Astonishment burst through her, spinning out like hot rays of sunshine, melting through the layers of sadness besieging her heart.

'Believe it, Eva, for it is the truth. I love you.' His voice rumbled out, gruff and confident. 'When I first saw you, cowering in the snowstorm, your foot caught in that godawful trap—I knew it then, but I refused to admit it. My heart was numb, destroyed, churned up by the thought that I had driven Sophie to kill herself, but after I met you, Eva, all that began to change. You have changed me. And you have my heart, my love, you have all of me, all that I am able to give you.'

Her hands crept up to his shoulders. 'I thought you hated me,' she whispered. 'An annoying encumbrance, holding you back. I thought you couldn't wait to be rid of me.'

His eyes shone over her, triumphant. 'Never. I have been so foolish. Stupid.'

'Oh, I wouldn't—' she began to protest.

He grinned at her. 'Don't you dare absolve me, Eva. Not after I have dragged you over half the countryside, ridden until you were half-dead in the saddle. I took your precious innocence…' He hesitated, eyes snaring hers, and she blushed at the memory. He sighed, ruefully. 'I have treated you abysmally and for that I am sorry.'

'I wanted to be with you,' she responded shyly. Her fingers twisted his hair at the base of his neck, the silky fronds tickling her wrists. 'It's all I have ever wanted. I love you, Bruin, with all my heart.'

He groaned at her simple admission, sliding his muscular arms around her, drawing her slight frame against his. His heart thudded against hers. He tilted his head, metallic eyes shimmering with unspoken promise, of a future bound with love and happiness, sealing his mouth to hers in a kiss that would bind them together, for ever.

Epilogue

Outside the great hall at Striguil, the snow continued to fall; flakes brushed the windows, drifting down like miniature puffs of cloud. The diamond-shaped glass panes rippled and shone in the light from the hall, hundreds of candles blazing out from wall niches and wrought-iron candlesticks. Inside, the glorious scent of winter-sweet filled the air; trailing garlands adorned window ledges and arches, the glossy evergreen leaves studded with tiny white flowers whose exquisite fragrance belied their size. An enormous fire crackled in the stone hearth, warming the crowds of people. Musicians, red-faced, fuelled by potent honey mead, played lively dance tunes on the fiddle and drum. The trestle tables had been pushed back; couples danced and laughed as they joined hands across the flagstone floor.

'I can't believe this is happening to me.' Eva turned to Bruin, heart overflowing with love for the man sitting at her side. Her wedding gown, heavy cream silk, glimmered in the candlelight. Pearls, sewn into the shape of flowers, decorated the curving neckline. Each pearl glowed with a lustrous patina, matching the beauty of

Eva's skin. Beneath her diaphanous veil, her ebony hair was loose, the shining tresses coiling down, pooling into her lap. Splaying her hand out across the pristine tablecloth, she stared hard at the gold band on her ring finger.

Following her frowning scrutiny, Bruin laughed. 'It is all real, you know.' His arm rested against her back; now, he squeezed her close, pulling her shoulder into the muscled hardness of his chest. 'Even the ring.' His brilliant eyes roamed over her, hot, possessive.

'I know.' Her cheek rubbed his shoulder. 'But I still can't shake the feeling that everything today has been like a dream. A wonderful, delicious dream.' Her gaze drifted over the thronging crowds, watching as the manservant from Deorham, Simon, steered Lady Sophie across the flagstones, a confident arm around her neat waist. Eva nodded in their direction. 'And that is certainly something I never thought to see.'

'You mean Simon de Chisholm? I have the impression he has always looked after Sophie,' Bruin replied. 'He told me that he watched out for her well-being where my brother was concerned. Sophie is happy now and so is young Arwin.' He searched for his small, bronze-haired nephew and found him running the length of the hall, giggling loudly, pursued by all three of Lady Katherine's children.

'And Katherine is content,' Eva added, her gaze alighting on the statuesque frame of her friend dancing with a dark-haired man. 'Her new husband is not the ogre we all imagined him to be. And he's fond of the children, as well.'

Bruin's hand covered hers, squeezing her fingers. 'And Striguil is yours again,' he murmured. Carved bone buttons secured his shirt sleeves around his wrists; his wedding tunic was of dark blue wool, moulded to his large frame, a leather belt pulling in the fabric about his slim hips. His bronze hair was tousled, loose strands brushing down across his forehead.

'And yours, too.' Tilting her chin up, she brushed her lips across the side of his mouth, a fleeting, sensual touch. His irises widened, black and knowing, flooding the silver of his eyes; the promise of the night captured in a single glance. A roar of appreciation rose from the dancing crowds, smiles flicking from bobbing heads towards the handsome couple. A blush stole across Eva's cheeks.

His chin grazed the top of her head. 'Even if we had nowhere to live, I wouldn't care,' he replied. 'All I want is the woman that I love, by my side.' He glanced along the table, across the shining faces of the knights and their ladies who had gathered to celebrate their wedding, across the sumptuous fabrics of their clothes, the sparkle of their jewels in sword hilts and circlets. His heart swelled with happiness, overflowing with hope for their future together, but most of all, with love for the woman in his arms. Eva, his darling wife, whom he would cherish for a lifetime.

* * * * *

If you enjoyed this story, you won't want to miss these other great reads from Meriel Fuller

CAPTURED BY THE WARRIOR
HER BATTLE-SCARRED KNIGHT
THE KNIGHT'S FUGITIVE LADY
INNOCENT'S CHAMPION
COMMANDED BY THE FRENCH DUKE